The Mamur Zapt
&
the Return of
the Carpet

The Mamur Zapt
&
the Return of
the Carpet

Michael Pearce

Poisoned Pen Press

Copyright © 1988 by Michael Pearce

First Trade Paperback 2001

10 9 8 7 6 5 4 3 2

Library of Congress Catalog Card Number: 2001090171

ISBN: 1-890208-77-9

Poisoned Pen Press
6962 E. First Ave. Ste. 103
Scottsdale, AZ 85251
www.poisonedpenpress.com
info@poisonedpenpress.com

Printed in the United States of America

Author's Note

Cairo, 1908. The heyday—or was it just past the heyday?—
of indirect British rule. Thirty years earlier the profligate
Ismail Pasha, Khedive of Egypt, had brought his country to
the edge of bankruptcy. The Western powers had stepped in
but at a price, and their yoke bore hard. In 1881 Egyptian
unrest became open rebellion. To safeguard its financial interests Britain sent in an army, crushed the rebels and
restored the Khedive, but from now on the Khedive gov-
erned in name only; the real ruler of Egypt was Cromer, the
British Agent and Consul-General. A complex apparatus of
control was introduced. There were British "advisers" at the
top of all the major ministries; the commander-in-chief of
the Egyptian Army, the Sirdar, was British; so were the
inspector-general of prisons, the commandants of the two
key police forces of Cairo and Alexandria, and of course the
Mamur Zapt, the head of the Political CID—the Secret
Police.

But by 1908 British rule was not as firmly based as it
looked. Other powers were growing jealous. France had
cultural links with Egypt which dated back to Napoleon and
had never forgiven the British for staying on after crushing
the Arabi rebellion. Many of Egypt's criminal procedures
were based upon the Code Napoléon, and the judicial

system in general followed French lines. This meant that investigation and prosecution were the responsibility not of the police but of the Department of Prosecutions of the Ministry of Justice; that is, of the Parquet.

Turkey was also jealous, for Egypt was still constitutionally a province of the Ottoman Empire, and the Khedive in theory owed allegiance to the Sultan of Istanbul.

And all the time the underground forces of Egyptian Nationalism were growing in strength and now, in 1908, were just beginning to assert themselves.

Egypt was a country of many potential masters. It had four completing legal systems, three principal languages and several religions, apart from Islam. It had many, many nationalities. It was a country ripe with ambiguities. A country bright with sunlight and dark with shadows. And in the shadows, among the ambiguities, worked the Mamur Zapt.

In this story I have tried to stay close to fact. The streets are those of Cairo in 1908. The terrorist "clubs" were a feature of the period, too. There really was a National newspaper called *al Liwa* and in 1908 Kitchener's famous screw-gun battery really did accompany the Return of the Carpet. There was even a Mamur Zapt, although perhaps he was not quite like this one.

Chapter 1

The Mamur Zapt was sitting in his office one morning when his orderly, Yussuf, burst into the room.

"Come quickly, effendi!" he said. "Bimbashi McPhee wants you at once. At once! Nuri Pasha has been killed!"

This was an exaggeration, for the attempt to assassinate the veteran politician had not succeeded; but Yussuf was not one for pedestrian detail.

However, along the corridor Owen could hear the assistant commandant's voice raised critically, so he put a paperweight on the estimates to prevent them from being blown all over the office by the fan, and rose reluctantly to his feet.

There was an Egyptian in McPhee's room. He was short and plump and apparently very agitated. McPhee was pouring him a glass of water, which he took with effusive thanks and much mopping of his brow. From behind the silk handkerchief steady brown eyes registered Owen's arrival.

"Ah!" said McPhee, catching sight of Owen as he turned: "Captain Cadwallader Owen."

This, too, was an exaggeration. A romantic Welsh mother had insisted on preserving a remote family connection through the middle name, and Owen had once made the mistake of signing his name in full in McPhee's presence.

The Scotsman, another romantic, had ever afterwards insisted on using both barrels.

"Do you know Fakhri Bey? No?"

They shook hands.

"Fakhri Bey was passing when it happened."

"I was in an arabeah," the Egyptian explained. "There was nothing I could do. So I told the driver to drive on and came straight here."

"I'm very glad you did," said McPhee. "We'll get there right away."

He picked up his sun helmet.

"In fact, if you'll excuse us—"

"Of course. Of course," the other protested.

They set off down the corridor.

"You don't want me, do you?" asked Owen.

Normally the Mamur Zapt, as head of the Political Branch, did not reckon to concern himself with routine killings.

"Certainly I do," said McPhee over his shoulder.

Owen would have preferred to have carried on with the estimates. They were not especially complex but required a certain attention, and he had set aside the morning for that purpose. His predecessor-but-one had been dismissed for corruption and Owen was sensitive on financial matters.

However, he collected his helmet and joined McPhee at the front of the building. The large square of the Bab el Khalk was empty of transport except for one carriage which Fakhri Bey was just getting into.

He stopped as he saw them.

"You would be very welcome to share my arabeah," he said.

"May we?" said McPhee. "There doesn't seem to be any other. It would be taking you back—"

"Not at all," said Fakhri. "It would be a pleasure."

The carriage was one of those with two horses and could take three passengers at a pinch. McPhee and Owen wedged themselves in around Fakhri, and the driver, after a great display of urgency, managed to get the horses going at a steady amble along the broad thoroughfare of the Sharia Mohammed Ali.

"And now," said Owen, "perhaps you could tell me exactly what happened where."

"Nuri Pasha was shot," said Fakhri. "It was dreadful. I am so sorry. He was a friend of mine, you know," he said, glancing sideways at Owen.

"A good chap," said McPhee supportively, but then McPhee considered many people to be good chaps whom Owen knew to be consummate rogues.

"And where did all this happen?" he asked.

"In the Place de l'Opéra," said Fakhri, "right in front of my eyes. I could not believe it. I could not believe it."

"You actually saw the shooting?" asked Owen, putting a heavy accent, and not too sceptical a one he hoped, on the word "saw."

"Yes," said Fakhri. "Yes, I did."

He hesitated.

"Or, at least, I thought I did. I was sure I did."

Again the sidelong glance at Owen.

"Now I am not so sure," he said.

"Come," said McPhee, sympathetic as usual. "You certainly did. You told me all about it."

"Yes," said Fakhri. "I know. And I told you what I thought I saw. But when Captain Car—" Fakhri mumbled a bit "—Owen asked me in that sharp way of his and I try to recall detail, what seemed clear suddenly becomes misty."

"Well," said Owen, brightening, "that's a start anyway."

The usual problem with Egyptian witnesses was not that they could not recall but that they recalled only too well.

"I expect you're used to this," said Fakhri. "The fallibility of witnesses? My legal friends, without exception, assure me that eyewitnesses are not to be trusted."

"It's a funny business," said Owen, "what you see and what you don't see."

"I thought I saw. Clearly."

"Perhaps you did. Start again. Where were you when all this was happening?"

"In an arabeah."

"Which was—precisely—where?"

"I had come down the Sharia el Maghrabi. I was just crossing the Place de l'Opéra."

"Past the statue?"

The statue of Ibrahim Pasha, the famous Egyptian general who had led his army to within a hundred miles of Istanbul, was a well-known Cairo landmark.

"Right by the statue. I was about to go down the side of the Ezbekiyeh Gardens."

"Fine. And you saw?"

"I saw Nuri Pasha. I think he had just come out of the Hotel Continental. He walked right out into the Place, looking for his arabeah. I think."

"About how far from you?"

"Twenty metres, perhaps."

"Anyway, you recognized him?"

"Oh yes. He is very distinctive. And I know him well. In fact, that was why I was watching him. To exchange greetings. If he saw me."

"Did he see you?"

"No. He was looking about and I thought he might see me."

"Go on."

"Well, I was watching him, and then suddenly there was a loud bang, and I saw Nuri Pasha stagger and put his arms up and fall, and I thought: That must have been a shot. Nuri Pasha must have been shot."

"The shot," said Owen, "sounded close to you?"

"Very close. It made the horses jump. The arabeah swerved. That was how I lost sight of the man."

"Tell me about the man."

Fakhri put his hands to his head.

"I am sorry," he said. "It is not clear."

"To the left or to the right of Nuri Pasha as you were looking at him?"

"To the right. But I didn't really see him. It was just that, as Nuri Pasha fell, in the corner of my eye I thought I saw someone move away."

"A blue galabeah?"

"Yes."

Fakhri grimaced. "Like all the other galabeahs," he said.

The long blue gown was the standard garment of the Cairo poor.

They exchanged smiles.

After a while, as Fakhri said nothing more, Owen prompted: "And then?"

"That was all," said Fakhri. "The arabeah swerved and I lost sight of Nuri Pasha. It was—oh, I suppose three or four minutes before I could look again."

"And then there was a crowd ten feet deep round Nuri Pasha and you couldn't see a thing."

"Yes," said Fakhri, surprised. "That's right. How did you know?"

☙

The crowd was still thick when they reached the Place de l'Opéra, although the incident must have happened at least half an hour before by the time they got there.

McPhee sprang out of the arabeah and shouldered his way into the throng. A constable appeared from nowhere and joined his efforts to the bimbashi's, laying about him with his truncheon. Reluctantly the ranks of the crowd parted and brought McPhee to where a man was lying stretched out in the grit and dust of the square.

"Make space! Make space!"

McPhee thrust the bystanders apart by main force and held them off.

"Why!" he said in disappointed tones. "This isn't Nuri Pasha! Who is this?"

"It is Ibrahim, sir," said a voice from the crowd. "He was wounded when Nuri Pasha was shot."

"And where is Nuri Pasha?"

"He was taken into the hotel, sir," said the constable.

"What sort of condition was he in?"

Seeing that the constable did not understand, McPhee changed his question.

"Was he alive or dead?"

Various voices from the crowd assured him that Nuri Pasha was (a) dead, (b) unhurt, (c) suffering from terrible injuries. Leaving McPhee to sort that out, Owen pushed his way back through the crowd.

To one side of the mêlée two constables were casually talking to a slight, spare Egyptian in a very handsome suit. He looked up as Owen approached.

"The Mamur Zapt? I did not expect to see you here in an affair of this sort. Mahmoud el Zaki. Parquet."

The Parquet was the Department of Prosecutions of the Ministry of Justice.

They shook hands.

"You were here very quickly," said Owen.

The Egyptian shrugged his shoulders. "Nuri Pasha is an important man," he said.

"How is Nuri Pasha?"

"Shaken."

"That all?"

"The shot did not touch him. It slightly grazed a lemonade-seller."

"No need for me," said Owen.

"No need for me either," said Mahmoud. "Though I expect I shall get the case now."

The Parquet, not the police, were responsible for investigation. It was clear that they already had the case in hand. The Ministry of Justice was nearer than the Bab el Khalk

and they must have sent a bright young man down as soon
as they had heard. There was nothing that Owen could do.
He pushed his way back through the crowd to where the
wounded lemonade-seller lay.

"Are you badly hurt?"

"I am dying," said the man.

There seemed no evidence of any wound.

"Where is your hurt?"

The man groaned but said nothing.

"In the bum, effendi," a woman said eagerly. "Look!"

She lifted the man's galabeah. The bullet had glanced along
the buttock, leaving a livid furrow.

"He will survive," said Owen.

The man was unconvinced.

"I am dying."

"This is not a houris you see," said the woman. "It is your
wife."

The man groaned again, louder. The crowd guffawed.

"Take heart, man," said Owen. "You might have been hit
in the front."

The woman looked up at him mock-demurely. She was a
villager and did not wear a veil.

"What difference would that have made, effendi?"

"None at all in his case," said a voice from the crowd.
"He has not been with his woman for weeks."

The wounded man sat up indignantly.

Owen moved away. There seemed very few casualties from
the shooting. Whoever it was had thoroughly bungled his job.

McPhee was talking to the man from the Parquet. He
signalled to Owen to come over.

"They think they've got the man," he said. "He was seized
as he tried to run away."

"Who by?" said Owen, surprised.

It was very rare for the ordinary populace to intervene in
an assault, which, as opposed to an injury or accident, they
tended to regard as a private matter.

"It's not so surprising," said the man from the Parquet. "Come and look."

He led them across the Place and into the Hotel Continental.

In a small storeroom at the back, guarded by a large, though apprehensive constable, an Arab lay prone on the floor.

He was completely unconscious. Mahmoud turned the head with his foot so that they could see the face. The eyelids rolled back to reveal white, drugged eyes.

McPhee dropped on one knee beside the man, bent over him and sniffed.

"Don't really need to," he said. "Smell it a mile away. Hashish."

He began searching the man methodically.

"I expect you've already done this," he said apologetically.

"Police job," said Mahmoud.

"And I don't expect they've done it," said McPhee.

Most of the ordinary constables were volunteers on a five-year contract and were recruited from those who had finished their conscript service, again five years, with the Egyptian Army. They tended to come from the poorer villages and were nearly all illiterate. They were paid three pounds a month.

"He wasn't like this when he was caught, surely?" said Owen, puzzled.

"Pretty well," said Mahmoud. "That's why they caught him. He more or less fell over."

"Then how—?"

"How did he fire the shot?" Mahmoud shrugged. "My guess is he took the hashish to stiffen himself up. He just about managed to fire the shot, and then it caught up with him. That's why he shot so poorly."

"Maybe," said Owen.

The other smiled.

"The other explanation is, of course, that he was drugged up to the hilt, someone else fired the shot—equally poorly— and then put the gun in his hand."

McPhee looked up. "The gun was definitely in his hand at some point."

He took up the Arab's limp hand, smelled it and then offered it to the other two.

"No, thanks," said Owen.

"Distinct smell of powder."

"I'm surprised you can pick it out among the other things."

McPhee let the hand drop and rose to his feet.

"Nothing else," he said.

"Did you find the gun?" Owen asked Mahmoud.

Mahmoud nodded. "On the ground," he said.

He signed to the constable, who went away and returned a moment later gingerly carrying a large revolver in a fold of dirty white cloth.

"Standard Service issue, I think," said McPhee, "but you'll know better than I."

He looked at Owen.

"New model," said Owen. "Only started being issued here last February. Wonder where he got that?"

"I'll have to check," said Mahmoud.

"You'll have something to go on at any rate," said McPhee. He was always pleased to put the Parquet in its place.

"More than that," said Owen. "I think we've got a witness for you."

Mahmoud looked at him inquiringly.

"Blue galabeah," Owen said to McPhee.

He turned to go.

"Have a word with Fakhri Bey," he said as they went.

ᏳᎲᎲᎧ

Afterwards, Owen and McPhee went to the Sporting Club for lunch, and then Owen had a swim. In the summer working hours were from eight-thirty till two. The whole city had a siesta then, from which it did not stir until about six o'clock. Then the shops reopened, the street stall-holders emerged from under their stalls, the open air cafés filled up, and the narrow streets hummed with life until nearly three in the morning.

Owen had got used to the pattern in India and it did not bother him. However, he never found it possible to sleep in the afternoon. Usually he read the papers at the club and then went for a swim in the club pool. The mothers with their children did not come until after four, so he had the pool to himself and could chug up and down practising the new crawl stroke.

Usually, too, he would return to his office about six and work for a couple of hours in the cool of the evening, undisturbed by clerks and orderlies, agents and petitioners. It was a good time for getting things done.

That evening he had intended to get to grips with the estimates, but when he arrived in his office he found a note on his desk from McPhee, asking him to drop along as soon as he got in.

"Oh! Hullo!" said McPhee when he stuck his head round the door. "Just as well you're here. The Old Man wants to see us."

Garvin, the professional policeman who had relatively recently been appointed commandant of the Cairo police, was, if anything, a little younger than McPhee, but McPhee always liked to refer to him in what Owen considered to be a prep-school manner. McPhee had spent twelve years teaching in the Egyptian equivalent of a minor public school before Garvin's idiosyncratic, and amateur, predecessor had recruited him as assistant commandant at the time of the corruption business.

The choice was not, in fact, as eccentric as might appear. McPhee was patently honest, a necessary qualification in the circumstances and one comparatively rare in worldly-wise Cairo; he spoke Arabic fluently, which was a prime prerequisite for the post so far as the British Agent, Cromer, was concerned; and he possessed boundless physical energy, which, although irritating at times, fitted him quite well for some of the tasks a policeman was called on to do.

He was, however, an amateur, and, Owen considered, would not have stood a cat's chance in hell of getting the job if Garvin had been making the appointment.

The same was probably true of his own appointment as Mamur Zapt, head of the Political Branch and the Secret Police.

McPhee himself had been responsible for this. The post of Mamur Zapt had become vacant at the time when McPhee, pending Garvin's arrival, had been appointed acting commandant. The post was considered too sensitive to be left unfilled for long and McPhee had been asked to advise the Minister. Not a professional soldier himself, he had been over-impressed by Owen's service on the North-West Frontier in India, and Owen's facility with languages had clinched the matter.

The shrewd, unsentimental Garvin, thought Owen, would have appointed neither of them; neither the eccentric McPhee nor the inexperienced Owen. He would probably have got on better, Owen thought, with the previous Mamur Zapt: the one who knew the underworld of Cairo just a little too well.

Now, when he and McPhee took up their accustomed chairs before the large desk, Owen felt the usual small-boy-about-to-be-disciplined feeling creeping up on him. He guessed that McPhee felt it, too, but they reacted in different ways. McPhee sat up ramrod-straight and barked, "Yes, sir!" Owen lolled back in what he suspected was an absurdly exaggerated manner and said nothing. He suspected that Garvin found him far too easy-going.

The suspicion was soon reinforced.

"Nuri Pasha," said Garvin.

"Nasty shock, sir," said McPhee. "But he's recovering. We have the man who did it."

"Oh," said Garvin.

McPhee described the circumstances.

Garvin did not seem much interested.

"So that's all buttoned up," McPhee concluded.

"Buttoned up?" Garvin regarded him incredulously. "You haven't bloody begun!"

He turned to the Mamur Zapt.

"Did you get any warning of this?"

"No."

"Why not?"

Owen thought that was an unfair question.

"We get any number of warnings," he began defensively. "Three or four a day—"

Garvin cut across him.

"Did you get one about this? About Nuri Pasha?"

"Not specifically," Owen admitted.

"Worrying."

"Nine-tenths of them are baloney."

"The other tenth isn't," said Garvin.

He brooded for a moment.

"What do you do about those? The ones that aren't baloney?"

"We check them all out," said Owen. "Baloney or no baloney. The ones that look as if they might have something in them we take action over."

"What action."

"Notify the appropriate people. Stick a man on. Stay with the source."

"Sometimes it works," said Garvin.

"It nearly always works," said McPhee loyally.

Garvin ignored him.

"But those are the cases where you hear something. You didn't even pick up a whisper this time?"

"No."

"Slip-up," said Garvin.

Owen fought back.

"Not necessarily," he said. "Anyone who's plotting an assassination isn't going to broadcast the fact. There may have been nothing to pick up."

"There's always something to pick up in Cairo," said Garvin dismissively.

He turned his attention back to McPhee.

"Buttoned up!" he repeated. "You haven't bloody even started! Whose man was he? What's behind this? What are they after?"

"The Parquet—" Owen began.

Garvin swung round on him.

"For Christ's sake!" he said. "Stop messing around! You know damned well this is nothing to do with them. It's political."

Garvin's eyes bored into his.

"So you'd better bloody get on with it," he said. "Mamur Zapt."

Chapter 2

Owen was at the Place de l'Opéra shortly before seven the following morning. Early though he was, the Parquet was there before him.

Mahmoud was surprised.

"The Mamur Zapt?" he said.

He broke into a smile.

"They have been leaning on you, too?"

"They told me to stop messing around and bloody get on with it," said Owen.

"*Moi aussi.*"

They both laughed.

"It must be political," said Mahmoud.

"What isn't?" said Owen.

"And big."

"Why?"

"Because you're here."

"I honestly don't know anything that makes it big," said Owen.

"Nuri Pasha?"

"I thought he'd retired from active politics."

"Those bastards never retire from active politics," said Mahmoud. He looked at Owen curiously. "Don't you know? Really?"

"No," said Owen.

"I don't really know, either," said Mahmoud. "I just assumed—" He broke off.

"What did you assume?"

Mahmoud hesitated.

"I've got no particular reason for assuming," he said at last. "I just took it for granted."

"What?"

"That it was to do with Denshawai."

"Why should it be to do with Denshawai?"

"Because Nuri Pasha was an under-secretary in the Ministry of Justice at that time."

The Denshawai Incident had happened in 1906, just before Owen was transferred to Egypt and took up the post of Mamur Zapt.

Some British soldiers had been marching from Cairo to Alexandria and en route five officers had gone to the village of Denshawai to shoot pigeons. Round ever Egyptian village were flocks of semi-wild pigeons kept for food and manure. No one was allowed to shoot them without permission from the head man of the village. The officers had misunderstood a guide who was with them and, thinking they were free to shoot, did so. The infuriated villagers had attacked the officers. Two had been wounded and one had died, of sunstroke it was thought, as he lay on the ground. The British-controlled Administration had taken exemplary action against the villagers. Four had been sentenced to death, others sent to prison, and seven had received fifty lashes.

The incident had sparked off widespread protests throughout Egypt. It had not been too popular with the new British Government, either. Word went that Cromer had been, in effect, forced out over the issue. He had been replaced as Consul-General by the more pliable Sir Eldon Gorst, something which hadn't, in the view of old hands, helped matters one little bit.

"Denshawai flavours most things," said Owen slowly. "I don't know that it is particularly important in this case. How closely was Nuri Pasha involved?"

"Not very," said Mahmoud. "Which is why my assumption may be quite wrong."

He looked around him.

"And also why," he went on breezily, "I should get on with my reconstruction before the remaining half million of the Cairo population arrive on the scene to help me."

The number of people on the Place was indeed beginning to grow. The first water-cart was coming down the Sharia el Maghrabi spraying water behind it to keep down the dust. The first forage camels were weaving their way along the Ezbekiyeh Gardens, great stacks bobbing precariously on their backs. The cab-men and donkey-boys lunched their animals on green forage, and from dawn a steady train of camels slouched over the Nile bridge to supply them. The first donkeys, laden with heavy blocks of ice wrapped in dirty sacking, were making their way to the hotels. People who had slept on the pavement, or on the wall next to the railings of the Gardens, or in the gutter (which was probably safer since they could not fall off) were beginning to stir. In the early morning it was sometimes quite difficult to get along because of the number of men lying about with their faces covered like corpses, sleeping as soundly as the dead. Now, as he watched some of the white or blue-gowned figures get to their feet, Owen was suddenly reminded of apocalyptic accounts of Judgement Day that he had heard from Welsh preachers. Not normally given to such visions himself, he thrust it out of his mind and concentrated on Mahmoud's reconstruction. The Parquet followed French practice and usually required a "reconstruction" of a crime by its investigators, and Owen, whose knowledge of standard police procedures was limited, was interested in seeing how Mahmoud approached it. Briskly, it appeared.

The Egyptian went over to a mark he had scuffed in the dust.

"Nuri Pasha," he said, "was about here, facing out across the Place towards the Ezbekiyeh Gardens."

"According to Fakhri?"

"And others."

Mahmoud pointed to where a man was relieving himself in the road.

"Fakhri's arabeah was about there."

"He would have had a good view," said Owen.

"Yes," said Mahmoud, "I think he did. Though between him and Nuri Pasha there were a lot of people."

"Did you find any of them?"

"Yes. The first they knew of it was a loud bang. They looked round to see Nuri Pasha falling—"

"Why was he falling?" asked Owen. "He wasn't hit."

"Don't know," said Mahmoud. "I'll have to ask him. Reflex, perhaps."

He darted back and affected to stumble.

"An old man," he said. "Dazed, winded and scared. Perhaps half-stunned. Anyway, he lay approximately here until about five hundred people took it upon themselves to carry him into the hotel."

"Who took the initiative?"

"As I was saying," said Mahmoud, "about five hundred of them. Each one says."

He looked up and down the road and then walked over to another mark.

"Meanwhile, an ordinary fellah who had attempted to run away immediately after the shot was seized and brought to the ground, or tripped, or just fell over, about here. Definite, because he stayed there, unconscious, till the police came and one constable, brighter than most, marked the spot."

"That's where he was taken," said Owen. "Where was he when he fired the shot?"

"Or when the shot was fired. Don't know. Fakhri Bey said he moved to the right, so if we move to the left—" He counted out four paces. "He might have been standing here."

"About twelve feet from Nuri."

"In which case," said Mahmoud, "why didn't he hit him?"

"It's more difficult than you might think," said Owen, "even at twelve feet. Especially if you've never fired a revolver before."

"Which might well have been the case," said Mahmoud. "Why is it so difficult?"

"It kicks back in your hand when you fire," said Owen. "If you're not holding it properly the barrel jerks upward."

"If the shot went upward," said Mahmoud, "how did it hit the lemonade-seller?"

"Could have ricocheted."

"Off what?"

Mahmoud moved back to where Nuri Pasha had been standing. Owen took up the position they had guessed at for the assailant.

"Off the statue," said Owen. "Maybe."

They went over to the statue of Ibrahim Pasha and examined it.

Mahmoud put his finger on a mark.

"Yes?" he said.

"Yes."

They became aware that a small crowd was watching them with interest.

"I think your half million is beginning to arrive," said Owen.

"It's unreal to reconstruct without a crowd," said Mahmoud. "It's impossible with one."

He walked across the Place to where Fakhri might have observed the scene from his arabeah. For a moment he stood there looking. Then he walked slowly back to Owen.

"Just fixing it in my mind," he said, "before I talk to them."

Two heavily laden brick carts emerged at the same time from adjoining streets and then continued across the Place abreast of each other. A car coming out of the Sharia el Teatro was obliged to brake suddenly and skidded across in front of two arabeahs which had just pulled out of the pavement. All three drivers jumped down from their vehicles and began to abuse the drivers of the brick carts, who themselves felt obliged to descend to the ground, the better to put their own point of view. Other vehicles came to a halt and other drivers joined in. Some Passover sheep, painted in stripes and with silver necklaces around their necks, which had been trotting peacefully along beside the Ezbekiyeh Gardens, abandoned the small boy who was herding them and wandered out into the middle of the traffic. In a moment all was confusion and uproar. The Place, that is, had returned to normal.

"That," said Mahmoud resignedly, "is that."

ᏯᎳᎵᎧ

The two had taken a liking to each other and Mahmoud, unusually for the Parquet, invited Owen to be present at his interrogation. It took place in the Police Headquarters at the Bab el Khalk. They were shown into a bare, green-painted room on the ground floor which looked out on to an enclosed square across which the prisoner was brought from his cell.

He looked dishevelled and his eyes were bloodshot but otherwise he seemed to have completely recovered from his heavy drugging. He looked at them aggressively as the police led him in. In Owen's experience a fellah, or peasant, caught for the first time in the toils of the alien law tended to respond either with truculent aggression or with helpless bewilderment. This one was truculent.

After the preliminaries Mahmoud got down to business.

"Your name?"

"Mustafa," the man growled.

"Where are you from?"

"El Deyna is my village," he said reluctantly.

El Deyna was a small village on the outskirts of old Cairo just beyond the Citadel.

"You have work in the fields," said Mahmoud. "What brought you to the city yesterday?"

"I came to kill Nuri Pasha," said the other uncompromisingly.

"And why did you want to kill Nuri Pasha?"

"He dishonoured my wife's sister."

"Your story will be checked," said Mahmoud.

He waited to see if this had any effect on the man but it did not.

"How did he dishonour your wife's sister?"

Mustafa did not reply. Mahmoud repeated the question. Again there was no response. The fellah just sat, brawny arms folded.

Mahmoud tried again.

"Others will tell us if you do not," he said.

The man just sat stubbornly there.

"Come, man," said Mahmoud, not unkindly. "We are only trying to get at the truth that lies behind this business."

"There is one truth for the rich," the villager said bitterly, "and another for the poor."

"The truth we seek," said Mahmoud, "is not necessarily that for the rich."

"The rich have all the weapons," the man said, "and you are one of the weapons."

Unexpectedly, Mahmoud seemed to flinch.

"I would not have it so," he said mildly.

The man had noticed Mahmoud's reaction. It seemed to mollify him.

"Nor I," he said, mildly, too. "I would not have it so."

He rubbed his unshaven chin.

"Others will tell you," he said. "My wife's family works in the fields for Nuri Pasha. One day Nuri went by. He saw my wife's sister. He said: "Tell her to bring some melons to the house." She brought the melons and a man took her in. He took her to a dark room and Nuri came to her."

"That was wrong," said Mahmoud, "but it was wrong also to try to kill for that."

"What was I to do?" the man said passionately. "I am a poor man and it is a big family. Now she is with child. Before, there was one mouth and she could work in the fields. A man wanted her and would have taken her at a low price. Now there are two mouths and she has been dishonoured. No one will take her now except at a large price. And how can I find a large price for her?"

Unconsciously he had laid his hand on the table palm uppermost as if he was pleading with Mahmoud.

"How?" he repeated vehemently. "How? I have children of my own."

Mahmoud leaned across the table and touched him sympathetically on the arm.

"There is worse, friend," he said. "How will they manage without you when you when you are gone?"

The passion went out of the man's face.

"There will be money," he said, and bowed his head, "without me."

"How can that be," asked Mahmoud softly, "when you have none?"

"Others will provide."

"What others? Your family?"

"Others."

Both sides seemed to consent to a natural pause, which lasted for several minutes. Owen was impressed. He knew that if he had been conducting the interrogation, in the distant English way, he would never have reached the man as Mahmoud had done.

Mahmoud leaned forward now and touched Mustafa on the sleeve.

"Tell me, brother," he said, "about your visit to the city yesterday."

"I went to the city," said the man, almost as if he was reciting, "and there were many people. I was one of a crowd. And I saw that bad one and I fired my gun at him. And he fell over, and I gave thanks to Allah."

"How did you know where to find the bad one?" asked Mahmoud.

The man frowned.

"I do not know," he admitted. "He was suddenly there before me."

"Someone told you, I expect," said Mahmoud.

The man did not pick this up.

"Have you been to the Place before?"

Mustafa shook his head.

"Never."

"And yet you knew where to find him," Mahmoud observed.

He waited, but again the man did not pick it up.

Mahmoud switched.

"Where did you get the gun?"

The man did not reply.

"Did the one who told you where to find the bad one also give you the revolver?"

Again there was no reply.

"If the rich have their weapons," said Mahmoud, "and I am one of them, you, too, are a weapon. Who is wielding you?"

"Not the rich!"

"When the tool is broken it is thrown away."

"I am not broken," said the man defiantly.

"As a tool you are broken. As a weapon."

"My task is done," said the man. "I am satisfied."

"Nuri is still alive."

The man looked at him, startled.

"Didn't you know? The shot missed."

"Is that the truth?"

"On the Book."

The man buried his face in his hands.

"I am a poor weapon."

"You have fed too much on the drug," said Mahmoud.

"It gave me the power," said the man from behind his hands.

"It took away your power."

The man shook his head.

"Who gave it to you?"

"A man."

"The same who gave you the gun?"

Again the shake of the head.

"The one who showed you where to find Nuri Pasha?"

The shaking had become continuous. Owen doubted now if it meant negation.

"The one who will provide for your family when you are gone?" Mahmoud went on inexorably.

The shaking stopped and the man raised his head.

"Inshallah," he said. "If God wills."

He would say no more and after several further attempts to resume the conversation Mahmoud ordered him to be returned to the cells.

☙

That afternoon they went to el Deyna. Mahmoud decided, on the spur of the moment, that he would like to talk to Mustafa's family. Then, equally on the spur of the moment, he decided he would ask Owen to go with him.

Owen accepted at once. He liked Mahmoud and, besides, he had grown sensitive enough to Arab style by now to know that if he did not respond with equal warmth it would immediately chill the relationship that was developing between them.

He was, however, a little surprised. Relations between the ministries were not normally as close as this. He wondered whether the invitation was solely the product of an impulse of friendliness. Mahmoud was no fool. Perhaps, operating alone in what might turn out to be politically sensitive areas, he felt the need to guard his back. If so, Owen could certainly sympathize with him.

They met after lunch at the Ataba el Khadra, the terminus for most of the Cairo tramways, and took a tram to the Citadel.

Although it was still relatively early in the afternoon, and extremely hot, the Ataba was, as always, full of people. The ordinary population of Cairo was still impressed by trams and treated them very seriously. To board a tram at the terminus meant forcing one's way through a mass of street-sellers, all concerned that the passengers might perish en route for lack of sustenance. Water-sellers, peanut-sellers, lemonade-sellers, Turkish-delight-sellers, sellers of tartlets, sweets and sherbet competed for custom.

The tram itself was, of course, crowded. Passengers hung over the driver in his cab and shared his agitation at the continual excesses of arabeah drivers. They bulged out of the tram itself and clung on to the steps. One or two hardy spirits climbed up on to the roof, from which they were dislodged with difficulty by a determined constable, only to be replaced by equally tenacious clamberers at the next stop.

Owen enjoyed all this, but even he had had enough, in the heat, by the time they got to the Citadel. They changed with relief into the small bus which would take them out into the country.

Here, too, there was difficulty in finding a seat. A large fellahin woman with a load of water-melons occupied the whole rear of the bus.

"Come, mother," said Mahmoud. "Move your fruit. They take up more space than people."

The woman started to move the melons and then looked up at Mahmoud.

"Why is the Englishman here?" she asked in Arabic, not thinking that Owen understood.

"He is with me," said Mahmoud.

"He should be in a motor-car," said the woman, "or in an arabeah."

The bus had fallen quiet.

Conscious that she held the stage, the woman reached over and picked up two large melons.

She showed them to the passengers.

"Two fine ones," she said.

She cast a sidelong glance at Owen.

"As big as your balls, Englishman," she added, giving the other passengers a wink.

"As big as they would need to be, woman," said Owen, "were I your husband."

The bus exploded with delighted laughter.

The woman moved her melons, with good grace now, having enjoyed the exchange as much as anyone else, and Owen and Mahmoud sat down.

In a way, it was nothing, but Owen had sensed a current of feeling in the bus that had surprised him. Most Englishmen in Egypt would have said that the country-dwelling fellahin were all right, that it was only in the city that there was trouble. He had defused the current so far as he was concerned and the atmosphere was now quite relaxed. But that it should exist at all was significant.

Mahmoud must have sensed the current, too, for throughout the rest of the journey he kept the conversation at the level of general chit-chat, in Arabic.

The village omda, or headman, showed them to Mustafa's house.

It was a mud brick house with three rooms and a ladder going up to the roof. The floor was beaten earth. In the first room, at night, a donkey and a water-buffalo lay down together. In the inner rooms the family lived, ate and slept. On the roof were the household stores and the rabbits.

There seemed to be at least eight or nine people in the inner rooms, two old people and six or seven children. When the omda explained the purpose of the visit, they all retreated into the furthest room, leaving Mustafa's wife alone with Mahmoud, Owen and the omda. She held her veil up in front of her face the whole time they were there.

They sat down cross-legged on the floor. After a moment Mahmoud began.

"Tell me about your husband," he said. "Is he a good man?"

There seemed to be a shy nod of assent.

"Does he beat you?"

Owen could not detect any response, but the omda said: "He is a good man. He beats her only when she deserves it."

"Your children: does he beat them?"

This time there was no mistaking the denial.

"Those old ones: are they your family or his?"

"One is hers. One is his," said the omda.

"Tell me about your sister," said Mahmoud.

The woman put the veil completely over her face and bowed her head down almost to her knees.

Mahmoud waited, but she said nothing.

"I am not here to judge," he said, "merely to know."

The woman bent her body to the left and right in agitation but could not bring herself to reply in speech.

"She is ashamed," said the omda. "Her family is dishonoured."

"And Mustafa felt this shame greatly?" asked Mahmoud.

The woman seemed to signify assent.

"He took it into his heart?"

More definite this time.

Mahmoud turned to the omda.

"He spoke about it? Some nurse a hurt in silence, others speak it out."

"He spoke it out," said the omda.

Mahmoud considered for a moment or two.

"It is hard to bear dishonour," he said at last, "but sometimes it is better to bear dishonour than to lift your hand against the great."

"True," said the omda neutrally, "but sometimes a dishonour is too great to be borne."

"Was that so with Mustafa?"

"I do not know," said the omda. "Mustafa is a good man."

Mahmoud turned back to the woman and shifted tack.

"Where is your sister staying?" he asked.

"With friends," said the omda.

"In her village or in this?"

"She will not show her face," said the omda, "either in her village or in this."

"What will happen when her child comes?" asked Mahmoud. "It is a lot to ask of friends."

The omda was silent. "I do not know," he said at last.

The woman broke in unexpectedly.

"She will stay with me," she said determinedly.

The omda looked troubled but said nothing.

"How will you manage?" asked Mahmoud.

"The way we have always managed," said the woman bitterly.

"It is hard for a woman to manage alone," said Mahmoud. "Even if she is used to it."

The eyes above the veil seemed to flash.

"When did your husband begin taking hashish?"

The omda made to answer but the woman cut across him.

"He has always taken hashish," she said, "a little."

"But recently," said Mahmoud, "he has started taking more."

Again the eyes seemed to register the remark, but otherwise there was no response.

"Where did he get it?"

"There are always those willing to sell," said the omda.

"Whom you know?"

The omda spread his hands. "Alas, no," he said.

"There are always those willing to sell," said Mahmoud. "At a price."

He leaned forward and addressed the woman directly.

"Money for hashish," he said, "comes at the cost of money for food. His family was hungry. Why did he buy hashish?"

"It made him strong," the woman said.

"Strong in the fields? Or strong in the bed?"

"In the bed," said the woman. "In the fields, too."

"He feared he was losing his strength in the bed?"

"Yes," said the woman.

Mahmoud looked across at Owen.

Owen knew what he was thinking. In villages of this sort bilharzia was rife. Among the symptoms of the disease in males was a kind of overall sensual lassitude which the fellahin often took for loss of sexual potency.

"Your husband has the worm?"

"Yes."

It was common for fellahin to take hashish to counter the lassitude. Ironically, it aggravated the very condition they feared.

In the room behind a small child began to cry. It was hushed by the grandmother but then began to cry again more determinedly. Another joined it.

The woman stirred.

Mahmoud put up his hand.

"One question more: in this last week your husband has come upon a great supply of the drug. Where did he get it from?"

"I do not know," said the woman.

"Have strangers been to the village?"

"No," said the omda.

Mahmoud ignored him.

"Has a stranger been to your house?"

"No."

"Has your husband talked to strangers?"

"I do not know."

"Has he spoken to you of the drug?"

"He never speaks to me of the drug," said the woman bitterly.

Mahmoud sat back and regarded the woman for a moment or two without speaking. Then he suddenly leaned forward.

"Listen to me," he said to the woman, speaking slowly and emphatically. "I believe your husband to be a foolish man and not a bad one. He is a tool in the hands of others. I promise you I will try to see that his punishment fits foolishness and not badness. But I need to know whose are the hands that hold the tool. Think about it. Think long and hard."

He turned to the omda.

"And you," he said, "think, too. Think doubly long and hard. Or else you will find yourself in trouble."

☙

A servant showed them through the house and out into the garden, where Nuri Pasha was waiting for them.

He was sitting in the shade of a large eucalyptus tree, a gold-topped cane between his knees and a rug about his shoulders. His head was resting on the back of the chair and from a distance it looked as if he was asleep, but as they drew nearer Owen saw that the apparently closed eyes were watching them carefully.

"Monsieur le Parquet! And—" the watchful eyes lingered a little on Owen—"le Mamur Zapt!"

Servants brought up wickerwork chairs.

"I was," said Nuri Pasha, "about to have a late tea. Would you care to join me? Or something stronger perhaps?"

"Thank you," said Owen. "Tea would be very welcome."

He did not know how strict a Muslim Mahmoud was.

Nuri, it was clear, was a very Europeanized Egyptian. He spoke English perfectly, though with a suggestion that he would rather be speaking French. He was dressed in a dark jacket and light, pin-striped trousers. His shirt was impeccably white and he wore a grey silk tie fastened with a large gold pin.

"Tea, then."

Already, across the lawn servants were bringing a table and teathings. The table was spread with an immaculate white cloth. The teapot was silver, the cups of bone china. One of the servants poured the tea and then retired into the background.

"Good," said Nuri, sipping his tea.

He put the cup back in the saucer.

"And now, what can I do for you two gentlemen?"

"If it would not distress you," said Mahmoud, "I would like to hear your account of what happened in the Place de l'Opéra."

"Of course, dear boy," said Nuri. "I am only too glad to be able to assist the Parquet. Especially," he smiled, "in the circumstances."

He seemed, however, to be in no hurry to begin. His eyes wandered across the flowerbeds to the other side of the lawn.

"Beautiful!" he whispered.

Owen thought at first that he was referring to the freesia or the stocks, or perhaps to the bougainvillaea in bloom along the wall which surrounded the garden, but as he followed the direction of Nuri's gaze he saw that the Pasha was looking at a young peasant girl who was walking along a raised path just beyond the wall with a tall jar on her head.

"Beautiful," breathed Nuri again.

"If I was younger," he said regretfully, "I'd send someone to fetch her. Those girls, when they are washed, are very good in bed. They regard an orgasm as a visitation from Allah. When I was young—"

He went into graphic detail.

The story came to an end and Nuri sat for a moment sunk in the memory of past pleasures.

Owen stretched out a hand towards the cucumber sandwiches. The shadow of a kite hawk fell on the table and he looked up hurriedly, but the hawk was wheeling far above. He helped himself to the sandwich. Sometimes, at the Sporting Club, the hawks would snatch the food out of your very hand.

Mahmoud ventured a little cough.

"The Place de l'Opéra," he murmured.

Nuri affected a start.

"I am so sorry," he said. "Monsieur le Parquet does right to recall us to our business." He looked at Mahmoud with a glint of amusement in his eyes. "I hope my reminiscences did not bore you?"

"Oh no," protested Mahmoud. "Not at all."

"Ah? Well, in that case perhaps you would like to hear about the peasant girl on one of my estates. She—"

He stopped with a grin.

"Or perhaps not. You are busy men. And it is not every day that one receives a visit from the Mamur Zapt."

"I shall enjoy reading your memoirs," said Owen.

"I am afraid," said Nuri, with real regret, "that the best bits have to be left out. Even in Egypt."

"The Place de l'Opéra," murmured Mahmoud doggedly.

"The Place de l'Opéra," said Nuri. "Just so."

Even then he shot off at a tangent.

"The case," he said. "How is it going?"

"All right," said Mahmoud, caught off guard. "We are making progress."

"Ah? What have you found out?"

"We are only at the beginning," said Mahmoud reluctantly.

"Nothing, then?"

"We are holding a man."

"The fellah?"

"Yes."

Nuri waved a dismissive hand.

"A tool," he said.

Mahmoud rallied determinedly.

"A number of points have emerged from my inquiries," he said, "some of which are interesting and which I would like to check. Against your account."

"Oh?" said Nuri. "What interesting points?"

"That, I shall not be altogether certain of until I have heard your account," said Mahmoud blandly.

Nuri threw up his hands with a laugh.

"You have beaten me!" he conceded. It was evidently his way to play games.

He signalled to one of the servants, who came up and rearranged the rug round the old man's shoulders.

"I will tell you what happened," said Nuri, "although I am afraid it will be a very sketchy account."

"Even that may help," said Mahmoud.

"Yes," said Nuri sceptically. "It may."

He leaned back in the chair and closed his eyes.

"I had been meeting colleagues—former colleagues, I should say—in the Hotel Continental. When the meeting was over I went to find my arabeah. It was not there, so I went out into the Place to look for it. Suddenly—" his eyes opened—"I saw a man in front of me raising a gun."

"How close?"

"From me to you. Perhaps a little more."

Mahmoud waited for Nuri to think back.

"And then?"

Nuri frowned.

"And then I don't know what happened."

"Were you conscious of the gun going off?"

"I heard a shot. Yes, I certainly heard a shot. And I fell down. Though whether before or after or at the same time I really cannot remember. Everything is very hazy."

"You may have dazed yourself in falling," said Mahmoud.

"The doctor thinks so," said Nuri. "He claims to detect a bruise on the back of my head. I must say, I am not conscious of it myself, but then, my livelihood does not depend on finding bumps on other people."

"You did see the man with the gun, though. Could you describe him?"

"Not very well. I saw him only fleetingly."

"Was he dressed in European clothes?"

Nuri looked at him. "I have heard the accounts of my would-be assassin," he said drily, "and you yourself confirmed that he was a fellah."

Mahmoud apologized.

"I was merely trying to prompt you to recall exactly what you saw," he said. "Was he young or old, for instance, what kind of galabeah was he wearing?"

"I do not," said Nuri Pasha, "bother to distinguish one fellah from another."

There was a little silence.

"In any case," said Nuri, "the fellah is not the one that matters. He is merely a tool."

"Have you any idea," asked Owen, "who might be using him as a tool?"

"I am afraid not."

"Can you think of anyone who would wish to kill you?"

Nuri looked at Owen with surprise.

"Mon cher," he said, *"Every*body wants to kill me. *Tout le monde."*

"Come," said Owen, "you have enemies enough, I am sure, anyone in your position is bound to, but there is a difference between having an enemy and having an enemy who wants to kill you."

"You are right," said Nuri Pasha, "if a trifle literal. I am plainly guilty of exaggeration. Let me try to be more accurate. Only half the population of Egypt wants to kill me. The other half would just be happy to see it happen." He laughed, and then put his hand on Owen's arm. "I joke, *mon cher*," he said, "but it is no joke really."

Owen nodded.

The word "Denshawai" did not need to be spoken.

Nuri's eyes wandered away again across the garden. The girl had gone, however.

"The fellah who tried to shoot you," said Mahmoud, "had a personal grudge against you."

"Oh yes," said Nuri.

"It appears you took a liking to his wife's sister—a peasant girl, like the one we saw. Only on that occasion you did send for her."

"Really?" said Nuri, without much interest. "If so, she would have been well paid."

"It is just that it gives a motive," said Mahmoud, "sufficient in itself. We do not necessarily have to look for an ulterior one. The affair, that is," he ended carefully, "may be merely a private one."

"Since when," asked Nuri, "has the Mamur Zapt been interested in affairs which are merely private?"

"Have you received any threatening letters?" asked Owen.

Nuri made a gesture of dismissal.

"*Mon cher!*" he said, almost reproachfully. "Dozens!"

"Recently? In the last two weeks?"

"I expect so," said Nuri. "It is not the part of my mail to which I give the greatest attention."

He looked at Owen.

"You would not expect a killer to give warning, surely?"

"It happens surprisingly often," said Owen.

Nuri laughed. "I expect it is the weakness for rhetoric characteristic of those engaged in politics," he said.

He glanced at Mahmoud.

"Especially Egyptian politics."

"Not just Egyptian," said Owen. "However, there is a different explanation. The terrorist clubs tend to contact their targets first. Especially," he added, looking directly at Nuri, "when they are trying to extort money."

Nuri shook his head.

"If they had asked for money I would probably have paid."

"You have received a communication, then?"

"I was speaking generally."

Nuri leaned back in his chair and called to one of his servants. The man disappeared into the house.

"You must speak to Ahmed," he said. "He deals with my mail."

A sulky young Egyptian came out of the house. He seemed to walk across the lawn deliberately slowly, placed himself directly in front of Nuri, with his back to Owen and Mahmoud, and said:

"Yes?"

"Mon cher," said Nuri reproachfully. "We have guests."

The young man deigned to throw them a glance.

"Interesting guests," said Nuri. *"Le Parquet et le Mamur Zapt."*

The glance the young man threw now was one of undisguised hostility.

Nuri sighed.

"Our guests were asking if I have received any threatening letters recently?"

"You always receive threatening letters," said the young man harshly. "Deservedly."

"I would like to see," said Owen, "any that have been received in the last three weeks."

The young man looked at Nuri.

"Please!" said Nuri. "If you have not already consigned them to the wastepaper basket as they deserve."

"Very well," said the young man, "if you wish."

He went off into the house.

Nuri regarded him fondly.

"My son," he said, "by a slave girl. He hates me."

Ahmed returned with a sheaf of papers which he gave to Nuri, who in turn passed them to Owen.

They were very much as Owen had expected: abusive letters from individuals, either badly written or in the ornate script of the bazaar letter-writer; scurrilous attacks by obscure radical organizations, darkly hinting that Nuri would get his deserts; savage denunciations by extremist religious groups, threatening retribution; and the expected extortionary letters from the new political "clubs" which had sprung up in such profusion in the last couple of years.

There were four letters in this last category and Owen found no "club" names among them that he did not recognize. This should make it comparatively easy to check them out.

He passed the sheaf on to Mahmoud.

"I'd like to keep them for a bit, if I may," he said.

"Of course."

"Can I go?" asked Ahmed.

Nuri looked at Owen.

"Unless the Mamur Zapt wishes for something else?" he said.

Owen shook his head. The young man turned away immediately.

Nuri sighed.

The interview came to an end soon after and a servant showed them out.

They went into the house through a large, cool room, all marble and tiles, in which several people were sitting with drinks in their hands.

Among them was Ahmed. As Owen and Mahmoud entered, he ostentatiously turned his back. The woman beside him looked up at Owen with amusement. Owen caught a glimpse of a strong, beaky face and dark hair.

The other guests treated them with polite indifference. They were for the most part elderly, wealthy, Europeanized.

In the upper levels of Cairene society it was fairly usual for women to be present and for alcohol to be served; but, Owen reflected, had any of the fundamentalist groups which had written to Nuri been watching, it would have added fuel to their denunciations.

He and Mahmoud walked back to the main street to find an arabeah. By mutual consent they walked slowly. In this wealthy suburb of Cairo the bougainvillaea spilled over the walls and the pepper trees and eucalyptus hung out across the road making it cool and shady. From the green recesses of the trees came a continuous purring and gurgling of doves.

"A clear-cut case," said Mahmoud. "Circumstantial evidence, motive, confession."

"Believe it?"

"Not for one moment," said Mahmoud.

Chapter 3

Owen could not give all his time to the Nuri Pasha affair. He had his ordinary work to do.

This morning it was the demonstration. One of his men had picked the rumour up in el Azhar, Cairo's great Islamic university. It was supposed to be taking place that afternoon once the sun had moved off the streets. Intelligently, the man was staying in the university so that he could keep an eye on developments. His reports came every hour. It looked as if the thing was definitely on.

According to his most recent information, the demonstration would take place in Abdin Square, in front of the Khedive's Palace. The students intended to march there in procession from the university. They would make their way in separate groups through the narrow mediaeval streets which surrounded el Azhar and assemble in the wider Bab Zouweleh before the Mouayad Mosque. Then they would march along the Sharia Taht er Rebaa, cross the Place Bab el Khalk and proceed past the Ecole Khediviale de Droit, at which point they would join the law students. From there it was a short step to Abdin Square.

"Mounted?" asked Nikos.

Nikos was the Mamur Zapt's official secretary, a sharp young Copt.

Owen nodded.

"With foot in reserve to mop up. I've already spoken to McPhee."

"I'll check," said Nikos, rolling up the street plan.

"And, just in case," said Owen, "I want both entrances to Abdin Square sealed off."

"Both?"

"The two on the eastern side. The Gami'a Abdin as well as the Bab el Khalk."

"It shouldn't be necessary," said Nikos.

"I know. But I don't want to risk any of them getting into Abdin Square."

Nikos inclined his head to show that he had understood. He reached across the desk, took some papers from the out-tray and stuffed them under his arm along with the street map.

"It means more men," he said. "Wouldn't a small mounted troop in the square do instead?"

"No. It would look bad."

Nikos raised dark eyebrows. "That worries you?"

"A bit," Owen conceded.

"The Khedive is hardly going to complain."

"He might," said Owen. "Just to be difficult."

Nikos made a dismissive gesture. He had a Cairene contempt for the powerless.

From along the corridor came the chink of cups and a strong aroma of coffee.

"It's not that, though," said Owen. "It's the way it might come across in the papers. The international ones, I mean."

Especially now, he thought, with the new Liberal Government in England feeling extremely sensitive about international opinion after the Denshawai business and trying to get out. He wondered how much Nikos knew. Enough, he suspected. Nikos wasn't stupid.

Nor, in fact, was the Khedive. He was adept at finding pretexts to cause diplomatic trouble. There were plenty ready to help him. France for one, which had never forgiven the British for the way they had stayed on after crushing the Arabi rebellion. Turkey for another. After all, Egypt was still in theory a province of the Ottoman Empire, with a head of state, the Khedive, who owed allegiance to the Sultan at Istanbul.

In theory. In practice, the British ran it, and Egypt's real ruler, for over thirty years now, had been the British Agent, first Cromer and now Gorst. The Khedive appointed his Ministers and they were responsible to him through the Prime Minister and Cabinet for their management of the Departments of State. But at the top of each great Ministry Cromer had put one of his men. They did not direct, they advised; but they expected their advice to be taken, and if it was not, well, there was always the Army: the British Army, not the Egyptian.

And then, of course, there was the Mamur Zapt.

That was the reality. But it did not mean that appearances could be dispensed with. Egypt was still in principle a sovereign state, the Khedive still an independent sovereign. The British presence needed explaining.

The British story was that they were there by invitation and on a temporary basis. They would withdraw once Egypt's finances were sorted out. Only they had been there for thirty years now.

His Majesty's Government thought it best, in the circumstances, to emphasize that the British role in Egypt was purely an advisory one. The British Agent merely suggested, never instructed; the "advisers" made "recommendations," not decisions; and the Army was kept off-stage. Appearances were important.

And so it would not do for the students to demonstrate outside the Palace. It would give all sorts of wrong impressions.

Nikos, of course, understood all this perfectly well. Indeed, like many sophisticated Cairenes, he rather enjoyed the ambiguities of the situation. Not all Egyptians, naturally, had such a developed taste for irony.

Curiously, the British themselves were not entirely at home with the position either. It was too complicated for the military and, even under Cromer's strong hand, there was always tension between the civil Administration, conscious of the diplomatic need to preserve appearances, and the Army, impatient to cut through the web of subtleties, evasions and unstated limitations.

The Mamur Zapt inhabited the shadow between the two.

"Keep McPhee informed," he told Nikos. "I'm going out later."

He had an appointment with Mahmoud.

As Nikos left he nearly collided in the doorway with Yussuf, who spun the tray away just in time. Clicking his tongue at the departing Nikos, he slid the tray on to Owen's desk.

"The bimbashi has a visitor," he announced. Yussuf was a great purveyor of news. "He told me to bring the cups."

Like McPhee, Owen had his own service-issue mug, which Yussuf now half-filled with coffee. When they had visitors a proper set of cups was produced.

"Oh," said Owen, and then, pretending interest so as not to hurt Yussuf's feelings, "who is he?"

"From the Palace, I think," said Yussuf, gratified. "The bimbashi looked unhappy."

McPhee always found relations with the Khedive's staff very difficult. On the one hand, he had great respect for royalty, even foreign royalty; on the other, he knew that not all the Khedive's requests were to be met. Some were acceptable to the British Agent, others were not, and McPhee lacked the political sense to know which was which. The adroit politicians of the Khedive's personal staff ran rings round him, forever laying traps which he was forever falling into.

Owen was responsible through Garvin directly to the British Agent and had little to do with the Khediviate, something for which he was very grateful.

On this occasion, however, he was unable to keep out. Shortly after he had heard Yussuf's slippers slapping away down the corridor, he heard them slap-slapping back. Yussuf appeared in the doorway.

"The Bimbashi would like you to join him," he recited.

He saw that Owen had not finished his coffee.

"I bring you a cup," he said.

The man from the Khedive was a Turk in his late fifties, with close-cropped hair and a grey, humourless face.

"Guzman Bey," said McPhee.

He introduced Owen as the Mamur Zapt. The other barely nodded. Owen returned the greeting as indifferently as it was given.

McPhee sat stiff and uncomfortable.

"It's about Nuri Pasha," he said to Owen. "The Khedive is very concerned."

"Naturally," said Owen.

"He would like to know what progress has been made."

"It's very early days yet," said Owen, "but I believe the Parquet have the matter well in hand."

"What progress?" said the man harshly.

"A man is held. He has confessed."

Guzman made a gesture of dismissal.

"The others?" he said.

"The Parquet has only just begun its investigations," Owen pointed out.

"The Parquet!" said the man impatiently. "And you? The Mamur Zapt?"

"The case is primarily the concern of the Parquet," said Owen. "I am interested only in security aspects."

"Precisely. That is what interests the Khedive."

"I am following the case," said Owen.

"No progress has been made?"

"As I said—" Owen began.

The man cut him short. "The British are responsible for security," he said to McPhee. "What sort of security is this when a statesman like Nuri Pasha is gunned down in the street?"

"He was not gunned down," said Owen.

"Thanks to Allah," said the man. "Not to you."

Owen was not going to be provoked.

"The Khedive has many valued friends and allies," he said evenly. "It is not easy to protect them all."

"Why should they need protection?" said the Turk. "That is the question you have to ask."

"That is the question the Khedive has to ask," said Owen, counter-attacking.

The man gave a short bark of a laugh.

"If he is not popular," he said, "then it is because he shares the unpopularity of the British."

Owen drank up his coffee.

"Ah," he said, "I am afraid that is a problem I cannot help you with." He stood up to go. "If you will excuse—"

"The Khedive wants reports."

"Reports?"

"Daily. On the progress you are making in tracking down Nuri Pasha's killers."

"That is a matter for the Parquet."

"And the Mamur Zapt. Or so you said."

"Security aspects only."

"Security," said the Turk, "is what the Khedive is especially interested in."

Owen pulled himself together.

"If the Khedive would genuinely like reports," he said, "then he shall certainly have them."

"Send them to me," said Guzman. "Directly."

"Very well," said Owen. "I'll see you get them directly from the Agent."

"The Khedive has spoken to the Agent. Directly to me. With a copy to the Agent."

Owen found the Turk watching him closely. He put on a charming smile.

"Of course," he said.

"Good!" said the Turk. "See to it." And he walked out.

McPhee swore softly to himself.

"See to it!" he reported. "I'll bloody see to him. Just wait till I get to Garvin!"

"He's very confident," said Owen. "He must have got it fixed already."

"I'll bloody unfix it, then. Or Garvin will. We can't have the Mamur Zapt reporting to the bloody Khedive or where the hell will we be?"

Owen was thinking.

"Gorst must have agreed."

"The stupid bastard!"

There was little liking among the old hands for the liberal Gorst.

"If he has agreed," said Owen, "Garvin will find it hard to get him to change his mind."

"Stupid bastard!" said McPhee again. He got up. "I'll go straight to Garvin."

"Don't let it worry you too much," said Owen.

McPhee stopped and turned and opened his mouth.

"If the Khedive wants reports," said Owen, "he can have them."

He winked deliberately.

"All the same," said McPhee, soothed, "it's the principle—"

Walking back down the corridor Owen thought that it was doubly advisable that no students should get into Abdin Square.

"Yes," said Mahmoud. "The Khedive has been on to us, too."

They were sitting outside an Arab café in one of the small streets off the Place Bab el Khalk. The café was tiny, with one dark inner room in which several Arabs were sitting smoking from nargilehs, the traditional native water pipe, with its hose and water-jar, too cumbersome to be carried around so hired out at cafés. Outside in the street was a solitary table drawn back into the shade of the wall. The café was midway between the Parquet and Owen's office off the Bab el Khalk: on neutral ground.

"Reports?"

Mahmoud nodded. "Daily."

"Why is he so worried?" asked Owen.

Mahmoud shrugged. "Perhaps he's scared. First Nuri, then him."

"There have been others," said Owen. "Why this sudden interest?"

"He knows something that we don't?" offered Mahmoud.

"If he does," said Owen, "he's not going to tell us."

"He has his own people," said Mahmoud.

"Guzman?"

"And others."

A forage mule made its way soporifically towards them. Its load was so huge as almost to span the narrow street. Owen wondered if they would have to move, but at the last moment the mule was twitched aside and the load, bowing almost to the ground, grazed the table.

They were meeting at Mahmoud's request. Later that morning he had rung Owen proposing a coffee before lunch.

Mahmoud waited until the mule had passed on down the street and then said: "I have been checking on the gun."

"Find anything?"

"Part of a consignment missing last March from the barracks at Kantara. They suspected a sergeant but nothing was ever proved. All they could get him for was negligence—he was in charge of the store. He's done six months and is due out about now."

"Probably sold them," said Owen.

Mahmoud nodded. "That's what they thought."

"No lead?"

"He wouldn't talk."

"He won't talk now," said Owen, "especially if he's due out."

"If he was told he'd be all right?"

"Out of the goodness of his heart? No chance."

"If he thought he was just shopping an Egyptian—" suggested Mahmoud tentatively.

His eyes met Owen's.

He could be right, Owen was forced to admit. In the obscure code of the ordinary Tommy, shopping a mere Egyptian might not count.

"Just worth trying."

"I was wondering—" began Mahmoud, and then hesitated.

Owen knew what he was thinking. It would have to be an Englishman and would probably need to be Army rather than civilian.

"Would you like me to have a go?"

"It might be best," said Mahmoud.

୧୧୧୧୬

Owen lunched at the Gezira and then, unusually, went back to his office. Late in the afternoon, when the sun's fierce heat had softened, he went again into the Place Bab el Khalk.

He was in a light linen suit and wore a tarboosh, the pot-like hat of the Egyptian, on his head. With his dark Celtic colouring and the years of sunburn he looked a Levantine of some sort. He carried an Arabic newspaper.

He chose a tea-stall on the eastern side of the Place and perched himself on a stool. The tea-seller brought him a glass of Russian tea.

From where he sat he could see along the Sharia Taht er Rebaa to where the massive battlemented walls of the Mosque el Mouayad rose on the left. One or two little bunches of black-gowned figures were already beginning to spill out on to the sharia. From somewhere behind the Mosque came a confined noise which, as he listened, began to settle down into a rhythmic chanting.

"*Wa-ta-ni. Wa-ta-ni. Wa-ta-ni.*"

The tea-seller came out from the other side of the counter and looked uneasily down the street.

"There will be trouble," he said.

On the pavement behind him a barber was shaving a plump, sleepy-looking Greek. The barber put his razor in the bowl beside the chair and came out on to the street also.

"Yes," he said, peering towards the mosque, "there will be trouble."

The Greek opened one eye. "What trouble?"

"Students," said the barber, wiping the soapsuds off his hands on to his gown.

"Again?" said the Greek. "What is it this time?"

"I don't know," said the barber. "What is it this time?" he called to a bean-seller at an adjoining stall.

The bean-seller was serving some hungry-looking students with bowls of ful madammas, red fava beans cooked in oil and garlic.

"What is it this time?" he asked of them.

"We don't know," said the students. "It is the students of el Azhar, not us."

"They are going to Abdin Square," volunteered one of the students, "to demonstrate against the Khedive."

"Much good that will do," said the bean-seller. "They will just get their heads busted."

"Someone has to," said the student.

"But not you," said the bean-seller firmly.

"You sound like my father," said the student.

"Your father and I," said the bean-seller, "are men of experience. Learn from us."

"Anyway, I cannot go with them today," said the student. "I have my exams tomorrow."

"Have not the el Azhar students exams also?" called the Greek.

The students shook their heads.

"They're not like us," they said.

Owen guessed them to be engineering students. Engineering, like other modern subjects, was studied at the governmental higher schools. At el Azhar, the great Islamic university of Cairo, the students studied only the Koran.

The students finished their bowls and left. The bean-seller began clearing away his stall. At the far end of the Taht er Rebaa a crowd was coming into view.

"You carry on shaving," the Greek ordered. "I don't want you running away before you've finished."

"Who is running away?" said the barber. "There is still plenty of time."

"I am running away," said the bean-seller. "Definitely."

At this time in the afternoon the Place Bab el Khalk was fairly empty. A few women, dressed in black and heavily veiled in this part of the city, were slip-slopping across the square, water-jars on heads, to fetch water for the evening meal. Men sat in the open air cafés or at the street-stalls drinking tea. Children played on the balconies, in the doorways, in the gutter.

The bean-seller apart, no one appeared to be paying much attention to the approaching demonstrators, though Owen knew they were well aware of them. When the time came, they would slip back off the streets—not too far, they wouldn't want to miss anything—and take refuge in the open-fronted shops or in the houses. Every balcony would be crowded.

He could pick out the head of the column distinctly now. They were marching in disciplined, purposeful fashion behind three large green banners and were setting a brisk pace. Behind them the Sharia was packed with black-gowned figures.

Some of the more nervous café-owners were beginning to fold up chairs and tables and move them indoors. Obliging customers picked up their own chairs and took them into the shops and doorways, where they sat down again and continued their absorbing conversations. There were no women on the street now, and children were being called inside.

The barber wiped the last suds from the Greek's face with a brave flourish.

The Greek felt his chin.

"Wait a minute," he said. "What about here?"

"Perfect," said the barber.

"Show me!" commanded the Greek.

The barber reluctantly produced a tin mirror and held it before him.

"It's lop-sided," complained the Greek. "You've done one side and not the other!"

"Both sides I have done," said the barber, casting an uneasy glance down the street. "It is just that one side of your face is longer than the other."

The Greek insisted, and the barber began to snip and scrape at the offending part.

The tea-seller lifted his huge brass urn off the counter and took it up an alleyway. Owen felt in his pocket for the necessary milliemes.

The procession was about a hundred yards away now. At this stage it was still fairly orderly. The students had formed up into ranks about twenty abreast and were marching in a disciplined column, though with the usual untidy fringe around the flanks, which would melt away at the first sign of trouble.

The barber dropped his scissors into a metal bowl with a clang and hurriedly pulled the protective cloth from off the Greek. The Greek stood up and began to wipe his face. The barber threw his things together and made off down a sidestreet. As he went, the Greek dropped some milliemes in the bowl.

Owen folded his newspaper and stepped back into the protective cover of a carpet shop. The shop was, like all the shops, without a front, but the carpets might prove a useful shield if things got really nasty.

The Greek came over and stood beside him.

"Not long now," he said.

The head of the procession entered the Place. Owen's professional eye picked out among the black gowns several figures in European clothes. These were almost certainly not students but full-time retainers of the various political parties, maintained by them to marshal their own meetings and break up those of their rivals.

As the column marched past, the students seemed to become progressively younger. El Azhar took students as young as thirteen, and some of the students at the back of the column could have been no more than fourteen or fifteen.

The procession was now strung out across the Place, the bulk of it in the open space in the middle and the head approaching the street which led up to Abdin Square.

An open car suddenly shot out of a street at right angles to the procession, cut across in front of it and stopped. In it was McPhee.

He stood up and waited for the marchers to halt. The four armed policemen in the car with him leaned over the side of the car and trained their rifles on the front row of the demonstrators.

The procession hesitated, wavered and then came to a stop. Those behind bumped into those in front, spread round the sides and formed a semi-circle around the car.

McPhee began to speak.

The crowd listened in silence for a brief moment and then started muttering. One or two shouts were heard, and then more, and the chanting started up again. The crowd began to press forward at the edges.

Owen saw the first missiles and heard the warning shots.

Then, to the right, came the sound of a bugle and Owen looked up, with the crowd, to see a troop of mounted policemen advancing at the trot.

This was the pride of the Cairo Police: all ex-Egyptian Army cavalry men all with long police service, experienced, tough and disciplined, mounted on best quality Syrian Arab stallions expertly trained for riot work.

They advanced in three rows, spaced out to give the men swinging room.

Each man had a long pick-axe handle tied to his right wrist by a leather thong.

At an order the handles were raised.

And then the troop was among the crowd. Handles rose and fell. The crowd opened up, and there were horses in the gaps, forcing them open still further. They split the crowd into fragments, and round each fragment the horses wheeled and circled, and the sticks rose and fell.

Whenever a group formed, the horses were on to them.

Students fell to the ground and either scrabbled away from the horses' hooves or lay motionless. All over the Place were little crumpled heaps.

And now there were very few groups, just people fleeing singly, and no matter how fast they fled, the horses always outpaced them.

All this while, McPhee had stayed in the car, watching. Now he signalled with his hand, and out of the street behind him emerged a mass of policemen on foot.

They spread out into a long, single line and began to work systematically across the Place.

Anyone who was standing they clubbed. Behind them, in an area of the Place which steadily became larger, there was no one standing at all, just people sitting, dazed, holding their heads, or black gowns stretched out.

The last groups broke and fled, harried by the horses.

"Very expertly done," said the Greek.

A student darted in among the stalls and tables close by them, a rider in hot pursuit. The student threw himself on the ground behind a stack of chairs. The horse halted and the policeman leaned over and hit the student once or twice with his stick. Then he rode away.

The student got to his feet, panting and sobbing. He looked back across the Place and saw the line of foot policemen approaching. In a second he had shot off again.

He reminded Owen of a hare on the run, the same heaving sides, panicked eyes, even, with his turban gone and his shaven head, the hare's laid-back ears.

Another student rushed along behind the row of deserted street-stalls. He brushed right past Owen and then doubled back up an alleyway.

"That one!" snapped Owen. "Follow him! Find out where he goes!"

Georgiades, the Greek, who was one of Owen's best agents, was gone in a flash.

The student was Nuri Pasha's secretary and son, the difficult Ahmed.

☙❧

The tea-seller put the urn back on his stall with a thump. Without asking, he drew a glass of tea and handed it to Owen.

"Watching," he said, "is thirsty work."

The only students on the square now were walking in ones and twos, sometimes supporting a third. Around the edges of the square, though, the foot police were still in action, prising out the students from their hiding-places among the stalls and chairs. Owen was pleased to see that McPhee had them well in hand. It was only too easy for them to get out of control in a situation such as this.

McPhee, helmetless and with his fair hair all over the place, was plainly enjoying himself. His face was lit up with excitement. It was not that he was a violent man; he just loved, as he would have put it, a bit of a scrap. Strange, thought Owen, for he was a civilian, an ex-teacher. On second thoughts perhaps it was not so strange.

He was using a cane, not a pick-handle. He had a revolver at his waist but had not drawn it throughout the whole business, even when he had been threatened in the car.

He was driving slowly round the square now, ostensibly chivvying the students, in fact, Owen noted, calling off his men.

At the far side of the Place the mounted troop had re-formed and was sitting at ease, the horses still excited and breathing heavily, pick-handles now hanging loosely again from the riders' wrists.

Georgiades reappeared.

He spotted the tea-seller and came up to the stall.

"Here is a man who deserves to be favoured of Fortune," he said, "the first man back on the street with his tea."

"I shall undoubtedly be rich," said the tea-seller, "but not yet."

He made Georgiades some mint tea. The Greek took the glass and stood casually by Owen.

"See how our friend is already rewarded!" he said to Owen. "Heads are the only thing damaged on the street today."

"And my head not among them," said the tea-seller.

He took the lid off the urn, looked inside and went to fetch some more water.

Georgiades turned so that he was looking out over the Place.

"Your little friend," he said quietly.

"Yes?" said Owen, equally quietly, and turning, too. They might have been discussing the demonstration.

"You saw where he went?"

Georgiades nodded.

"Not far."

Owen waited. A student limped past.

"Where did he go?"

"To a newspaper office."

"He would!" said Owen. "Which?"

"Al Liwa"

"Might have guessed," said Owen, recalling the chanting he had heard. *Al Liwa* was the recently established organ of the National, or Hisb-el-Watani, Party.

"They'd have heard, anyway," said Georgiades, thinking Owen was worried about the paper's reaction to the breaking up of the demonstration.

"It's not that," said Owen.

He told Georgiades about Nuri Pasha. With another agent he might not have been so forthcoming. The Greek, however, was reliable.

"Funny friends the boy has," said Georgiades, "for a son of Nuri Pasha."

"He hates his father," said Owen, "or so his father told me."

"His father is not very popular with the Nationalists either," said Georgiades, touching his chin where the barber had skimped.

"Yes. Interesting, isn't it?"

"Want me to put a man on him?"

"Not yet. You've got someone on the *al Liwa* offices?"

"Selim. He's quite bright."

"OK. Tell him to keep an eye open for young Ahmed."

Georgiades nodded.

"I'll do a bit of digging, too," he said.

The tea-seller returned, piloting a small boy staggering under the weight of a huge water-jar. Georgiades drained his glass.

"May the streets be full of trouble!" he said to the tea-seller. "So that you can make your fortune."

"Thank you," said the tea-seller, "for your kind wishes."

Chapter 4

Owen had arranged for the sergeant to be brought to the Kasr el Nil barracks and the following morning he went down to interrogate him.

He met Mahmoud at the bridge and they walked into the barracks together.

The guards at the main gate eyed the Egyptian curiously but non-committally and pointed out the administration block, a large, old-fashioned building with lattices and sentry-boxes.

Their way to it took them past a vast, sanded parade ground on which soldiers were drilling. A squad approached them along the edge of the square. As it passed, the drilling sergeant gave them an eyes-right. Owen, who was in Army uniform, acknowledged with a salute. His eye took in their hot, strained faces. New from England, he thought; and fairly new to the Army, too, judging by their awkwardness.

The sentry-boxes and lattices were touched up with white, but inside the administration block everything was a darker, more restful green. A huge three-bladed fan rotated above the heads of the clerks bent at their desks in the orderly room.

One of the clerks collected the passes from Owen and disappeared into an inner room. A moment or two later a corporal came out with them in his hand, greeted Owen and called to a bearer squatting on the floor by the door. The man hurried out.

"It's all laid on, sir," said the corporal. "The escort got in about half an hour ago and is waiting in the guard-room. They'll bring him over directly."

"Fine," said Owen. "Have you got a suitable room?"

"There's one we normally use for this sort of thing," said the corporal. "I'll take you, sir."

He registered Mahmoud's presence.

"Mr. el Zaki," said Owen. "From the Parquet."

"Good morning, sir," said the corporal politely.

"I'd like him to listen in."

"Oh," said the corporal, and hesitated. "A bit difficult, sir," he said, after a moment.

"I don't want anything too special," said Owen. "Is there a room next door? Yes? Well, stick a chair in that and leave the door open. That should be enough."

"Yes, sir," said the corporal, but looked unhappy. His eyes sent desperate signals to Owen, which Owen refused to read. He knew very well what the trouble was. The Army guarded its privileges jealously. One of those was that its soldiers were subject to no legal processes but its own. It would not allow its men to be brought before any civilians, much less Egyptian civilians.

"Mr. el Zaki will not be actually present," he pointed out helpfully.

"I—I know, sir," said the corporal, thinking hard.

"You have the passes."

"Yes, sir." The corporal glanced at them uncomfortably. "They—they don't actually say, sir—" he began with a rush and then stopped.

"They wouldn't," said Owen. He was on tricky ground. He could not insist. "But they do authorize Mr. el Zaki to come with me. And the reason for that is plain, Corporal," he added, with just a little amount of stress, pulling his rank.

"Yes, sir," the corporal responded automatically to the inflection, "of course sir."

"Then—?"

The corporal made up his mind.

"I'll have to check, sir," he said. "Sorry, sir," he added apologetically.

He went off along the corridor. Because of the heat all the rooms had their doors open, and so Owen was able to hear very clearly the explosion at the far end of the building.

"A bloody Gyppy? Certainly not!"

Heavy footsteps hurried down the corridor and a flushed major burst into the room.

"What the—" he began, and then, seeing Mahmoud, stopped.

Even the Army had to make some effort to keep up appearances.

"Would you step this way, Captain?" he said stiffly, and stalked off up the corridor.

In his room he wheeled on Owen.

"What the bloody hell do you think you're doing?"

"I'd like el Zaki to listen in."

"He can't. I'm not having one of our men questioned by a bloody native."

"He's a member of the Parquet, for Christ's sake!"

"Still a bloody native as far as I'm concerned," said the major, "and I'm not having him question one of our men."

"Who the hell said anything about him questioning anybody? I'm questioning. He's listening."

"Same thing."

"It's not the same thing. He'll be in a separate room. All I want is the doors open."

"Can't be done," said the major flatly.

"I'd like it done."

The major's cheeks tightened.

"Would you, now," he said sarcastically. "And just who the hell are you?"

"I'm the Mamur Zapt," said Owen. "And I've got authorization to interrogate, and I'd like to bloody get on with it."

The major looked at him hard. Then he went across to his desk and sat down.

"You're the Mamur Zapt, are you?" He spoke with distaste.

"That's right," said Owen. "OK?"

"You can question him," said the major, with a stress on the "you." "He can't."

"I don't want him to question. I want him to listen."

"He can't."

"I want facilities made available for him to listen in."

The major looked at the papers on his desk.

"It doesn't say anything about that here," he said.

"It doesn't have to."

"For something like this," said the major, "I'd need authorization."

"You don't usually."

"I do this time," said the major. He thought for a moment and then smiled. "Yes," he said, "that's right. For something like this I'd need special authorization. In writing."

"That would be too late. The man's coming out on Thursday."

"Pity!"

Owen considered going over the major's head, directly to the commander-in-chief. He knew one of the Sirdar's aides-de-camp.

The major must have seen him look at the telephone, for he said: "I'd need it in writing. From the Sirdar. Personally."

It would take too long. Even if he got through to John, John would need time to clear it.

The major was watching him. "OK?" he said.

"Not OK," said Owen.

"Dear, dear!"

"There's a certain amount of rush on."

"Difficult."

"Could be," said Owen. "For you."

"Why me?" The major raised eyebrows.

"If things go wrong."

"Why should they?"

Owen carried on as if he hadn't heard.

"Especially if it came out why they went wrong."

"I'll risk that."

All the same the major must have felt a little uneasy, for he said: "You won't get anything out of him. Not if he's coming out on Thursday."

"I'll risk that," said Owen. "It's just that I'd like el Zaki to listen in."

"Didn't you hear?" asked the major. "In writing. From the Sirdar. Personally."

Owen sighed.

"Anything else I can do for you?" asked the major.

"No," said Owen. "Not yet."

He turned to go, then stopped.

"Oh, just one thing—"

"Yes?"

"Major…?"

"Brooker," said the major. "Major Brooker."

"Thank you," said Owen. "That was it."

⚬⚬⚬

"It wasn't my fault, sir," the ex-sergeant said. "I trusted those bloody Gyppies. That bloody 'Assan. He'd got it all figured out. He had his mates outside. 'Course, I was wrong to trust him. That was my mistake."

Ingenuous blue eyes met Owen's. Owen, who did not believe a word of it, decided to play along.

"Tell me about this Hassan," he said.

"Bloody orderly, sir. Used to run messages. 'Ere, there and everywhere. Kept his eyes open. Didn't miss much."

"You think he tipped somebody off?"

"Or let them in, sir. There was a skylight found open. You know, I'd been looking at that bloody skylight a couple of days before. There was only a simple catch on it and I thought to myself: Anyone could open that. But I didn't bother much because it was so small. I thought: Nobody can get in there. But do you know what I think, sir? The way it was done?"

He leaned forward confidentially.

"They slipped in one of those walads. A boy. Probably stripped him naked and greased him all over. Seen it done. At Ismailia. Bloody gang of kids. Went all through the mess. Watches, cash, even your bloody handkerchief. The little bastards. But they got too cocky and the guards caught one of them. Brought the little bugger to me. I caught hold of him and was going to teach him a thing or two but he slipped through my hands. That's how I knew he was greased. Didn't do him much good. The guard caught him with the rifle butt."

"And you think that's what may have happened here?"

"Can't swear to it, sir. But the skylight was open the morning after, and it was only big enough for a kid."

"Could be," Owen agreed.

"'Course, it was my fault, sir," said the man. "I admit that. I should have kept my eyes open. I made a mistake. But I've paid for it."

The weathered, experienced face, which retained a sunburn despite nearly a year's confinement, assumed a virtuous expression.

An old hand at the game, thought Owen. Twenty-five years in the Army, fifteen of them in India. There was not much he didn't know. Three times reduced, each time made up again. Crafty, plausible, he would know how to make himself useful. How willing would he be to be useful now?

"Pity to get into trouble just because of a Gyppy," he said aloud.

"I know, sir," said the ex-sergeant, as if ruefully. "I could have kicked myself."

"It's easy done," said Owen.

"My mistake was to trust the bleeders. I treated them decent. That 'Assan was a useful bloke. Smart. He did me a favour or two, and I did him a few. Used to give him fags. And not say nothing if I caught him smoking in the armoury." He grimaced. "Should have. That was my mistake."

"In the armoury?"

"I know, sir. I dare say that's what gave him the idea."

Thin trickles of sweat ran down on either side of the man's nose. There was no fan in the room and it was very hot. The one window, high up in the wall, was shuttered. The door was closed.

"Did he ever talk?"

"'Assan? He went missing that night."

Very convenient, thought Owen. And part of it might even be true. They might well have used the skylight, might even have slipped a boy in, as the man had said. Only, of course, he knew more about it than he had let on. How much did he know? Not much, if it was just a matter of money passing and agreement to turn a blind eye. Hassan could even have been the go-between. In which case the ex-sergeant would not know anyone else.

Owen looked through the file in front of him. One of the times the ex-sergeant had been reduced was for selling Army equipment. Not weaponry—the Army took that seriously. Odds and ends from the stores. At least, that was all they had caught him for. The chances were that he had flogged quite a lot more. And once a seller...The idea might have come to him again. He had been running a woman in Ismailia and had needed the cash. He might have approached somebody. There was always a ready market for weapons. He might have known someone. Worth a try.

Owen studied the face opposite him. Shrewd, Army-wise, hard. A drinker's face. Little red veins beneath the tan, tell-tale puffiness below the eyes. In certain circumstances, thought Owen, I could crack this man.

But not easily. Not here, and probably not now. He was sitting there at ease. He knew he was coming out on Thursday. All he had to do was to sit tight and say nothing. There was no way of putting him under pressure.

Outside in the corridor he heard the guards' feet shuffling. It would take too long to break the man, and before then he would have been interrupted.

He had to find a way of getting the man to cooperate. He might be willing if he thought there was something in it for him.

"You've been reduced before," said Owen. "Three times."

"Yes, sir," said the man equably.

"Gets harder."

The man gave a little shrug.

Used to it, thought Owen.

"How much longer have you got?" he asked.

The man looked slightly surprised.

"To serve, sir? Four years."

"Time enough to get made up again," said Owen. "It would be nice to go out with a bit of money in your pocket."

The man looked at him cautiously, but his interest was aroused.

"Help me," said Owen, "and I might help you."

He waited.

After a moment, the man responded.

"Exactly how could I help you, sir?"

"A name. All I want is a name."

The man rubbed his chin. There was a faint rasp. In the heat it was never possible to shave closely.

"'Assan is the only name I can think of, sir."

"Sure?"

The blue eyes met his blandly.

"Yes, sir. Afraid so, sir."

"I'm not really interested in your case," said Owen. "I'm interested in another. And if I got a name, that could be really helpful."

"I'd like to help, sir," said the man. "But 'Assan is the only name I can think of."

"Go on thinking," said Owen, "and let me know if another name comes into your head."

He turned through the papers in the file.

"After all," he said casually, without looking up, "it's only a Gyppy."

He went on turning through the papers. No reply came. He had not really expected one.

He took a card from his pocket.

"If you want to get in touch with me," he said, "later—and, remember, one word will do—that's where you'll find me."

The man took the card and fingered it gingerly.

"Mamur Zapt," he said, stumbling a little. He raised his head. "What's that, sir? Civilian?"

"No," said Owen. "Special."

"Sorry, sir. No offence."

After a moment he said: "'Course, it couldn't be, you being in uniform. It was just that 'Mamur' bit."

Owen closed the file and sat back. He had done what he could. Whether the seed he had planted would bear fruit remained to be seen.

"A mamur is just a district officer," he said. "Not the same thing at all."

"Of course not, sir."

Judging that the interrogation was over he became relaxed, even garrulous.

"I know, sir. I ran into one of them once, at Ismailia. We'd gone off for the day, a few of us. Filled a boat with bottles of beer and set out along the coast. We come to this place, and the bloody boatman hops over the side. We thought he was just doing something to do with the boat, but the bugger never came back. We just sat there, waiting and drinking. We'd had a few already by this time. Anyway, after a bit we runs out of bottles so we gets out of the boat to go looking for some more when we runs into this mamur. One of my mates hits him, but we're all so bloody pissed by then we can't really hit anyone, and suddenly they're all around us and we're in the local caracol."

Owen laughed.

The man nodded in acknowledgement and pulled a face.

"Christ!" he said. "That was something, I can tell you. A real hole. The place was stuffed full of dirty Arabs, about twenty of them in a space that would do eight, and then us as well. The pong! Jesus! Shit everywhere. You were standing in it. Pitch black. No bloody windows, just a wooden grating for a door. No air. Hot as hell. All them bodies packed together. Christ! I've been in some rough places, but that scared the shit out of me. We were in there for a day and half. Bloody Military didn't get there till the next morning. And then, do you know what they did? Those bastards just came and looked at us through the grating and went away laughing! Didn't come back till they'd had a drink. "That'll bloody teach you!" they said. It did too, and all. Wouldn't want to go through that again."

ᘓᘏᘎᘏᘎ

The café stood at the corner of the Ataba el Khadra, just at the point where Muski Street, coming up from the old quarter, emerged on the squares and gardens of the European part of Cairo.

Owen had chosen a table out on the pavement, from where he could see both down Muski Street, with its open-fronted shops and goods spilling out into the road, and across the Ataba.

At this time in the evening the Ataba was lit by scores of lamps, which hung from the trees, from the railings, from shop-signs and from house-fronts, even, incongruously, from the street-lights themselves. In their soft light, round the edges of the square, the donkey-boys and cab-men gambled, drank tea and talked, forming little conversation groups which drew in passers-by and drove pedestrians into the middle of the Place, where they competed with the arabeahs and buses and trams and carts and camels and donkeys and brought traffic to a standstill.

Everywhere, even out in the middle of the thoroughfare, were street-stalls: stalls for nougat, for Turkish delight, for Arab sugar, for small cucumbers and oranges, for spectacles, leather boots and slippers, for cheap turquoises, for roses, for carnations, for Sudanese beads made in England, for sandalwood workboxes and Smyrna figs, for tea, for coffee, for the chestnuts being roasted around the foot of the trees.

And everywhere, too, were people. The women, in the shapeless dark gowns and black veils, were going home. But the men were appearing in all their finery to stroll around the streets and sit in the cafés. Here and there were desert Arabs in beautiful robes of spotless white and black, and a rather larger number of blue-gowned country Arabs from Der el Bahari. But for the most part the men were dressed in European style, apart from their handsome tarbooshes. All, however, had magnificent boots, which the shoe-brown boys fought to shine whenever an owner sat down in a café.

Owen enjoyed it. He lived alone, and in the evening, when he was not at the club or at the opera, he would often sit in a café. When he had first come to Egypt he had done it deliberately, often going to a café with his Arabic teacher after a lesson to drink coffee and to talk. His teacher, the Aalim Aziz, had instructed him in far more than the language during those civilized discussions of all aspects of the Arab past and present, discussions which continued late into the night and usually finished with everyone in the café involved.

In his first six months in Egypt Owen had gone to Aziz for instruction every day; and afterwards, when by usual European standards he spoke the language well, he would still meet him at least twice a week, not so much now for formal instruction as to continue discussion with one who had become a friend. Even now, when his work tended to isolate him, he still met Aziz regularly.

Having acquired the taste for café society, Owen kept it. Indeed, it was one of the things that made him prefer Egypt to India. Unlike many English Arabists, he was a man of the city rather than the desert. It was common among the British in Egypt to regard the urban Egyptian as a corrupted, degenerate version of the more sympathetic traditional Bedouin. Owen, on the other hand, was more at home with the young, educated, urban Egyptian, with people like Mahmoud.

He was waiting for Mahmoud now. After their experience that morning at the barracks, he had been anxious to contact Mahmoud at once to apologize. But when he had rung up Mahmoud to suggest a meeting he had found him off-hand, unwilling. Owen had pressed, however, and in the end, reluctantly, the Egyptian had agreed.

They had arranged to meet in the café that evening. Instinctively Owen felt that to be better. If they had met at the Bab el Khalk or at the Parquet he had a feeling that Mahmoud would have retreated into his shell. In the more natural atmosphere of the café they might do better.

But when Mahmoud arrived, the strategy did not seem to work. Owen apologized for the morning. Mahmoud brushed it aside. It was nothing, he said. How had the interview with the sergeant gone? When Owen told him, he brushed that aside, too. He hadn't really expected anything different. Owen had done what he could, and he, Mahmoud, was grateful. The man was coming out on Thursday and couldn't really be expected to talk. It was not Owen's fault.

Which was all very well, but Owen knew that things weren't right. When they had first met, and throughout the whole of the day they had spent together, they had got on unusually well. Owen had taken an immediate liking to the Egyptian and he felt that Mahmoud had taken a liking to him. He had found himself responding sympathetically to the Egyptian and understanding what he was after without it needing to be spelt out, and he had felt that Mahmoud was reading him in the same way. This evening, though, there was none of that. Mahmoud was unfailingly courteous, but something was missing. The outgoing friendliness that had characterized him previously seemed to have gone.

In the time that he had been in Egypt Owen had got used to the way in which Arab relationships varied in intensity. Arabs seemed to blow hot and blow cold. They invested their relationships with more emotion than did the stolid English and so their relationships were more volatile. Owen could understand this; perhaps, he told himself wryly, because the Welsh were not altogether dissimilar. Perhaps, more particularly, his own intuitive nature made him especially sensitive to such things.

In an effort to put Mahmoud more at ease, he switched into Arabic. Mahmoud switched back into English.

The conversation was at the level of exchanging commonplaces. Owen knew that when Mahmoud had finished his coffee he would go.

Some shoe-boys were larking about near their table. One of them threw a brush at another. The brush missed and fell under the table. The boy scurried to retrieve it and almost upset their coffee. They grabbed at the table together and cursed simultaneously. The boy fled laughing, chased by a furious waiter. Owen smiled, and thought he saw an answering flicker on Mahmoud's face.

Deliberately he moved his chair round so that he sat beside Mahmoud, closer to him. Arab conventions of personal territory were different from European ones. What to an Englishman seemed keeping a proper distance, to an Arab seemed cold and unfriendly.

"Your day has been hard?" he asked sympathetically.

At last he got a real response.

Mahmoud looked round at him.

"Not as hard as yours yesterday," he said bitterly. "Although perhaps you did not find it so."

Owen knew that Mahmoud was referring to the students. The remark surprised him. He knew, of course, that this kind of political policing was resented by Egyptians, but had thought that as a member of the Parquet Mahmoud must have come to terms with it. He wondered suddenly what Mahmoud's own political position was. A bright young Parquet lawyer on the rise might well have political ambitions; and if he did, they might well be on the Nationalist side.

"I was not involved directly," he said slowly, "although of course I knew of it."

"Perhaps I should not have spoken," said Mahmoud.

"No, that's all right," said Owen. He smiled. "It's just that I am trying to think of an answer."

He pondered for a moment and then decided to go for honesty.

"The answer is," he said, "that I did not find it hard. It was regrettable, certainly, but a necessity. Given the situation in Egypt. Of course, you may not want to grant the situation. I would understand that."

A little to his surprise, Mahmoud seemed to find the answer satisfactory. He relaxed visibly and waved to the waiter for more coffee.

"I appreciate your answer," he said. "And in case you're wondering, let me tell you I personally am not a revolutionary. Nationalist, yes, reforming, even radical, yes; but not a revolutionary. I would like the British out. But meanwhile…" He sighed. "Meanwhile, for you and for me, there are necessities."

He paused while the waiter filled their cups.

"However," he said, "I must tell you I would not want to grant the situation."

"That," said Owen, "I can quite understand."

He brooded a little.

"I can understand," he said presently, "a bit at any rate, because I myself am not English."

"Not English?" said Mahmoud, astonished.

"Welsh."

"Welsh? *Pays Galles?*"

Owen nodded.

"I have never met anyone from Wales before," said Mahmoud.

"You probably wouldn't know if you had. They're very like Englishmen. Smaller, darker. Not enough to stand out. But there is a difference. In the part of Wales I come from," said Owen, "most people do not speak English."

"*Vraiment?*"

Mahmoud hesitated.

"But—you speak English very well. How—?"

"We spoke both Welsh and English at home," said Owen. "My father normally spoke English. He wanted me to grow up to be an Englishman. My mother spoke Welsh."

"And she wanted you to grow up to be a Welshman?" asked Mahmoud.

"Probably," said Owen, laughing. "She was hopelessly romantic. She wanted Wales to be an independent country again."

"And that seems romantic to you?"

"In the case of Wales, yes."

Mahmoud considered.

"In the case of Egypt, too," he said at length. "Romantic. Definitely romantic."

☾⁂☽

Their rapport quite restored, they continued happily drinking coffee.

At the other end of the café a party broke up with the usual prolonged Arabic farewells. Most of the party went off together across the square, but one of them made his way along the pavement in their direction, skirting the gambling and waving aside the shoe-boys. As he passed their table his eye caught Owen's. It was Fakhri.

He stopped in his tracks.

"The Mamur Zapt?" he cried. "And—" taking in Mahmoud— "the Parquet? Together? There must have been a revolution! And no one has told me!"

"Come and join us," Owen invited, "and we'll tell you."

Fakhri dropped into a chair.

"I don't want to interrupt you," he said, "unless you're talking business."

"Business and pleasure. Mostly pleasure."

"Ah," said Fakhri, waving a hand back at the dispersed party. "Like me. Pleasure and business. Mostly business."

"What is your business?" asked Owen curiously.

"He has not heard," said Fakhri sorrowfully.

"Fakhri Bey is a distinguished editor," said Mahmoud.

"Oh, *that* Fakhri!" said Owen, whose own business was to know the political press. "My apologies. I read your editorials with pleasure. Sometimes."

"I am afraid you may not read tomorrow's with pleasure," said Fakhri.

"The students?" Owen shrugged.

"Quite so," said Fakhri. "Let us forget about them."

He and Owen both waved for more coffee simultaneously.

"At least what you say," said Owen, "will be less predictable than what I read in *al Liwa*."

Fakhri made a face.

"They say everything at the top of their voice," he said. "There is no light and shade."

"What's happening at *al Liwa*," asked Owen, "now that Mustafa Kamil has died?"

Mustafa Kamil, the brilliant young politician who had built up the National Party virtually from scratch, had died a month or two previously, from a heart attack.

"They have not sorted themselves out yet. All the top posts keep changing, the editorship among them."

"The complexion of the paper doesn't, though," said Owen.

"It could. It depends on who wins control of the party. If it's el Gazzari it will become very religious. Crazily so. If it's Jemal it will go in for heavy doses of revolutionary theory." Owen sighed. "Neither will make it more readable," he said. "They lack your touch."

Fakhri tried not to look pleased.

"See how expertly he works," he said to Mahmoud. "This is how the Mamur Zapt gets the press eating out of his hand."

"The Egyptian press," said Owen, "is the most independent in the world. Unfortunately."

They all laughed.

A boy went past sprinkling water to keep down the dust. Fakhri pulled his legs back hurriedly. For a little while there was the lovely, distinctive smell of wet sand.

"How is Nuri Pasha?" asked Fakhri. "I called on him two days ago to express my sympathy but his Berberine told me that he was talking to you."

"He is well," said Mahmoud.

"Praise be to God!" said Fakhri automatically.

He hesitated.

"And how are you getting on—?" He broke off. "Perhaps I shouldn't ask!"

His laugh allowed the brush-off; but he cocked his head attentively, inviting information.

Owen decided to play.

"We hold the man, of course," he said.

"Ah, yes, but—"

"Those behind?"

Fakhri nodded.

"Not yet."

Fakhri affected, or showed, disappointment.

Owen decided to try a move of his own.

"The attempt did not come as a surprise to you," he said, more as a statement than a question.

"No," said Fakhri. "It did not."

"Denshawai?"

"Of course."

"Just Denshawai?"

Fakhri looked surprised.

"So far as I know," he said.

"The reason why I ask," said Owen, "is that he doesn't seem to have been directly involved."

"More directly than he likes to pretend now," said Fakhri.

"OK. But surely a minor figure?"

"The civil servant responsible was only a minor figure and he was the first to be shot."

"I always thought that was in the heat of the moment when the sentences were first announced," said Owen. Then, after a pause: "You said 'first'?"

"Yes," said Fakhri, "I did."

"You think there are more to come?"

"All Cairo," said Fakhri, "thinks there are more to come."

He glanced at his watch.

"I really must go," he said, getting to his feet. "I have to see the first copy as it comes off the press."

"I shall read it tomorrow with interest," said Owen.

"If I were you," said Fakhri, "I would read tomorrow's *al Liwa* also. I think you will find that full of interest, too."

Chapter 5

When Nikos arrived in the office the next morning he found Owen already there, finishing a memo. It read:

The Mamur Zapt has received unconfirmed reports of a disturbing increase in the number of thefts from military installations in recent months. These include thefts of guns, ammunition and other equipment which could be used for offensive purposes. Clearly there could be serious implications for civil security if these got into the wrong hands. Unfortunately, such thefts are treated purely as an internal matter by Military Security and not reported to the Mamur Zapt, with the result that he has been unable to investigate the possibility of links with known terrorist organizations or establish whether a pattern is emerging. No analysis has been made by Military Security. In view of the possible threat to civil order and the likelihood that senior civil and military personnel could be at risk, it is recommended that:

1. an independent investigation be carried out as a matter of urgency into current security at military installations.

2. the Mamur Zapt be informed within twenty-four hours whenever a theft of arms occurs and given a full account of the circumstances in which the theft occurred.

3. Military Security be instructed to supply the Mamur Zapt with a complete list of thefts which had occurred over the past year.

"What's all this?" said Nikos, reading it through. "'Unconfirmed Reports?' Where did you get all this stuff from? It's not come through the office."

"No," Owen agreed.

"Of course, you've a right to use alternative channels," said Nikos huffily.

"I haven't been using alternative channels," said Owen. "I made it up."

"You what?"

"Made it up. To fix that bastard, Brooker," Owen explained.

"It isn't true?"

"Now look what you've done!" said Georgiades, who had come into the room at the same time as Nikos. "You've shocked him! Poor, innocent soul!" he said to Nikos, resting a fatherly hand on him.

"Never mind my innocent soul!" snapped Nikos. "What the hell is going on?"

Nikos rarely swore.

"I've told you," said Owen reasonably.

"You're doing this just to get even with Brooker?"

Owen nodded. Since coming to Egypt he had discovered that he had something of a bent for administrative politics.

Nikos took a moment to gather himself together.

"All right, then," he said, dumping the day's newspapers on Owen's desk.

"I hope you know what you are doing," he said, as he went out.

"So this is how one gets to be Mamur Zapt!" said Georgiades. He shook his head, marvelling. "Ah, what a thing it is to lack scruple! I've often wondered what it is that's been holding me back."

He followed Nikos off down the corridor chuckling.

Owen turned his attention to the newspapers. Every morning when he got in he read them all: all the Arabic ones, all the French ones and all the English ones, that is. Georgiades read the Greek ones and Nikos the Coptic, Armenian and Italian ones. Owen's legal adviser read the Turkish ones, which were especially important. Another experienced man read the Jewish ones.

Nikos also read the London *Times*, the *Morning Post* and the *Illustrated London News*, although Owen assured him they were of no help at all.

Owen read for "feel" only. The papers would be read again, more thoroughly, by the censors, who would pick up cases where action was unavoidable and alert him to anything he had missed. Owen himself seldom remembered detail. His concern was rather to take the political temperature of the city.

To do that meant taking several temperatures, not one. Cairo was a polyglot city of many communities. The bulk of its population, as elsewhere in Egypt, spoke Egyptian Arabic. But there were also sizeable communities of Greeks, Italians, French, Syrians, Armenians, English, Jews and Turks. The Turks had an importance out of proportion to their numbers because until recently they had supplied the ruling class and occupied most of the administrative and military positions. The language of administration, and certainly of the law, tended, however to be French, although English was taking over. French, too, was the language of upper-class Cairenes, reflecting their many links with French culture and society. Well-to-do Cairenes sent their children to French schools. Their wives looked naturally to Paris for their fashions. They themselves not only spoke French but thought French.

To move with ease in Cairo society you really needed a command of three languages: Arabic, French and English. The polished young men about the British Agent managed this without difficulty. Many of the other British administrations were fairly at home in Arabic at least. Only the Army, lacking both Arabic and French, was completely isolated linguistically; linguistically, and therefore socially.

Owen's own Arabic was excellent, his French fair only, though a girl in Alexandria the previous year had improved it considerably.

He read over the Arabic papers, keeping an eye open especially for anything that would support what Fakhri had said the night before. He found nothing to suggest that Fakhri's foreboding was generally, or even widely shared. However, that did not make him discount Fakhri's words altogether. The Egyptian might well be reflecting faithfully the views of the part of upper-middle-class Cairene society with which he was familiar. Such people might well see themselves as potential targets for attack and he might well be registering accurately their apprehension. So long as such views were restricted to them Owen did not mind. What would concern him would be if they showed signs of spreading to other people. Put ideas in people's heads, Garvin might have said, and there's always a chance that they will act on them.

He read, therefore, Fakhri's own paper with particular care. It was an intellectual weekly with a fairly limited circulation, and in itself hardly likely to stir a man's adrenalin. However, it was well known. Other journalists and, indeed, other editors might well read it; and if they read it they might take things from it.

Like most Cairo editors, however, Fakhri knew exactly where to draw the line. In the present number he had drawn it with a finesse that earned Owen's professional admiration. The connection between Nuri and the Denshawai Incident was made, but circumspectly and in the most general of terms. Even the account of the student demonstration, which occupied most of the front page, was handled in a way to which it was difficult to take exception. Legal exception, that was. Exception might well be taken on other grounds. The account itself was sharp to the point of viciousness and the editorial, which commented on it, provocative to the limits of admissibility. The writing did not, however, actually step over the line which divided it from the inflammatory and defamatory.

Not so *al Liwa*, which, like Fakhri's paper, covered the demonstration at considerable length. Most of the length in *al Liwa's* case was due to passages of extended vituperation which were saved—if they were saved—from being defamatory only by their generalness and imprecision. Owen skipped through the bloodsucking imperialists bit, noted with pleasure that the Sirdar was being blamed for the whole thing—incorrectly, since the Army had nothing to do with it—and was amused to find that the original target of the demonstration was quite lost sight of: the article ended by inviting the Khedive to march with the demonstrators.

Owen wondered how much Ahmed had contributed or whether, indeed, he had written it entirely.

However, that was not the only interesting article the paper contained. Buried on an inside page was another article which, Owen began to suspect, was the article which Fakhri had really wanted him to see.

It was about Mustafa, Nuri's would-be assassin, and was called MUSTAFA'S MISTAKE. The mistake, according to the article, lay in Mustafa's thinking that his was a personal wrong which could be remedied by private action. In fact, it was an instance of a general problem, that of landlord-fellahin relations, and the only way to put that right was through political action. Baldly—and the article was anything but bald—that meant joining the Nationalist Party. This, the paper assured its readers, Mustafa had been on the brink of doing when, alas, he had been carried away by the sight of his enemy. Only the day before he had spoken at a public meeting organized by the Nationalist Party in his village. He had been one of many willing to stand up and testify to the wrongs the fellahin were suffering. Although he had not—yet—formally joined the Nationalist Party, it would stand by him. His hand, the article concluded with a flourish, may have held the gun but it was the landlords themselves who had pulled the trigger.

Owen read it through again, thought for a moment and then reached for the telephone.

"It's true," said Mahmoud. "He was there. He did speak. I checked."

Mahmoud had been in court all day. Like Owen, he could not give all his time to the Nuri affair, important though it might be. A hearing had been scheduled for that day in connection with another case, and as he had been responsible for drawing up the *procès-verbal* he had had to attend. Unusually, the Parquet's analysis had been challenged and Mahmoud had had to spend the morning defending it and the afternoon—while, he pointed out to the clerk of the court, the judges were having their siesta—revising his submission. He was in a jaundiced frame of mind by the time he got back to his office, late in the afternoon, to find Owen's message waiting for him. They had arranged to meet that evening, which gave him an opportunity to get his men to do a quick, independent check. First reports had come back to him before he set out.

"Someone must have heard him speak," said Owen, "and thought they could use him."

Mahmoud nodded. "It's a possibility. I'll get my man to check if anyone talked to him afterwards."

"He would have been angry. He might have spoken with a lot of force. Enough to attract attention."

"I'll get it checked."

Owen, who had had a long, hot day too, had proposed a walk along the river bank before finding a café. It was dark by this time and the street-lamps were on. It ought to be getting cool. They turned along a promenade beneath the palms.

"If someone heard him," said Owen presently, "they were there, too. Who else was at the meeting?"

"The whole village. It was one of a series of meetings the Nationalists have been holding in that area."

"Not just the village," said Owen.

"No? Who are you thinking of?"

"The Nationalists must have sent some people."

There was a little pause.

"Yes," said Mahmoud, rather distantly, "yes, they must have."

"We ought to find out who they were."

Then, as Mahmoud did not reply at all, Owen looked round at him. Mahmoud's face had gone wooden.

Something had upset him. Owen wondered if it was anything he had done. Perhaps Mahmoud was fed up with Owen telling him his business.

"Just a thought," he said apologetically. "I dare say you've got it all in hand."

Mahmoud did not respond. Owen racked his brains to see what he'd done wrong.

"Not my business, perhaps," he said. "Sorry!"

In the poor light of the street-lamps he could not see whether Mahmoud acknowledged his apology. He began to grow a little irritated. Mahmoud had been all right when they met. A little hot and bothered after his day in court, perhaps. Why had he suddenly become all huffy?

A thought struck him. Surely Mahmoud did not think he was trying to use him? That Owen wanted him to compile a list of active Nationalists which the Mamur Zapt might then make use of for other purposes?

"I hope you don't think I'm trying to get some names out of you," he said angrily.

Mahmoud grimaced. It was clear that was exactly what he did think.

Owen was furious. How could Mahmoud suppose that! After the friendship that had sprung up between them! It was unjust and unfair. He had taken Mahmoud to be a reasonable man. But this was so unreasonable...

Just like a bloody Egyptian. He had met this sort of thing before. You would be getting on all right with them one minute and then the next minute something would happen and they would be quite different. They would go all wooden, just as Mahmoud had done, and you wouldn't be able to get any sense out of them. He hadn't thought Mahmoud was like that, though. He had seemed all right. Why was he getting himself in a stew over something as trivial as this? It wasn't as if it was going to make any difference. If Owen wanted the names he would bloody well get them. His own men would get the lot within twenty-four hours. Why was Mahmoud being so absurdly stuffy?

Then another thought struck him. Perhaps it wasn't so trivial to Mahmoud, after all. Owen remembered his earlier speculations about Mahmoud's politics. He had admitted he was a Nationalist himself. Whose side was he on?

And then a faint warning bell began to tinkle. It manifested itself as a growing unease which started just at the time that he said to himself, "Just like a bloody Egyptian." As soon as you started saying things like that you were talking like an Old Hand. Owen had not got on with the Old Hands in India and when he had transferred to Egypt he had sworn to himself that he would never become like them. And here he was! "Bloody native" would be next.

In this case, too, natural antagonism was reinforced by family upbringing. Owen was unusual among Army officers in having been brought up as a Welsh Liberal; and he could hear his mother's soft voice in the background saying firmly: "Not a native, dear; an Eastern gentleman." His Welsh Liberalism had been somewhat tempered by the Army but,

having lost his parents early, he adhered all the more strongly
to his mother's teaching, especially when it came to personal
relations. Every man, from the highest to the lowest, of whatever race or colour or creed, was to be treated as a gentleman;
every woman as a lady.

Except bloody Brooker, he told himself.

He began to simmer down. Perhaps he was overreacting.
Mahmoud had made perfectly clear what his political position
was, and it was a completely respectable one. And it was not
unreasonable that he should be worried about putting a list
of Nationalist sympathizers into the hands of the Mamur
Zapt. He might even have used it.

That thought quite shocked him. Would he really have
used it? he asked himself. Well, yes, he might, he was forced
to admit. It was his job, after all. In that case Mahmoud was
not being so unreasonable. In fact, he was not being unreasonable at all. Just properly cautious.

He stole a glance at Mahmoud. His face was stiff and
unyielding. This was an issue of principle for him and he
was not going to give way.

Owen could see the bridge ahead of them. That was where
the promenade came to an end, and unless something
happened that was where the walk would come to an end.

Owen knew that he was the one who would have to do
something. The trouble was that he couldn't think what.

Just before they got to the bridge he stopped and turned,
forcing Mahmoud to look at him.

"I've been thinking," he said.

"Yes?" Mahmoud was wary but not completely distant.

"I've been trying to think of a way forward," Owen said,
"one acceptable to both of us."

Mahmoud was interested, and because he was interested
his face lost some of its woodenness.

"Let me try this on you: my people make a list and your
people make a list. You check everyone whether they are on

my list or on your list. If they're on your list and not on mine you don't have to tell me—unless you want to."

Mahmoud's face cleared at once.

"I would be happy with that," he said. "I would be very happy with that."

෴

"Of course," said Mahmoud, "it may not be political anyway."

They were sitting in a café, one of the few Arab ones in this European part of the city.

"What else could it be?"

"Well, let me try something on you," Mahmoud said. "Someone besides Mustafa has got a personal grudge. Perhaps even for the same reason—Nuri can't leave women alone."

"And set Mustafa up?"

"Yes. That way they would get their revenge and not get caught. If it worked."

"No real evidence," said Owen.

"No real evidence for it being political," Mahmoud pointed out.

"Yes, but—"

"You've got a feel?" Mahmoud laughed. "So have I. I'm just being a good boy and checking out all the possibilities. Like they taught me in college."

Owen laughed, too, more comfortable now.

"There you are!" he said. "That's where you have the advantage!"

Mahmoud looked at him curiously.

"You didn't go to college? They didn't train you?"

"Not for this," said Owen.

"The English prefer amateurs," said Mahmoud.

He meant it consolingly, Owen knew, but the remark jarred. That was how many Egyptians saw it, he knew. Most of them, if they were in the professions, had received a formal training, either in Cairo or in France.

Mahmoud, quite at ease now, took a sip of coffee and then sat thinking.

"There's no real evidence for either," he said, going back to his original line of thought. "Like you, I incline to the political. But there's one thing that bothers me. If it's political. Ordinary politicians are not going to be involved. It's got to be extremists. But if it's them there's something funny about it. Why are they using Mustafa?"

"If it's a 'club' they'll have people of their own, you mean."

"Yes. People who know what they're doing."

"Not all the 'clubs' are as professional as you imagine," Owen pointed out. He was something of an expert on such matters. "The ones based in the universities, for instance. That," he said, "is why they usually don't last very long."

He wondered immediately whether this would upset Mahmoud again and looked at him a trifle anxiously.

Mahmoud caught the look and burst out laughing.

"We're going to have a job, aren't we?" he said. "Almost any ground is dangerous! However—" he leaned forward and gently touched Owen on the sleeve in a gesture that was very Arab—"I'm not always so unreasonable!"

He thought again.

"It's the gun," he said. "That's what makes me think it must be a 'club.' And one of the more professional ones. Ordinary fellahin like Mustafa don't get near such things. If they bought a gun—if they could afford to—it would be of the pigeon-shooting sort. A shotgun for scaring the birds. A rifle that came with Napoleon. Not the latest issue to the British Army."

"Could you buy one? If you had plenty of money? If you were that other-man-with-a-grudge, for instance?"

Mahmoud shook his head. "Not unless you knew somebody."

"You can't rule that out as a possibility."

"You can for Mustafa. He's never been out of the village."

Mahmoud brooded a little.

"And that's the problem," he said presently. "You see, if you can get hold of a gun like that and you want someone killed, why go to Mustafa? There's a gap. Between the professionals behind the scenes and the very far from professional man who's supposed to do the actual work."

Two shoe-shine boys came round the corner and launched themselves immediately at their feet. They both tucked their feet under their chairs and Mahmoud waved the boys away.

"And there's another thing," he said. "The hashish."

"They gave him too much."

"Yes."

Mahmoud looked at Owen.

"You know what I think?"

"Tell me."

"It all sounds terribly amateur."

"Yes," said Owen. "Like me."

Although Owen had told Mahmoud about the article in *al Liwa* he had kept back one piece of information. Now, as they walked back towards the centre of the city, he said:

"I know someone who was at the meeting, in the village. This person hates Nuri, is a Nationalist, is, I would say, a bit incompetent and from what I have heard would be quite likely to sympathize with Mustafa."

"You should join the Parquet," said Mahmoud, surprised. "Who is he?"

"The person who wrote the article in *al Liwa*."

"Whose identity you have already checked."

"Yes," said Owen. "Ahmed."

☙

One of the Mamur Zapt's privileges was a box at the Opera. At first Owen had been a little surprised. But no, it was not an imaginative bribe. It was a perfectly genuine prerequisite of office and Owen soon began to make regular use of it. Although he came from a musical family and a Welsh village with a deep-rooted musical culture, he had never been to the opera before he came to Egypt. Soon after taking up his position, however, he went to a performance of *Aïda*, which had been written, of course, specially for the Opera House at Cairo, and was hooked. He went to every new performance during the season. Indeed, he went several times and had recently made a resolution to cut down his attendances at the Opera House to twice a week.

Coming back from the Opera House that evening he passed an Arab café in which some young men were sitting. They were in high spirits and had probably been drinking. As Owen approached, one of them said something to the others and there was a burst of derisive laughter, almost certainly at Owen's expense. Then, as he continued past, one of the others, in an obvious attempt to outdo, leaned out into the street and shouted something abusive almost directly up into Owen's face, cursing, as is the Arab custom, not Owen himself but his father.

Without stopping and, indeed, without thinking, Owen at once replied that he would certainly have returned the compliment had his addresser only been in the position to inform him which of his mother's two-and-ninety admirers his father had been.

There was an instant of shocked silence behind him and then, almost immediately, the rush of feet.

Owen cursed his over-ready tongue. One thing the Agent would not tolerate was brawling in the street with Egyptians.

The footsteps came up to him and he braced himself.

And then a hand was placed gently on his arm and a voice said politely: "Please, please. I am so sorry. I did not think for one moment that you knew Arabic, still less the correct Arabic abuse. We are all very sorry. Please come and join us for some coffee and let us try and convince you that we are not as boorish as we appear."

Two contrite young men looked at him pleadingly. Owen could not resist and went back with them to the table where a space was quickly made for him.

The rest of the café looked on with approval, having enjoyed, in typical Arab fashion, both the abuse and the courtesy.

The men apologized. They were, they explained, filling in time before going to a party. They had been talking politics and one of their number had been carried away. It was not said, but Owen guessed, that the topics had included the British in Egypt. The conversation turned tactfully in another direction.

They inquired how Owen came by his Arabic and when he mentioned his teacher it turned out that two of them knew him. This reassured Owen, for the Aalim was not one to waste his time with fools.

Indeed, they were far from fools. They were all journalists, it appeared, working for the most part on arts pages. One of them was introduced as a playwright.

Owen said he had been to the Arab theatre but found the plays excessively melodramatic.

"That's us," said one of the men. "All Arabs are melodramatic."

"No, it's not," said the playwright. "We're dramatic. It's the plays that are melodramatic. They're just bad."

"Perhaps you will improve the standard," said Owen.

"Gamal's latest play is good," one of the men said.

"Is it on somewhere? Can I see it?"

They all roared with laughter.

"Alas, no!" said Gamal. "But when it is put on I shall send you a special invitation."

Owen said he had just been to the opera. They asked him how it compared with opera in Europe. He was obliged to admit that the only opera he had seen had been in Egypt. Two of the journalists had seen opera in Paris. They thought Cairo opera provincial.

The conversation ran on merrily. Some time later Owen glanced at his watch. It was well past two. Opera finished late in Cairo; parties started even later, evidently.

The thought occurred to one or two of the others and they rose to go. Owen got up, too, and began to say his farewells. His acquaintances were aghast that he should be leaving them so early. They insisted that he came to the party with them.

Owen was taking this to be mere Arab politeness when the playwright linked his arm in Owen's and began to urge him determinedly along the street.

"A little while," he coaxed, "just a little, little while."

"We want you to meet our friends," they said.

The house was a traditional Mameluke house. It went up in tiers. The first tier was just a high blank wall with a decorated archway entrance. Above this a row of corbels allowed the first floor to project a couple of feet over the street, in the manner of sixteenth-century houses in England. And above this again a triple row of oriels carried out into the street a further two feet. There was no glass, of course, but all the windows were heavily screened with fine traditional woodwork.

Through the archway was a courtyard with a fountain and some people sitting round it. They belonged to the party, but most of the guests were inside, in a mandar'ah, or reception room, opening off the courtyard.

The mandar'ah had a sunken marble floor paved with black and white marble and little pieces of fine red tile. In the centre of the floor was a fountain playing into a small shallow pool lined with coloured marbles like the floor.

A number of people stood about the room in groups, talking. Other groups reclined on large, fat, multi-coloured, leather cushions. Some had Western-style drinks in their hand. Quite a few were drinking coffee. All were talking.

At the far end of the room was a dais with large cushions. This was where the host normally sat, along with his most honoured guests. There was a group on it now, sprawled about on the cushions, all talking animatedly.

Two of Owen's acquaintances went off to find their host. They returned leading him triumphantly.

He was Fakhri.

He recovered at once, grasped Owen's hand in both his own and embraced him.

"It would take too long to explain," said Owen.

However, his friends were determined to explain, and Fakhri got the general picture.

"But we have met already!"

"You have?"

Fakhri bore Owen away.

"Whisky?" he said. "Or coffee?"

"I would say coffee but I have had so much already—"

"Whisky, then. For me also. After such surprises—"

"Sorry," said Owen.

"Such nice surprises. I take it you are not on duty?"

"Far from it," said Owen, with conviction.

"Then enjoy your evening. Come! I will introduce you—"

But another group of guests arrived, who solicited Fakhri's attention. Owen went off to find his acquaintances. The playwright was in a little group about the fountain. Owen started across to join him.

The party was Western-style. That is, women were present. There were Syrians, Jews, Armenians, Greeks, Tripolitans and Levantines generally; there were scarcely any Egyptians. None were unattached. That would have been flouting convention too far.

One of them Owen recognized. It was the girl he had noticed at Nuri's. She looked up and caught his eye.

"Why," she said, smiling, *"le Mamur Zapt."*

Fakhri appeared, hot and bothered from greeting three lots of guests simultaneously.

"You know each other?" he said. "Captain Carwall—" he mumbled the word "—Owen."

"What?" said the girl.

"Owen."

"I know," said the girl. *"Le Mamur Zapt."*

Fakhri looked at Owen a little anxiously.

"Pas ce soir," said Owen.

"Ah!" said the girl. "You are Mamur Zapt only sometimes. That is imaginative." She turned to Fakhri. "Don't you think," she asked, "that it is one of the weaknesses of the British that they can usually be only themselves?"

"It is one of their strengths," said Fakhri. "They never doubt that they are right."

"While we doubt all the time. Perhaps. But it is a weakness, too. The world is not so simple."

"Cairo is not so simple, either," said Fakhri, with a sidelong glance at Owen.

He slipped off to greet some new arrivals.

"I saw you the other day at Nuri's," said Owen.

"My father," said the girl.

"Nuri is your father?"

"Oui."

He considered her. Something in the face, perhaps? A strong face, not a pretty one. But the figure was willowy, unlike Nuri's barrel-like one.

"You must take after your mother."

"In more ways than one."

"How is she?" asked Owen. "The attack on your father must have been a great shock."

"She is dead."

"I am sorry."

"It was a long time ago."

The girl looked out into the courtyard where the fountain caught the moonlight.

"I think they loved each other," she said suddenly. "They never married, of course. She wouldn't go in his harem."

Seeing that Owen was trying to work it out, she said: "My mother was Firdus."

She saw he was still puzzled.

"The courtesan. You wouldn't know, but she was famous."

"And obviously beautiful."

The girl regarded him sceptically.

"She was, as a matter of fact. But that is not one of the things I have inherited from her."

"I don't know," said Owen. "Is Ahmed your brother?" he asked.

"Half-brother. His mother was a woman in the harem."

"We met him at your father's that day."

"*C'est un vrai imbécile, celui-là,*" said the girl dismissively.

"He doesn't like the British."

"You can't expect originality from him."

Owen laughed.

"He doesn't seem to care greatly for your father, either," he said.

"Naturally," said the girl. "None of us do. We are angry for our mothers."

"You are," said Owen. "Is Ahmed?"

She shrugged her shoulders. "Ahmed is just angry," she said.

Then she looked hard at him.

"Why do you ask?"

"Interested," said Owen.

"Surely you don't think—" She began to laugh. "It's too ridiculous," she said.

"Is it?"

"If you knew Ahmed—" She broke off. "Why," she said, "you sound just like the Mamur Zapt."

And turned on her heel and walked away.

Owen rejoined the group around the playwright. They were talking now about the way in which old parts of Cairo were being torn down to make way for new buildings in the European style. Was this progress or was it deterioration? The debate continued happily and vehemently.

A little later in the evening, or morning, Fakhri detached him.

"I would like you to meet one of my colleagues," he said, and led Owen over to a little group in one corner. Two earnest young men were addressing a somewhat gloomy middle-aged man, who looked up with relief when he saw Fakhri approaching.

"*Mon cher!*" he said.

They shook hands and embraced.

"I have been here all night and not had a word with you!"

"It was good of you to come," said Fakhri. "Have you put it to bed?"

The man glanced at his watch.

"The first copies will be coming off in an hour," he said. "I shall have to go soon."

"Not before you have had some more coffee," said Fakhri, and clapped his hands.

A splendid suffragi, or waiter, in a spotless white gown and a red sash around his middle appeared at once with a coffee-pot.

"You need it to keep awake," said Fakhri. "Anyway, why do you have to be there? Can't they manage without you?"

"No," said the man gloomily. "It will all be wrongly set, the columns won't be straight and some of it is bound to be transposed."

"They used to be all right," said Fakhri. "Well, fairly all right."

"They were always hopeless," said the man, "and now they're worse."

"Daouad always sees the gloomy side of things," Fakhri said to Owen. "However, it is true that things are not easy for him."

"Not easy," said Daouad, roused. "I'll say they're not easy! You don't know what problems are!" he said to Fakhri.

He turned to Owen.

"There's no direction! Not since Kamil died. They're all at each other's throats, el Gazzari, Jemal, Yussuf, Abdul Murr. And I'm in the middle! If I print something that Jemal likes, el Gazzari won't have it. If I put in one of Gazzari's huge sermons, Jemal comes to me and says it has to go or his people won't distribute it."

He gulped his coffee.

"That's why I have to be there," he said to Fakhri. "It was all right when I left the office but who knows what they've done since? They'll have pulled articles out, pushed articles in—"

Fakhri patted him on the shoulder. "Only a man like you could cope," he said.

Owen knew now why Fakhri had introduced him. Daouad was the editor of *al Liwa*.

"Working to so many people is impossible," he said sympathetically.

"It is," Daouad agreed fervently.

"And they are so extreme! They won't compromise at all."

"Not one bit," agreed Daouad.

"I don't know how you manage. Is there any sign of someone getting control?"

"That might be worse," said Daouad gloomily. "If it's el Gazzari, I couldn't go on. I can't even talk to him. And Jemal wouldn't be much better. They never listen to me!" he complained to Fakhri.

"They couldn't do without you," said Fakhri.

"What about Abdul Murr?" he asked.

"He's got more sense," Daouad conceded. "I could work with him."

"I would have thought there was a chance of Abdul Murr," said Fakhri. "In the end both Jemal and el Gazzari must see that things can't go on like this. Someone has to be in charge. Abdul Murr is a reasonable man. They can both work with him, even if they can't work with each other."

"He's too moderate for both of them."

"It may have to come to that," Fakhri insisted. "There has to be compromise. Even they must see that!"

"They might see it," said Daouad, "but others won't."

"If they see it, the others will have to."

Daouad pursed his lips. "There are others who are even more difficult," he said. "Compared with them, el Gazzari and Jemal are reason itself."

"Then," said Fakhri, "you certainly do have problems."

"Fakhri doesn't really care if I have problems," Daouad said to Owen. "He's on the other side."

"There are lots of other sides," said Fakhri. His cheeks crinkled with laughter. "Anyway," he said, "of course I am! I like to hear of your problems. It makes me forget mine for a little."

"How I envy you. Fakhri," said Daouad. "There's only one boss in your place and that's you. In my place there are ten bosses and none of them is me."

"I can't believe there's anyone worse than Jemal and el Gazzari," said Owen.

"Oh, there is!" said Daouad with great conviction.

"There can't be!" said Owen. "Who?"

Daouad started to speak, then stopped.

"There just are," he said.

Owen shook his head, affecting disbelief.

"Some of el Gazzari's factions are impossible," Fakhri said to Owen.

"And some of Jemal's," said Daouad.

Fakhri chuckled. "And Daouad is not going to tell us which of them he's thinking of!"

"That's right," said Daouad. "I'm not."

"I promise I won't print what you say," said Fakhri.

"It's not that that worries me," said Daouad darkly.

"What is it that worries you?" asked Owen.

Daouad looked at his watch.

"I've got to go," he said.

"At any rate," said Fakhri, "there's one worry that I've got and you haven't."

"What's that?" asked Daouad.

"Money," said Fakhri.

"Oh, money," said Daouad, shrugging his shoulders.

"Just so," said Fakhri. "But if you're independent like me—"

"I am independent," muttered Daouad touchily.

"—you've always got to be thinking about it. One big fine would close me down."

"They can close you down without doing that," said Daouad.

They talked for a little while longer about the difficulties of the censorship. Owen knew he was being got at, but he did not mind. Fakhri was being very helpful. He had certainly earned something. The question was, what did he want? At one point Owen had thought he was angling for a bribe. That could be arranged. But perhaps Fakhri had in mind something less directly financial: greater tolerance if he stepped over the line, perhaps. That, too, was possible.

Daouad looked at his watch again. He shook hands with Owen and Fakhri escorted him to the door. Owen wondered whether he could decently leave himself.

A voice behind him said: "No arts pages in *al Liwa.*"

It was one of his friends from earlier in the evening.

"A pity," said Owen, "especially from your point of view."

"It would be a better paper if it did have them. It's too one-track at the moment. Boring."

"That's because Daouad is boring," said another of the earlier party, joining them.

"It's not just that. Even if he wanted to, he couldn't."

"El Gazzari?" hazarded Owen.

The other two exchanged grimaces.

"Not that Jemal's any better," one of them said.

"A pity," said Owen again. "Fakhri says they've got plenty of money."

"He would. He's envious."

"Where do they get it from?" Owen asked. "Party funds?"

"Ah-ha." One of the young men laid a finger along his nose and winked. The other called to a group standing next to them. "Zeinab!"

A girl turned round. It was the one Owen had spoken to earlier.

"What is it?" she said, coming across to them.

"We want to know where *al Liwa* gets its money from."

"Why ask me?"

"We thought Raoul might know."

"Then ask him," she said, and walked off.

A tall, distinguished-looking Syrian with silvery-grey hair came over.

"What's the matter?" he said.

"We thought you could help us," they said. "We want to know where *al Liwa* gets its money from."

The Syrian looked annoyed. "Why should I know?"

"You're so friendly with *al Liwa*."

"I'm friendly with everybody," the Syrian said.

"I wish you were friendly with Fakhri," one of the young men said. "Then I could have a bigger column."

"There's no money in newspapers," the Syrian said.

"Except what people put into them," one of the young men said.

The Syrian looked at him steadily. "I don't put money into papers," he said. "I stick to business."

He rejoined the people he had been talking to previously. A little later, Owen saw him leaving, with the girl.

Chapter 6

Understandably, Owen got into the office late the next day. Nikos and Georgiades were waiting for him.

Nikos cocked an eyebrow.

"How are you feeling?" asked Georgiades.

"Fragile," said Owen.

"Serve you right," said Nikos vindictively. He had not forgiven Owen the business about the memo.

Georgiades clucked his tongue disapprovingly at Nikos and led Owen into his office.

"Coffee!" he shouted to Yussuf. "Coffee quickly! The man is dying!"

Yussuf scuttled into the room and poured out a large mug of coffee. He watched sympathetically as Owen did his best to wrap himself round it: cradling it in his hands and letting the warmth move up his arms, sucking in the aroma and then taking a sip and letting it transform itself into a glow in the pit of his stomach.

Georgiades took some, too; in case it was catching, he informed Yussuf.

Owen had not really drunk much the night before. One seldom did at Egyptian parties, even Europeanized ones. However, he had not left Fakhri's until it had gone four and had had only three hours' sleep.

He put the mug back on his desk and motioned to Georgiades to draw up his usual chair.

"OK," he said. "Tell me about Ahmed, then."

"Nineteen," said Georgiades, "a student. Second year at the law school. Not very good at his studies. A certain native wit, his teachers think, but inconsistent. Not very well organized. His work doesn't get done. Too many distractions."

"Like?"

"Politics. Spends too much time hanging around Nationalist headquarters. Attends meetings. Distributes leaflets."

"Speaks?"

"No. Gets tied up. His emotion outruns his thinking."

"Heart's in the right place but head isn't."

"That's the sort of thing."

"And how did he come to fall into these bad habits?"

"Before he went to law school his father sent him to Turkey for six months. The idea was for him to make contacts which might be useful to him later. Business, a bit, but mostly the kind of contacts that would help him with the Khedive. Nuri's good at that kind of lobbying. Anyway, apparently Ahmed didn't spend much time talking to the kind of people Nuri wanted him to talk to. Instead, he fell in with a group of Young Turks—officers in the Army, stationed at Stamboul. He got to talking politics with them. They were very keen on getting some change in things. Too keen. They got put down by the Secret Police and Ahmed had to leave the country in a hurry. Nuri wasn't very pleased."

"And then he came home to Egypt and thought he'd carry on where they left off?"

"That's the general idea."

"Young Turk, is he?"

"Not really. More Young Egyptian."

"Never met that."

"Treasure it," Georgiades invited. "You might not meet it again. He's on his own, this boy."

"What's his position? Who's he against, for a start?"

"The British."

"I'd spotted that."

"The Khedive. The Government. The University. His father. The owner of the café. He's anti most things."

"Pro anything?"

"Pro the big ideals," said Georgiades. "Like, me. Including Pan-Islam. Unlike me."

"Religious, then?"

Georgiades shook his head.

"Come on!" said Owen. "He's got to be if he's Pan-Islam!"

"The boy's confused."

"How can you be secular and Pan-Islam?"

"I told you, the boy's position is unique."

"What the hell!"

"He has a vision," said Georgiades, "of a worldwide brotherhood of Arab Nationalists. Big, like I said. Only misty."

"Anyone else share this vision?"

"Only me," said Georgiades. "He couldn't persuade the others in the café."

Big, sympathetic brown eyes met Owen's. Georgiades was a marvellous listener. People would tell him anything: their troubles, their hopes, their dreams, their worries; the difficulties they had at work, the problems they had with wife, husband, parents, children. Out it would all come pouring. It was one of the things that made him such a good agent.

"Adopting for the moment a more limited perspective," said Owen, "who does he tie up with? Not el Gazzari, evidently. Jemal?"

"Not Jemal either. He's quarrelled with Jemal. He did offer Jemal his services but Jemal made some unflattering remark. About rich landlords' sons, I believe."

"His father *is* a rich landlord," said Owen. "Is he a rich son?"

"I don't think he has much money," said Georgiades. "Nuri keeps him on a tight rein. He doesn't trust him."

"I'll bet that helps their relationship."

Owen thought for a moment.

"All the same," he said, "Nuri keeps him on as his secretary."

"In a funny way," said Georgiades, "I think he loves him. Anyway," he added, "the secretarying is pretty nominal."

The room was dark and cool. Heavy slatted wooden shutters kept light and heat out. They were opened only in the evening when the air had become cooler.

"Nuri loves him," Owen said. "Does he love Nuri, though?"

"Not according to Nuri."

"But according to Ahmed?"

"Well," said Georgiades, "the boy is misunderstood."

"Really he loves his father?"

"Sure," said Georgiades, "and hates him."

He eased himself back on his chair to free his trousers, which were sticking to the seat.

"But not enough to kill him," he said, "if that's what you were thinking. He's not the sort."

"That's what his sister said. Half-sister."

"You been doing research into the family, too? Well, that's right. He hasn't got the steel."

"The job was bungled," said Owen.

"That raises the question," said Georgiades, "of what the job was."

Their eyes met.

"True," said Owen. "Interesting."

Nikos stuck his head into the room.

"Have you shown it him yet?"

"What?"

Georgiades took a scrumpled piece of paper out of his pocket and put it on the desk in front of Owen. It was a handbill such as are given out at political meetings. It was in

Arabic and the heading, printed bold at both the top and the bottom of the page, was DEATH TO THE SIRDAR.

"He was giving these out to students at the law school yesterday," said Georgiades. "He had a couple of hundred of them."

"Did you take them off him?"

"Just the one. Do you want me to anything about the others?"

"Too late now," said Nikos. "You should have taken them all while you were at it."

"But that would have given me away," protested Georgiades. "He thinks I'm a supporter. The only one."

Nikos sniffed. "They'll be all over the law school by now."

"You'd be surprised at the indifference of people," Georgiades said. "Business was not exactly brisk. If you want me to—" he said, turning to Owen.

"No. It's not worth bothering."

Owen picked up the handbill and examined it. Seditious leaflets were as common in Cairo as pornographic postcards. It was impossible to control them all and Owen usually contented himself with confiscating a sample and destroying the printer's type. In the case of leaflets considered inflammatory, however, the working rule was to suppress the run completely. There was not much doubt that this one was inflammatory, but if it had already been distributed it was too late.

"Have you come across any more of these?" he asked.

"No."

"It's funny no one else is distributing them," said Nikos.

"Perhaps he's the only one dumb enough?" suggested Georgiades.

"That might mean the printer's not got a proper distribution system set up yet," said Nikos, disregarding him. He took the handbill from Owen. "I don't recognize the printer," he said. "Do you?" he asked Georgiades.

Georgiades shook his head. "He's new."

"That fits," said Nikos.

"How did he get in touch with Ahmed?" asked Owen.

"Or Ahmed with him," said Georgiades. "An interesting question." He looked at Owen. "Want me to find who printed this?"

"Yes," said Owen, "and when you do find him, don't do anything."

"You don't want me to call on him?" asked Georgiades, surprised.

"Not immediately. Not yet. Put a man on him. Not too obviously."

He could easily accommodate it within his budget. In Cairo it was the bribes that were expensive. The men came cheap.

☙

Georgiades and Nikos had hardly left when Nikos was back on the phone.

"I've got a call for you," he said. "Guzman. He wants to talk to you about thefts from Army barracks."

He cackled loudly and put Guzman through.

"What is this I hear about dangerous lapses in military security?" said the harsh voice.

"I don't know what you hear," said Owen. "Do tell me."

"Your memo to the British Agent—"

"I didn't know you were on the circulation list," said Owen.

"You should have put me on," said Guzman. "The Khedive is interested."

"Purely internal matter," said Owen smoothly.

"Internal? Where threats to security are concerned? Perhaps to the Khedive himself? You yourself speak of risk to important people."

"Not the Khedive, surely?"

He wondered how Guzman had got hold of the memo. By the same means as Owen got hold of the Khedive's internal memos, he supposed. Still, it was disquieting.

"What are you doing about it?" asked Guzman.

"Setting up appropriate liaison machinery, reviewing existing security arrangements, replacing where appropriate by new ones—that sort of thing," said Owen.

"About time, too!" snapped the Turk.

"That is, of course, what the memo argues."

"But you are responsible for security."

"Oh no," said Owen. "Not military security. I suggest you talk to the Sirdar."

And he'll bloody sort you out, he said under his breath.

"I shall," said Guzman. "Meanwhile, how are you getting on with your own investigations?"

"Fine," said Owen. "Fine, thanks."

"Have you arrested the murderers yet?"

"What murderers did you have in mind?" asked Owen.

"The Nuri murderers. That *is* your responsibility, isn't it?" the Turk added sarcastically.

"Afraid not. The Parquet. The police," Owen said airily.

"And Security?"

"There are, indeed, security aspects," said Owen. "I'm looking into those. Hence my memo."

There was a silence at the other end of the phone. Owen wondered whether Guzman had rung off. He was about to put the phone down when the Turk spoke again.

"The Khedive would appreciate more cooperation from the Mamur Zapt."

Owen took that, correctly, for a threat.

"You can assure the Khedive of our fullest cooperation," he said heartily.

Again there was a pause.

"I have not had your report yet," said Guzman.

"That's strange!" said Owen. "I sent it off."

"To me?"

"Of course. Perhaps it's stuck in your front office?"

"Or yours. Or perhaps you haven't written it."

"Oh no," said Owen. "I have certainly written it. I think."

"I shall complain to the Agent," said Guzman, and rang off. Owen sighed.

Nikos, who had been listening throughout, rang through again.

"Why didn't you put him on to Brooker?" he asked.

༄

In this outer part of Cairo the houses were single-storey. A low mud brick wall screened them and their women from the outside world. Beyond the houses was the desert, flat, grey, empty, except for a few wisps of thorn bushes.

Mahmoud met Owen in the open square where the buses turned.

"I thought it better like this," he said. "Otherwise you'd never find it."

He led Owen up a dark alley which narrowed and bent and doubled back on itself and soon lost its identity in a maze of other alleys threading through and connecting the houses. In the poorer suburbs there were no roads. The alleys were the only approach and these were thick with mud and refuse and excrement.

In the dark Owen could not see, but he could smell, and as he stumbled along, his feet skidding and squashing, he could guess. There were, too, the little scurries of rats.

The only light was from the sky. Out here there was no reflected glare from the city's lights and you could see the stars clearly. The sky seemed quite light compared with the dark shadows of the alleys.

Occasionally you heard people beyond the walls and often there was the smell of cooking. Once or twice the voices came from the roofs where the people had taken their beds and lay out in the evening cool.

The alleys became narrower and the walls poorer and more dilapidated. There were gaps in them where bricks had fallen away and not been repaired. You could see the spaces against the sky.

Some of the bricks had fallen into the alleyways and there were heaps of rubble and other stuff that Owen had to climb over or wade through.

They came out into what at first Owen thought was a small square but in fact was a space where a house had fallen down. He heard Mahmoud talking to someone and then felt Mahmoud's hand on his arm gently guiding him along a wall. There was a small doorway in the wall, or perhaps it was just a gap. Mahmoud slipped through it and drew Owen after him.

They were in a small yard. Over to one side there was a little oil lamp on the ground, around which some women were squatting. They looked up as Mahmoud approached but did not move away, as women usually would. They wore no veils, and in the light from the lamp Owen could see they were Berberines, their faces marked and tattooed with the tribal scars.

He followed Mahmoud into the house. There was just the single room. In one corner there was a low fire from which the smoke wavered up uncertainly to a hole in the roof, first wandering about the room and filling the air with its acrid fumes. On the floor was another oil lamp, and beside it two people were sitting, one of them a policeman. The other man looked up. He was gaunt and emaciated and plainly uneasy.

Mahmoud muttered something and the policeman left the room. They squatted down opposite the other man.

The smell of excrement was strong in the air. So was another smell, heavy, sickly, sweet. Owen recognized it to be hashish.

The man waited patiently.

Eventually Mahmoud said: "You travel the villages?"

"Iwa," said the man. "Yes, effendi."

"You take them the drug?"

"Yes, effendi."

"Do you take them just *the* drug, or do you also take them the one that chills?"

The man's face twitched slightly. "Sometimes I take them the one that chills," he said in a low voice. He put out his hand pleadingly.

"But not often, effendi. Sometimes—just for a rich omda—that is all."

"It is bad," said Mahmoud sternly. "It is bad. Nevertheless, that is not our concern tonight. Our concern is with something other. Tell us about the other and we shall not ask questions about this. Do you understand?"

"I understand, effendi," said the man submissively.

"Good. Then let us begin with what you have already said. You travel the villages with the drug."

"Yes, effendi."

"Among them the village that we know."

"Yes, effendi."

"And at that village you sell the drug."

"Yes, effendi."

"To all the men? Do most of the villagers buy?"

"Most of them. They work hard, effendi. This year there is little food. It fills their stomachs," the man said quietly.

"And among the men," said Mahmoud, "you sell to the one we spoke of?"

"Yes, effendi."

"Every time? Or most times?"

"Since Ramadan," said the man, "every time."

"Little or much?"

"Little, effendi."

The man looked at Mahmoud.

"He is a good man, effendi," he said. "He would not take it from his children."

"So he bought only a little. But not last time."

"Last time," said the man, "he wanted more."

"Why was that? Did he say?"

"He said that one had given him the means to right a great wrong and that he wished to strengthen himself that he might accomplish it."

"And what did you say?"

"I warned him, effendi." The man spoke passionately, pleadingly.

"I warned him. I said, 'The world is full of wrongs. Try to right them and the world turns over. Better leave it as it is.'"

"And he said?"

The man looked down. "He said, effendi, that a drug-seller was without honour."

The lamp flickered and the shadows jumped suddenly. Then the flame steadied and they returned to their place.

The man raised his eyes again.

"I warned him," he said. "I told him that the one who had given him the means was a wrongdoer, for his was not the grudge. That troubled him. He said the one who had given him the means did not know what he intended. I asked him how could that be? But he would say no more."

"And you said no more?"

"And I said no more."

"He had the money."

"He had the money," the man agreed.

He looked down at the lamp. Mahmoud waited. The silence continued for some minutes. Owen was not used to squatting and desperately wanted to stretch, but he knew that the silence was important and dared not break it.

Eventually the man looked up.

"I think I saw the man, effendi," he said diffidently, "the wrongdoer."

"How was that?" asked Mahmoud mildly, almost without interest.

"It was the day of the meeting," said the man. "Afterwards I saw one from outside the village talking to him. And then again the next day. I stayed in the village that night," he explained.

"This one from outside the village," said Mahmoud, "was he young or old?"

"Young, effendi," said the man immediately. "Not much more than a boy."

"Rich or poor?"

"Rich. One of the well-to-do."

"If we showed a man to you," said Mahmoud, "could you tell us if it was he?"

The man looked at him with alarm. "Effendi, I dare not!" he said. "They would kill me!"

"They?" asked Owen. It was the only time he spoke.

"When one acts in a thing like this," said the man, "one does not act alone."

"The man was not alone, then?" said Mahmoud.

"When I saw him he was alone," the drug-seller said. "I spoke without meaning."

"If you saw him," said Mahmoud, "you would know him."

"I would know him," the man agreed wretchedly. "But, effendi—"

"Peace!" said Mahmoud. "We will bring you where you will see him but he will not see you. No one will ever know. I swear it."

"Effendi—" began the man desperately.

"Enough!" Mahmoud held up his hand.

"Do this thing for us," he said, "which no one shall ever know about, and you shall go in peace. Do not do this thing, and you will never go."

The man subsided, shrank into himself. Mahmoud rose. He put his hand gently on the man's shoulder.

"It will soon be over, friend," he said. "Go in peace."

"Salaam Aleikham," said the man, but automatically.

Owen followed Mahmoud out into the courtyard. The two policemen came across and waited expectantly. Mahmoud spoke to them for a couple of minutes and then they went into the house. They emerged with the slight figure of the drug-seller between them. Owen and Mahmoud set out along the alleyway with the others following close behind. In this part of the city it was better to travel as a party. When they reached the space and light of the main road Mahmoud spoke to the constables again and then they went off separately, on foot. He and Owen walked slowly back to where Owen had left his arabeah.

"We're going to find it's Ahmed, aren't we?" said Owen.

"It begins to look like that."

They walked a little way in silence.

Then Mahmoud said: "I must say, I am a little surprised."

Owen told him what Georgiades had found out about Nuri's son and secretary. Mahmoud listened with interest.

"It fits together," he said. "Mustafa and the Nationalists, Mustafa and Ahmed. Ahmed and the extremists among the Nationalists, if that leaflet really means anything. Those most likely to want to kill Nuri."

Which made it all the more surprising the next day when one of Owen's men reported that Nuri and Ahmed had been seen visiting *al Liwa*'s offices: together.

Chapter 7

"It's got to be protection," said Georgiades and Nikos together.

"He's a rich man," said Georgiades.

"A natural target," Nikos concurred.

"I wouldn't be surprised if several of the clubs were on to him," said Georgiades.

"They are," said Owen. "I've seen their letters."

"There you are, then."

"And checked them out."

"You got nothing?"

"Nothing."

"Did you check the right ones?" asked Georgiades.

"I checked the ones I was given," said Owen, and stopped.

"Given by Nuri's secretary," he said. "Ahmed."

"Yes," said Nikos, "well…"

"It wouldn't have made any difference," said Georgiades. "He wouldn't have given it you, anyway. And, sure as hell, he won't give it to you now."

"Nuri must know," said Owen.

"Do you think he would tell, though?"

"He told me about the other ones."

"Did he?" asked Nikos.

Owen shrugged. "He made no difficulty about showing me the letters."

"Some of them."

"Did he tell you whether he'd paid them off?" asked Georgiades.

"No," said Owen. "He rather gave me the impression he disregarded them."

"He would," said Nikos.

"Do you think he pays?"

"Of course," said Nikos.

"Invariably," said Georgiades.

"Everybody does," said Nikos.

"Then why did they try to kill him?"

"Did they try to kill him?" asked Georgiades.

Owen looked at him. "Are you suggesting they didn't?"

Georgiades spread his hands.

"Try this," he said, "for size. He didn't respond at once. So they tried to frighten him."

"Mustafa tried to kill him."

"It went wrong," said Georgiades.

"Why did it go wrong?" asked Nikos.

"Because they used that moron Ahmed as a go-between. He set it up wrongly."

"Ahmed would try to extort money from his own father?" asked Owen.

Georgiades spread his hands again, palms up, open as the Cairo day.

"Why not?" he said. "Better than trying to kill him."

Owen frowned. "It makes sense," he said. "Some sense. Neither you nor Zeinab thought he was of the stuff that killers are made of."

"Who is this Zeinab?" asked Nikos.

"A girl," Georgiades told him. "He's been doing some research of his own."

"He's been writing some memos of his own, too," said Nikos, still unforgiving.

"But there remains the difficulty," said Owen, disregarding them, "that the societies, or most of them, are professional and Ahmed is a bungling amateur. Why does a professional use an amateur?"

"Because he's Nuri's son?" offered Nikos.

"I still don't see—"

"It adds to the pleasure," said Nikos. "Their pleasure. To use the son against the father," he explained patiently.

"Now you've shocked *him*," said Georgiades to Nikos. "Anyway, I can think of another explanation."

"What's that?"

"They wanted to give him something to do. Always hanging around. Get him out of their hair."

"I prefer that explanation," Owen said to Nikos.

Nikos smiled, worldly-wise.

"We're still left with the old question, though," said Owen. "Who's 'they'?"

"We know the answer now, don't we?" asked Georgiades.

"Do we?"

"The ones Nuri and Ahmed went to see at *al Liwa*."

But that was strange. For the person Nuri and Ahmed had talked to at *al Liwa*, they later learned from their agent, was Abdul Murr.

⚬⚬⚬

Much to Owen's surprise, for he had neither expected nor intended the memo to have such an effect, there were three other responses besides Guzman's to the memo that day.

The next came at lunch-time. Owen had gone as usual to the club and as he was going in to the dining-room someone hailed him through the open door of the bar.

It was one of the Consul-General's bright young men, a personal friend.

"Hello, Gareth," he said. "Can I catch you for a minute?"

He led Owen out on to the verandah and they sat down at a table where they were unlikely to be disturbed.

"It's about that memo of yours," he said, "the one about lapses in military security."

"Look, Paul—" Owen began hastily.

"The Old Man's concerned. He had the SPG in first thing this morning. Told him a thing or two. And not before time, I must say! The Army behaves as if it's on a bloody island of its own. Has its own procedures, won't talk to anyone else, won't even listen to anyone else. Thinks it knows it all and in reality knows bloody nothing! The Egyptians mightn't be here at all as far as it's concerned. And much the same goes for the Civil Branch. We might as well not exist. The Army goes clumping in with its bloody great big boots. Half our time is spent trying to make up for the damage it's already bloody caused and the other half trying to anticipate what it's going to cock up next. Liaison—you talk about liaison in your mem—Jesus! they can't even spell the word!"

"Some of them particularly," said Owen, pleased.

"You're dead right! Military Security in particular. Mind you, you get all the dummos in that. A fine pig's ear they've been making of things! Supplying arms and ammunition to half the bloody population. And making a few bob out of it on the side, I'll bet. Those bloody Army storesmen are about as straight as a corkscrew—an implement with which they are all too familiar."

"Now, now, Paul," said Owen. "They drink beer."

"You're bloody right they do! No wonder the place is a desert. Anything liquid they bloody consume."

"The trouble is," said Owen, "the Sirdar will never do anything."

"Oh yes he will. This time. The Agent was on to him directly. He's at risk, too. Great minds think alike for once."

"You reckon the memo might have some effect?"

"It already has. Sirdar's already kicked some people up the ass."

"He has?" said Owen happily.

"He certainly has."

Paul leaned forward and spoke a trifle more quietly but just as vehemently.

"And with bloody good reason," he said. "Because do you know what came out? The Old Man demanded to know if anything had been stolen recently. The SPG had to tell him. And—can you believe it? It turned out that a box of grenades had vanished from Kantara barracks only last Tuesday! Grenades! A box! Jesus!"

"Kantara?" said Owen. "That's interesting."

"Is it? Well, perhaps it is to you. I must say, Gareth, they're pretty impressed with you. Timely prescience, the Agent called it. Even the Sirdar thought it was damn good intelligence work."

"Well, there you are," said Owen modestly.

"But what interests *me*," said Paul, "was that it was a whole bloody box. Could cause absolute havoc if they start chucking a few of those around. And it's just when we've got all the festivals coming up! We've got the Carpet next week and the place will be stiff with notables all hanging around for someone to take a pot shot at. Even the Khedive has been persuaded to come to receive the plaudits of his loyal and appreciative subjects. And I'm organizing our side! Christ!"

"The Agent?"

"*And* the Sirdar!"

"McPhee's very good," said Owen.

"He'll have to be," said Paul gloomily, "if the Army is issuing arms to the whole population of Egypt."

ᴑᴡᴡᴑ

"Is this real?" asked Garvin.

He had an unfortunate way of going to the heart of things.

"I am afraid it is, sir," said Owen, straightforward and thanking his lucky stars for the conversation at lunch-time. "A box of grenades went missing from Kantara only this week."

"I know," said Garvin. "The Sirdar told me." He still looked sceptical. "I must say I was a little surprised at your memo. I hadn't noticed any build-up. Still, I dare say you rely on information which does not come through in the ordinary way."

He looked down at the papers in front of him. Garvin's distaste for paper-pushing was well known.

"That's right, sir," said Owen immediately. He felt he was sounding too much like McPhee. "And a lot of it of very dubious quality. But when it all points in one direction—"

"And this did?"

"Enough to risk a judgement," said Owen.

Surprisingly, Garvin seemed satisfied.

"Well," he said, "it seems to have been a good judgement. Both the Agent and the Sirdar are pleased with you. And that doesn't happen often."

One of the reasons for that, Owen felt like saying, was that neither of them was particularly anxious to hear about the Mamur Zapt's activities; and Garvin usually thought it politic not to enlighten them.

"The only trouble is," said Garvin, "that now they'll expect you to do something."

"I've outlined several things in my memo—" Owen began.

Garvin brushed this aside.

"About the grenades," he said.

The conversation was beginning to take an unprofitable direction.

"Isn't that rather Military Security's pigeon?" Owen asked.

"Not any longer. The grenades are out of the camp, aren't they?"

Owen was forced to admit that this was so.

"They'll have to give me some information," he said.

"They will. This time."

"We'd never even have heard about the grenades if it had not been for my memo," he said, still hoping to deflect Garvin back to safer paths.

"Probably not," Garvin agreed cheerfully.

"Still," he said, "with your contacts—You must have had something to go on in writing your memo."

The scepticism had definitely returned.

"Of course," Owen agreed hastily. "Of course."

"However," he went on after a moment, "nothing on this, I'm afraid."

"It will all fit in," said Garvin, relaxed. "Never underrate your sources." It was a favourite maxim of his.

"No," said Owen.

A suffragi brought in some papers for Garvin to sign. He read them carefully and signed deliberately. Although he had been to Cambridge he always gave the impression that writing came hard to him.

"All I've got to go on at the moment," said Owen, "is that they were taken from Kantara. I'm interested in Kantara for another reason. That's where the gun came from which was used against Nuri Pasha."

He told Garvin about the sergeant. Garvin was not very concerned.

"Probably happening all the time," he said. "They probably all do it."

"And they all know where to take it to," said Owen.

"Yes," Garvin admitted. "There is that."

"Military Security haven't done anything about that angle," said Owen, still hoping.

"Nor have we," said Garvin. "You'd better start."

ᘓᗢᘐ

Owen returned unhappily to his room. This did not appear to be working out as he had hoped.

There was a message on his desk to ring one of the Sirdar's aides.

"Hello, John," he said.

"Gareth? That you? Thank goodness for that. I've got to go out this evening—the Sirdar's holding a reception—and I wanted to catch you first. It's about that memo."

"Yes?" said Owen, warily now.

"What's going on?"

"I'm trying to shake that bugger, Brooker."

"Reasonable. He needs shaking. But why bring the whole firmament down as well?"

"Have you got caught up in it?" asked Owen. "Sorry if you have."

"Oh, that's all right," said the other. "I'm not directly involved. The thing is, though, that I've been talking to Paul, and he's reminded me that we've got this blasted Carpet thing on next week. I've got to be holding the Sirdar's hand at the time and I don't want to be fending off grenades while I'm doing it."

"You've got the other hand free," said Owen.

"Thank you. Oh thank you."

"It'll be all right," said Owen. "McPhee's quite sound."

"He's thick as a post. And erratic as well."

"He's OK at this sort of thing. Anyway, we'll double up security all round."

"The Sirdar thinks something extra is needed."

"Such as?"

"Don't know. You're the one who's supposed to have ideas on things like that. The Sirdar thinks you're smart."

"I am, I am."

"He doesn't want just a routine operation this time. I must say I'm right with him."

"I'll speak to McPhee."

"You're the one in charge."

"No, I'm not. I'm sort of in the background," Owen explained.

"Not this time. Haven't you heard?"

Owen's heart began to sink.

"No," he said. "Tell me."

"Sorry to be the one to break the news. Thought it would have got through by now."

"It hasn't."

"Well, the Sirdar wanted security augmented. He offered the Army. The Agent said no thanks. Wisely. The Sirdar said this was a special situation. The police couldn't be expected to cope with terrorism. The Agent thought there was something in that. They decided that what was needed was someone who knew about that sort of thing. You. Congratulations."

"Christ!" said Owen.

"Help me catch the grenades, then?"

"I'll throw the bloody grenades," said Owen.

John roared with laughter.

"At any rate," he said, "you'll be spared the assistance of Military Security. Unless you want it. I offer you Brooker."

"That stupid bastard! It's all his fault," said Owen unfairly.

"If he gets in your hair anymore," John offered, "tell me. I'll get him posted to Equatoria."

"Those grenades were taken from Kantara."

"Where that sergeant was?" He whistled. "Pity you couldn't squeeze something out of him. He's coming out today, you know."

"Is he? The lucky bastard."

"He'll be celebrating tonight. And every night for the next week, I shouldn't wonder."

"He won't talk now."

"No? Couldn't you frighten him somehow?"

Owen suddenly had an idea.

⁂

To the north of the Ezbekiyeh Gardens were the streets of ill repute. The chief of these was the Sharia Wagh el Birket, one side of which was taken up by the apartments of the wealthier courtesans. The apartments rose in tiers over the street, each with its balcony, over which its occupants hung in negligees of virgin white.

on the balconies but busy inside. However, customers
still coming and going. Small groups of scarlet Tommies
d together staggered down the street singing drunkenly.
n they got past the more selective establishments hands
ld very soon pull them into alleyways. As well, however,
e were the usual Cairene clients; too many of them.

"We'll wait," Owen said.

By three the street was empty. The last Tommies had been
allowed up. The traffic now was out of the houses and not
to them. The balconies were empty. The pimps were gone.
Owen signed with his hand.

Georgiades went up to the door and knocked upon it. A
ttle shutter opened at eye level. Apparently Georgiades
atisfied scrutiny, for the door was opened a crack. Someone
big was standing inside. Owen saw Georgiades look up at
him as he was talking. The door would be on a chain. It was
easier to get it right open.

Owen saw some money change hands.

There was the sound of the chain being taken off.
Georgiades stepped inside. A man fell suddenly against the
door. One of the big Sudanis with Owen pulled him outside
and hit him with his truncheon. Georgiades was holding the
door open with his shoulders. The other Sudanis piled in.

Owen stepped in after them. A man was lying by the door
dazed and holding his head. Two of the Sudanis were grap-
pling with a huge Berberine. As Owen entered he saw the
Berberine subside.

Georgiades had pushed on ahead. They were in a small,
dark hall at the end of which was a door. He flung the door
open. Beyond it was a large sunken room with couches and
divans on which people were lying in various states of undress.
There were glasses and bottles on the floor and one or two of
the men were smoking from nargilehs.

A woman sprang up. She was wearing a long purple dress
and her face was heavily made up. She called something and

The opposite side of the street wa
arches were little cafés where strong l
customers sat at tables on the pavement,
ing, and looking across at the balconies c
to time one would make up his mind anc

At the far end of the street the cafés ga
Unlike the ones opposite, they were dark a
enter, and many people did, you knocked
and waited to be admitted.

It was to one of these that the sergeant ha
reeling from the liquor he had previously consum
had an informant inside who reported regu
sergeant's progress, which was from drunk to fig
to maudlin to blind drunk and finally to stupor.
evening, in the intervals between drinking, he h
the needs of his flesh with the help of willing assis
had even more willingly relieved him of coin, wal
and other valuables.

"Did you get his belt?" asked Owen.

Georgiades held up a standard military belt.

"They did! Good!" said Owen with satisfaction.

Soldiers often sold their belts for drink. Since belt
military equipment they could then be charged w
different set of offences under military law.

He took the belt and inspected it almost as a matte
course. It was an offence to file the edges and point of
buckle; the belt made a nasty weapon in a brawl. Offic
were required to check belts regularly. Owen looked to see
there was evidence of filing. There was.

"We'll keep that," he said to Georgiades.

He might be able to use it later.

Georgiades put the belt on under his trousers.

"When do you want to go in?" he asked.

Owen checked his watch. It was not long after two in the
morning. The street was still quite busy. The houris were no

two men came out of an inner room holding thick sticks with spikes on them. Georgiades showed them his gun and they stopped. A Sudani hit one of the men across the arm with his truncheon. Then there was a crack and the spiked stick fell to the floor. The man doubled up, holding his arm. The other man ran off. The Sudani followed him.

Some of the people on the couches started getting up.

"Stay where you are!" Georgiades commanded.

He looked round the room. The sergeant wasn't there.

"Upstairs!" he said, and nodded to the Sudanis.

The madam advanced on him, her eyes blazing.

"What is this?" she said. "Who are you?"

Georgiades ignored her.

She caught one of the Sudanis as he went by.

"Who is this?" she hissed.

"The Mamur Zapt," said the man, and went out through the door.

The woman saw Owen.

"*Vous êtes le Mamur Zapt?*"

"*Oui, madame.*"

"*Qu'est ce que vous faîtes ici?*" she demanded, and launched on a bitter tirade. Owen pushed her away.

The people on the couches sat frozen. One of the girls began to cry.

Georgiades came in.

"He's upstairs," he said.

Owen followed him. There was a small landing at the top of the stairs which gave on to a series of rooms. Georgiades went into one of these.

There was a large bed with no covers. On it were two women, one black, one white, both naked, and the sergeant, dressed only in a shirt. He was trying to sit up.

"What the hell's this?" he said thickly.

Georgiades looked at Owen. Owen nodded.

"Get the cuffs on him," he said.

A big Sudani yanked the sergeant off the bed in a single movement. The sergeant swore and stood swaying. Georgiades snapped the cuffs on. The sergeant looked at them, bewildered. He had difficulty in focusing his eyes.

One of the girls gestured at his trousers, which had been flung over a chair.

"Take too long," said Georgiades.

The girl shrugged, curled herself up and lay there watching.

The Sudanis started hustling the sergeant out. As they got him to the door he suddenly bent over and vomited.

They had to wait while he leaned against the door post groaning and retching.

The madam came up the stairs.

"I will complain," she said. "You have no right."

Her eyes took in the sergeant.

"Pig!" she said. "*Cochon.*"

In one of the rooms off the landing a woman cried out.

The sergeant brought himself upright. His eyes suddenly focused on Owen.

"Seen you before," he muttered.

One of the Sudanis pulled at him. The sergeant shook him off.

"Who the hell are you?" he said. "Seen you before."

Two Sudanis got a grip on him and began to drag him down the stairs.

"*Mon dieu!*" said the madam. "*C'est affreux!*" She tried to intercept Owen. "I will tell the consul," she said. "You cannot do this."

The sergeant collapsed at the bottom of the stairs, white-faced and groaning.

"Take him out!" said Georgiades.

One of the Sudanis caught hold of the sergeant by the collar and tried to haul him upright. The collar tore and the sergeant fell back. Another Sudani picked him up by the armpits and propped him against the stairs. The sergeant looked about him, confused.

"Seen you before," he said.

The Sudanis pulled him towards the door. Half way across the room he was sick again.

"*Cochon! Cochon!*" the madam cried.

A grey-haired man came in through the door. He was wearing a silk dressing-gown and had plainly just got out of bed.

"I protest!" he said. "These are Syrian citizens!"

"This one?" asked Georgiades, pointing to the sergeant.

"That one, too," said the grey-haired man.

"He's a British soldier," said Georgiades.

The sergeant lifted his head. "I fucking am," he said.

He wrenched himself free from the Sudanis, put his head down and charged at the grey-haired man. Georgiades tripped him up and the Sudanis fell on top of him.

"Get him out, for Christ's sake," said Owen.

The Sudanis picked themselves up. The sergeant lay motionless on the floor. Another Sudani came across and helped them to carry him out.

The madam caught the grey-haired man by the sleeve and whispered to him. He came up to Owen.

"I protest!" he said. "This is a gross infringement of our nation's rights under the Capitulations."

"Who are you?" asked Owen.

The man drew himself up. "I am a member of the Syrian consular staff."

He fumbled in the pocket of his dressing-gown and produced a printed slip.

"Here is my card," he said with dignity.

Owen ignored it.

"I am the Mamur Zapt," he said. "I have right of entry into all premises."

"Under protest," said the man. "My country does not accept that interpretation."

"Too bad," said Owen, and turned away.

The sergeant was out of the house now.

"I shall complain to the Agent," said the grey-haired man. "This is Syrian territory and these are Syrian subjects."

He had to earn his money. Half the brothels in Cairo, and all the gambling saloons, retained a tame consular official to use in case of emergencies. Under the Capitulations, privileges granted to European powers by successive Ottoman rulers, foreigners were granted immunity from Egyptian law. They could not even be charged unless it could be proved that they had committed an offence not under Egyptian law but in terms of the law of their own native countries. Since nationality was elastic at the best of times in the Levant, it was very hard to convict anyone at all; except, of course, for the poorer Egyptians.

It was a system which commercially inclined Cairenes knew exactly how to turn to advantage, and which drove Garvin and McPhee to despair.

"One of them is a British subject," said Owen, "and he has been robbed."

He followed Georgiades out of the house. They had given the Sudanis enough time now to be well on their way.

Beneath the Mamur Zapt's office was a whole row of cells, but Owen did not want the sergeant put in one of them. He was taken instead to a public prison in the Hosh Sharkawiyeh. Owen had chosen it because it was a caracol, a traditional native lock-up. It consisted of a single long room. There were no windows, just two narrow slits high up for ventilation. Most air and what light there was came in through the heavy wooden bars of the grille-like door, through which prisoners could look up at the busy street outside. The prison stood at the corner of an old square and had either been deliberately built to be below ground level or else, like some of the other buildings in the square, had been constructed at a time when the level was generally lower.

There were fifteen prisoners in the cell, not many by Egyptian standards, but crowded enough. Foetid air reached up to Owen as the keeper unbolted the door. Some of the inmates had been confined for the same reason as the sergeant, and, mixed with the stale air, there was a strong smell of excrement and vomit.

The Sudanis threw the sergeant in and helped the keeper to slide back the heavy bolts.

"The Army is not going to like this," said Georgiades.

"No," agreed Owen, "it is not."

Before they left he gave certain instructions to the keeper. They were to see the sergeant had water, to give him bread, to keep an eye open in case there was trouble between him and the other prisoners, but otherwise on no account to interfere.

That should be enough, thought Owen.

ஒ௰௲ல

Owen went home and slept late. When he got in to the office the next morning Nikos was already at his desk.

"There's someone to see you," he said. "A friend of yours. He's been waiting a long time."

"Oh," said Owen. "Where is he?"

Nikos pointed along the corridor. From McPhee's room came the sound of voices. McPhee's. Guzman's.

"If that bugger doesn't get off my back," said Owen, "I'll bloody fix him."

"The way you did Brooker?" asked Nikos, keeping his eyes firmly on the papers in front of him.

Owen went into his office. A little later McPhee stuck his head in, looking hot and bothered.

"Guzman Bey is here," he said. "He's got a complaint."

"Another?"

Owen put his pencil down, closed the file he was working on and rose to greet Guzman as McPhee ushered him in.

"Captain Owen!" Guzman spoke without preamble. "I wish to protest!"

"Really?" said Owen. "What about?"

"Your high-handed action last night. The Khedive has received a formal complaint from the Syrian ambassador."

"On what grounds?"

"That you forcibly and illegally entered premises belonging to a Syrian citizen—"

"A brothel."

"—and abducted a guest present on the premises."

"A customer. A British subject."

"A British soldier. Characteristically engaged."

"But British. And therefore no concern of the ambassador's."

Nor of the Khedive's, he nearly added.

"Syrian rights have been infringed. That is the concern of the ambassador."

Owen reflected. He could simply tell Guzman to go and jump in the Nile. Or he could be more politic. In Cairo it was nearly always best to be more politic. He adopted a reasonable tone.

"At the time of entry the premises were not known to be foreign," he said. "They were known only to be a particularly vicious brothel. I must say, I find it a little surprising that the ambassador should be defending the rights of someone engaged in conducting such a place!"

"Perhaps," said Guzman drily, "he was unaware of the use to which the premises were put."

Owen was not sure that the words were meant ironically. Guzman spoke as flatly as he usually did; but was there a glint of humour? If so, it did not survive long.

"The fact remains," said Guzman, "that Syrian rights *have* been infringed and the Khedive embarrassed."

Owen decided to be politic still.

"If the Khedive has been embarrassed," he said smoothly, "it was, of course, inadvertently on our part. I hope you will convey my personal apologies."

Guzman was taken aback by this; indeed he appeared slightly put out. He hesitated, as if uncertain about prolonging the interview, and then said, almost tentatively: "The soldier—?"

"Will be dealt with by the Army," said Owen heartily.

He edged towards the door. Guzman, however, ignored the hint.

"But will he?" he asked suddenly.

"Will he—"

"Be dealt with by the Army?"

"Of course."

"Will it," said Guzman meaningfully, "get the chance?"

Owen was caught slightly off balance.

"I don't quite follow you."

"I understand," said Guzman, "that the man is still in your custody."

"Ah yes," said Owen, recovering, "but that is only temporarily."

"How temporary?"

"Very temporary," said Owen firmly. He was not going to be steam-rollered by Guzman.

"May I ask why you are holding him?"

"I just want to ask him a few questions."

"About—?"

"Oh, military matters," he said vaguely, edging further towards the door.

"Military matters?" Guzman looked puzzled. "But surely that is the concern of the Army?"

Owen realized that he had been cornered again.

"Some are my concern," he said off-handedly.

"Ah! Security!"

Owen smiled politely, and uninformatively. He took up a stance by the door. Guzman did not appear to notice. He seemed sunk in thought.

"This man you are holding—"

"Yes?"

"What precisely—?"

"I am afraid I am not at liberty to tell you that."

Guzman was still thinking.

"Was he at the Kantara barracks?" he asked.

Owen continued to smile politely but did not reply.

Guzman thought again. Then he made up his mind.

"I would like to see him," he said abruptly.

"That," said Owen, "would not be possible."

After Guzman had gone, Nikos came back into the room.

"That was odd," he said. "Why is he so interested?"

"In the sergeant, you mean? Don't know. For the same reason as us, perhaps."

"Perhaps," said Nikos, and went away again still looking thoughtful.

Owen opened his file and worked steadily till lunch. Then he went to the club. In the cloakroom he ran into his friend John, the Sirdar's aide.

"I don't want to be seen with you!" his friend said, pretending flight.

"Why not?"

"You're always doing horrid things to the Army."

"What am I doing now?"

"Kidnapping its soldiers. Or so I am informed."

Owen was surprised.

"Christ! That's quick!" he said. "Who informed you?"

"Someone from the Khediviate."

"Really?" A nasty suspicion dawned in Owen's mind. "You don't, by chance, happen to know his name?"

"He was unwilling to give it but I extracted it. Guzman."

"Guzman! The bastard!"

"You do seem to be having trouble with your acquaintances," said John.

"When did you get the message?"

"About an hour ago."

"He must have rung as soon as he got out of my office. The bastard!"

"I take it," said John, drying his hands, "that the poor kidnapped soldier is a certain ex-sergeant from Kantara?"

"You take it rightly."

"In that case," said John, "I wish to know no more. What I can tell you in confidence is that unfortunately I was unable to pass the message on before lunch as I was so busy. Naturally I shall inform my superiors as soon as possible. However, it may be that I shall be detained at lunch by someone who insists on buying me a drink and so I shall miss the afternoon mail with my memo. In which case it would only reach them tomorrow morning."

"You're a pal," said Owen.

"Would it help?"

"It would. It really would."

"Mind! Till tomorrow only!"

"That should be long enough."

"In any case," said John, "it would be bad for the Sirdar's digestion if he was told that sort of thing just after lunch."

"We wouldn't want that to happen. But now, about your own digestion—?"

"A drink would go down very nicely. Yes, please."

Owen called in at the office after his swim. Nikos was still there. "I don't understand it," he said when Owen told him about Guzman's message. "Why would he do a thing like that?"

"Because he's a nasty bastard, that's why!" said Owen with feeling.

Nikos shook his head. "That wouldn't be the only reason."

"What other reason could there be?"

"I don't know," said Nikos.

Owen left him thinking and went on into his own room. Nikos hated things to be untidy, unexplained. He would worry at this like a terrier with a bone.

Some time later he came into Owen's room.

"Maybe he's afraid," he said.

"Afraid? What of?"

"You. Talking to the sergeant. He thinks you might find out something."

"But why tip off the Army?"

"So that you get less time to talk."

He collected the papers from Owen's out-tray and went back into the main office. When Owen looked in half an hour later he had gone home.

Owen himself worked on till well after midnight. Then he called for the sergeant. The sergeant had been in the caracol for over twenty-four hours now; and this time he gave Owen the name he wanted.

Chapter 8

"I think we ought to go in," said McPhee.

"There's no real evidence," Garvin objected. "Nothing to link him with the grenades."

"There's plenty to link him with other stuff."

"Plenty?"

"That sergeant said it was a recognized route. They've been using that chap for years."

"If what the sergeant says is true," said Garvin, "and we know him to be a liar."

"He wasn't lying this time," said Owen.

"It's the lead we wanted," said McPhee. "What are we waiting for?"

"We're waiting for something real," said Garvin.

"Isn't the box something real?"

"There are boxes going in and out of that place all the time."

"Ali says he knows those and it wasn't one of them," said Owen.

"How can he know all the boxes? What about a new supplier?"

"He was sure."

"Might be anything," said Garvin dismissively. "A new hat for his wife, goods for the shop. We can't go in just on the word of a street beggar."

"And of a sergeant," said McPhee.

"A convicted criminal. Lying to save his skin."

"Not to save his skin," Owen pointed out.

"All right, then," said Garvin. "Lying because he's been terrified out of his wits. And that's something else I want to speak to you about."

"We wouldn't have found out any other way," said McPhee loyally, and bore without flinching the look Garvin gave him.

"The question is," said Garvin, "now that we've got some real information—"

Owen did not like the way Garvin kept emphasizing the word "real" today.

"—how do we use it? Wouldn't it be best simply to put a man on the shop and keep it under surveillance?"

"We don't have the time," said Owen. "The Carpet's next week."

"Suppose the grenades are still on their way?" asked Garvin. "Suppose they haven't got there yet? Don't we just scare whoever-it-is off?"

"Suppose they've already passed through?" said Owen.

"Well," said Garvin, "in that case we've lost them already. Going in wouldn't help."

"We might pick up something," said McPhee.

"And at least we'd know," said Owen.

"Suppose they're there all the time," said McPhee, "while we're mucking around."

"And suppose they'll soon be not there," added Owen, "if we go on mucking around. Boxes come out as well as go in."

"Yes," said Garvin. "I'll admit that's a worry."

He rested his chin on his hand and thought.

"All the same," he said, "it's not much to go on. If it wasn't grenades I wouldn't look at it."

"But it is grenades," said McPhee, "and the Carpet is next week."

"We don't know—" Garvin began, and then stopped. He thought for a little longer and then he looked at Owen.

"OK," he said, "you can go in. But on your head be it."

It was a typical Garvin ending and Owen wanted to ask what he meant, though he had an uneasy feeling that he knew what was meant. McPhee, however, was pleased.

"Good, sir," he said. "When?"

"This afternoon," said Owen, "when everybody's asleep."

"Not tonight?" asked Garvin.

"You can see better in the day," said Owen.

Garvin shrugged.

"All right, then," he said. "Only you'll have to move fast. He's a Syrian and he'll have someone round from the consulate in a flash of lightning. You won't even get a chance to question him."

"I'll see I get a chance to question him," said Owen.

⁕

Soon after two, when the sun had driven people from the streets and most Cairenes were settling deeply into their siesta, Owen's men went in.

The shutters had been half drawn across the front of the shop to give shade and to symbolize recess but there was a gap in the middle through which the men stepped. An assistant was asleep on the floor, curled up among the brassware. He opened his eyes as the men came in, blinked and then sat bolt upright. One of the men picked him up by the scruff of the neck and put him in a corner, where he was soon joined by two other startled and sleepy assistants brought through from the separate servants' quarters at the rear of the house.

The family lived above the shop. The first floor contained the dining-room and a surprisingly luxurious living-room, with a tiled floor and heavy, rich carpets on the walls. Above these were the bedrooms, where the man whose name Owen had been given slept with his wife and their five children. Above this again was the room at the front with five latticed windows where the wife's mother slept and spent most of her days, together with a warren of small storerooms.

Georgiades went straight to these, reasoning that the grenades would most likely be stored in the private part of the house and in a room rarely used by the family. Abdul Kassem, one of his most experienced men, went through to the back of the shop where goods awaiting unpacking or despatch were stored and began to search meticulously through the boxes.

The other men fanned out through the house. The first thing was to station a man at every intersection, where one floor gave on to another, or one set of rooms to an independent suite. In that way if anyone made a panic move in one particular direction he would be remarked and intercepted. After that the men began to move efficiently through each room.

McPhee, nominally under Owen's orders for the occasion, since the police did not possess right of entry without a warrant but the Mamur Zapt did, began to ferret around the shop itself, poking his stick particularly under the heavy shelving which supported the goods.

The shop was half way along the Musky and catered for both native Egyptians and tourists. The Egyptians came for the fine brassware: the elegant ewers called ibreek, which the Arabs used for pouring water over the hands, the little basins and water-strainers which went with them, old brass coffee-pots, coffee saucepans, coffee-trays, coffee-cups and coffee-mills, fine brasswork for the nargileh pipes, chased brass lantern-ends, brass open-work toilet boxes, incense-burners, inkpots, scales—all of good old patterns and workmanship. The tourists came for the brass boxes and bowls inlaid with silver, the spangled Assiut shawls, the harem embroideries, the cloisonné umbrella handles—a special attraction—Persian pottery, enamel and lacquer, silver-gilt parodies of jewels from the graves of Pharaohs, old, illuminated Korans and pieces of Crusader armour.

Plenty of capital tied up here, thought Owen, and plenty of money to buy other things as well.

He heard raised voices on the floor above, and a moment later flat slippers descending the stairs.

A man appeared. A Syrian.

"Qu'est-ce que vous faîtes ici, monsieur?" he began hotly as soon as he saw McPhee. The Scot waved him on to Owen and continued searching.

The Syrian was in a blue silk dressing-gown and red leather slippers. Although his house had been broken into in the middle of his siesta and interlopers were downstairs he had taken the time to smooth himself down and make himself presentable.

He repeated the question to Owen and then, registering the nationality, switched to English.

"What is the meaning of this?" he demanded. "I am a Syrian citizen. This is an outrage."

He was thin, middle-aged, grey-haired. The hair was brushed very flat and oiled. There were grey shadows under his eyes, not so much, Owen thought, because he had been disturbed in the middle of his sleep, as that it was a permanent feature of his face, which would always look haggard, worried.

"Where is your authority?" he demanded. "Have you a warrant?"

Owen noticed that he had understood at once that this was a police raid.

"I am the Mamur Zapt," he said. "I do not need a warrant."

"The Mamur Zapt!"

Owen caught the momentary flash of concern.

"I demand that a member of my consul's staff be present! I am a Syrian citizen."

"In time," said Owen, and turned away. He did not want to talk to the Syrian until he had something with which to shake him. Like the grenades, for example. But there was no sign yet of any success in the search.

He thought it likely that the Syrian had already succeeded in getting a message out of the house to whatever consular representative it was that he had in his pocket. Owen had posted a couple of men outside to guard against this happening but guessed that the Syrian had made provision for such an eventuality. It would take some time, however, for the man from the consulate to arrive. He could wait a few minutes.

"Let us go upstairs," he said.

The Syrian looked puzzled and then suddenly acquiesced. Perhaps he thought Owen was going to ask for a bribe. That was probably the way the previous Mamur Zapt had done things.

As they went upstairs Owen said to McPhee: "If anyone comes from the consulate keep him busy as long as you can. Ask him to prove his status. Ask him if he's got the right place. You know."

McPhee knew. He was less good at these things, however, than Owen, and a resolute official would soon brush his way past him. It would earn Owen a few minutes, though.

The Syrian went ahead of him into the living-room. Owen deliberately held back.

"I shall be with you in a moment," he said, and then continued upstairs to the next floor.

"Keep him down there," he instructed his man on the stairs.

Georgiades came out of one of the doors wiping the sweat from his face. He shook his head as he saw Owen.

"Nothing yet," he said.

He went into another room.

Owen lingered on the small landing. He knew better than to interfere with the search. Georgiades and his people were all experienced at that sort of thing and there was a pattern to it which he would only disrupt. Georgiades had once told him, too, that there were cultural differences in the way people hid things. Greeks hid things in one sort of place,

Arabs in another. Obviously he had not yet found out where Syrians hid things.

Owen could hear the Syrian's voice raised in protest. He knew he would have to go down and talk to him. The man from the consulate might soon be here.

The Syrian was at the bottom of the stairs, his way up barred by one of Owen's men. Both fell back as Owen came down the stairs. Owen pushed past them and went on into the living-room. He sat down on one of the low divans and motioned to the Syrian to sit on another before him.

Everything in the room was low, the divans, the tables, even the lamps. There were no chairs. There were no sideboards or shelves, no wall furniture of any kind to detract from the sumptuous carpets on the walls. On some of the little tables that were scattered around beside the divans there were fine boxes and bowls, all of silver.

A door opened at the far end of the room and a woman's face looked in. The Syrian waved her irritably away. She looked worried.

The Syrian himself had lost his apprehension and was waiting, almost confidently, for Owen to begin. Owen guessed that he was still thinking in terms of a bribe.

Owen decided he would try to shake him.

"You sometimes have British soldiers among your customers," he said, more as a statement than a question.

The Syrian looked slightly puzzled.

"Not often," he said. "The pay is not good,"

"Among your suppliers," said Owen.

"No," said the Syrian, too quickly, "no, I don't think so."

After a moment he said: "I deal mostly in brassware and silverware. With a few things for the tourists. If an officer's wife, perhaps, brought me a family heirloom I might consider that. But I don't really deal in English things."

"Do you keep a list of customers?"

"In my head," said the Syrian. "Only in my head."

Owen wondered whether it would be worth going through the books. Georgiades would not have time, though. McPhee could do it but Owen wanted him in the shop to take care of the man from the consulate. None of the other men would be any good. In any case it would probably be pointless. It would be as the Syrian said; the customers who mattered would be in his head.

The Syrian still waited expectantly.

"You don't deal in anything else?" Owen asked. "Arms, for instance?"

For the tiniest flicker of a second Owen thought he saw the face register. Then it returned to its normal impassivity.

"No," said the Syrian. "I don't deal in arms. Except—" he smiled. "—Crusaders' arms. Was that what you meant?"

Owen ignored him. He desperately needed something from Georgiades if he was to make anything out of this exchange. Out of the whole raid, for that matter. They had staked everything on being able to find something incriminating. If not the grenades, then at least something. Now it all seemed to be evaporating.

The Syrian's air of expectancy had disappeared. He now knew what Owen had come for. Knew, and was not bothered.

"And now I have to ask you," said the Syrian, "to what do I owe this outrageous visit?"

Owen said nothing.

The Syrian leaned forward even more confidently.

"Even the Mamur Zapt," he said with emphasis, "cannot get away with this!"

And now Owen's ears caught what perhaps the Syrian had already heard. A new voice had entered into debate with McPhee downstairs.

"I shall complain to my consul," said the Syrian. "It is not just as a private citizen but also as a foreign national that I have rights."

Georgiades appeared at the door.

"Wait there!" said Owen to the Syrian. Outside, Georgiades showed him two revolvers, new, still heavily greased from the store, of the same type as the one used by Mustafa.

"That's all," said Georgiades apologetically.

"Every little helps," said Owen, "and it helps quite a bit just at the moment."

He went back into the room.

"My people have found British Army equipment," he said coldly. "Stolen from British Army installations. Now in your possession."

The Syrian spread his hands. "The guns?" he said. "They were stolen? The man swore they had been officially disposed of as surplus to Army needs."

"New ones?"

The Syrian shrugged apologetically. "I am afraid I do not know new ones from old ones. I am not a military man, I bought them for protection. I have a lot of valuable silver."

Owen could hear the man from the consulate coming up the stairs.

"I am sorry if I have done something illegal," said the Syrian, "but I hardly think it warrants an invasion on this scale."

"This is an outrage," began the consular official as Owen brushed past him. "I shall complain—"

A grim-faced McPhee was waiting downstairs. They left the shop without a word. Outside, a small crowd had gathered, sensing that something exciting was going on.

"Make way! Make way!" snapped McPhee, still upset.

The bright white glare of the street was dazzling after the cool darkness of the house and they stopped momentarily to adjust.

Georgiades came running round the corner.

"The roof!" he shouted. "The roof!"

He plunged back into the shop. Two of his men rushed in after him.

Abdul Kassem appeared from a sidestreet.

"There's a man on the roof!" he said, and doubled back.

Owen ran after him, closely followed by McPhee, closely followed by the entire crowd.

The sidestreet bent round into a wide square from which they could look back at the roofline.

At first they could see nothing.

Abdul Kassem pulled them to one side and pointed.

"There! There!"

Half obscured by the small minaret of a mosque they saw a man on the flat roof of one of the houses. He appeared to be dragging something.

"That's him!" cried McPhee exultantly. He pulled out his revolver.

"Don't shoot, for Christ's sake!" said Owen. "It's grenades up there!"

Another man suddenly appeared on a roof some way to the right of the first man. It was Georgiades. He began running across the roofs. Two other men emerged and raced after him.

The first man disappeared behind a parapet.

"He could come down anywhere!" said Owen in agony.

He looked around. He still had four men with him.

"You take those two," he said to McPhee, "and try and get round behind him on that side. I'll take the others!"

McPhee ran off instantly.

Abdul Kassem did not wait for Owen but set off through the back-streets on the near side.

They soon lost sight of the roofs.

"Christ!" said Owen again. "He could come down anywhere."

They came out into a long street which ran roughly parallel to the man's course.

"You stay here," Owen said to the other constable. "You can see the whole street."

He himself ran on after Abdul Kassem. The Egyptian was much better than he was at this sort of thing. He knew, or was able to sense, the pattern of the tiny, twisting streets. Owen knew he was holding him back.

"You go on," he gasped. "Try and get in front of him."

Abdul Kassem shot off.

Owen came to a corner and stopped. His heart was pounding and his eyes were blinded with sweat. He took out a handkerchief to wipe his face and tried to think. There was no point in just running aimlessly along the street. He needed to know where the man was. He had a vague sense of him being to the right and heading northward, but in this warren of tiny streets forever twisting back on themselves that did not help much.

He walked along until he came to a square and then tried to look up at the roofs, but the square was small and the houses which surrounded it so high that he could see very little. He needed to be up higher.

At the corner of the square was a little mosque with a minaret rising above it. He ran over to it and tried to go in but the door was heavily bolted. Still, the idea was a good one, and as he ran on he kept his eye open for a mosque that was not barred.

The street narrowed still further and then opened out into a kind of piazza which did not seem to have any way out of it. Exactly opposite him was a sebil, a fountain-house, whose steeply curved sides, guarded with grilles of intricate metal-work, rose up high to an arcaded upper storey. It was approached by a sweeping flight of steps with an ornate marble balustrade.

Without stopping to think, Owen ran straight up the steps. At the top, set in among the arcades where it would be cool, was an open recess obviously used as a kuttub, a place where little children received their first lessons in the Koran. The kuttub was empty, but an old man lay sleeping against a pillar.

Besides him another flight of stairs, much narrower, led up to the roof. Owen leaped up them and came out on to the flat top of the arcades.

To one side, behind him, he could see out over modern Cairo as far as the Nile and the brown desert beyond it. To the other was the fantastic skyline of old Cairo, with its minarets and cupolas, the high towers of the mosques, the arcades and domes of the old houses, and in among them the flat spaces where people came up to take the evening air.

Now, with the sun still very hot, the roofs were deserted. There was no movement, anywhere.

He felt a hand plucking at his sleeve. It was the old man. Owen could see now that he was blind. He had found him by hearing alone.

"I will show you the way down, father," he said.

But the old man could get down without his aid. He kept asking Owen what he wanted. Owen explained lamely that he was looking out over the roofs in search of a thief. The old man shook his head, whether in disbelief or commiseration at the world's iniquity. He kept touching Owen's arm. He was obviously puzzled. Something about Owen, the accent, perhaps just the bodily presence, told him that Owen was a foreigner.

Owen apologized again, excused himself, and descended to the ground. Half way down he met a black-veiled woman carrying a bowl for the old man. She shrank back against the wall as Owen passed.

Little streets, so little they were hardly streets, ran off from the piazza on every side. There seemed nothing to tell one from another. It came over Owen how pointless it was trying to intercept a man in this maze.

He made his way back to the Syrian's shop.

McPhee arrived at almost the same moment.

"Like looking for a needle in a haystack," he said. "Useless!"

One of the men who had been with Georgiades on the roof came out of the shop carrying a large box.

"Thank Christ for that!" said McPhee. "At least we've got something."

A moment later Georgiades himself appeared. He was mopping his face with a large blue handkerchief.

"The next time we do this," he said to Owen, "it had better be in the cooler part of the day."

"You didn't get him," said Owen.

Georgiades shook his head regretfully.

"No," he said. "What a waste! After running over the roofs of half Cairo!"

He looked down at the big box.

"We got this, though," he said. "When I got close to him he put it down and ran."

The Syrian came out of the shop with the man from the consulate in attendance.

"This your property?" asked Owen, indicating the box.

"Yes," said the man from the consulate.

"I have never seen it on my life before," declared the Syrian solemnly.

"It's a box of grenades," said Owen.

"You heard my client," said the man from the consulate. "He has never seen this in his life before. You have made a mistake."

"And so have you," said McPhee, taking the Syrian by the arm.

"What are you doing?" said the man from the consulate, stepping between them.

"Taking him to the police headquarters," said McPhee.

"You cannot do that," said the man from the consulate. "He is a Syrian citizen."

"Caught redhanded," said McPhee indignantly, "with the arms in his possession."

"He knows nothing about the arms!" said the man from the consulate. "Someone else had put them there!"

"Oh, yes," said McPhee sarcastically. "Who?"

"I don't know," said the man from the consulate. "It's not my job to find out. It's your job."

"We have found out," said McPhee.

"I don't know about that," said the man. "It would have to be tested in a court."

"That's exactly what I'm planning," said McPhee.

"A Consular Court," said the man.

"A Consular Court?" said McPhee incredulously. "The man's been caught with arms in his possession."

"A Mixed Tribunal, then."

Even when a foreigner could be proved to have transgressed against the law of his own country he had the right to be tried by his own Consular Court. Where there was a dispute between foreigners, or between foreigners and Egyptians, the case was heard by a Mixed Tribunal, on which the majority of the judges were foreign. But that applied only to civil cases, and it had yet to be established whether this fell into that category. It almost certainly did not.

"Anyway," said the man from the consulate, "you certainly cannot arrest him."

"We'll see about that," said McPhee grimly, producing a pair of handcuffs.

"I protest!" said the consular official. "My client is a native Syrian and is outside your jurisdiction."

Owen was tempted to let McPhee go ahead. At any rate, it might give the Syrian a shaking. But it was not worth the trouble. They would have to release him at once.

"Leave him for the time being," he said to McPhee. "We shall be taking this up," he said to the official.

It was possible, in certain circumstances, which included a threat to security, to expel a foreigner from the country; but it took a long time.

"I shall be taking this up, too," said the man. "This is a gross invasion of Syrian territory. I shall be lodging an official complaint."

"Do!" said Owen.

The consular official took the Syrian by the arm and they went back into the shop. McPhee was purple with fury.

"It makes you lose heart," said Georgiades.

"We've got the grenades anyway," said Owen.

"Not all of them," said Georgiades.

"What?"

"Haven't you looked?" He flipped back the top of the box. Three grenades were missing.

McPhee swore.

"When did he take them?" asked Owen. "Or were they missing before?"

"I think he took them when he left the box," said Georgiades. "He seemed to fumble inside the box. The lid was open when I got there."

McPhee and Owen exchanged glances. Three was enough. Enough with the Carpet coming on.

"Got nowhere," said Owen.

"Could be worse," said McPhee. "At least we've got these. You did well," he said to Georgiades.

Georgiades shrugged. He was as disappointed as they were.

One of the constables shouldered the box and they started off along the street. Owen felt too depressed to say anything.

They had just turned the corner when there was a shout behind them. A small boy came running up.

"Ya effendi!" he hailed Owen.

"What is it?"

"I bring a message," he panted, "from Abdul Kassem."

Owen turned sharply. He had forgotten about Abdul Kassem.

"What is it?"

The boy hung back.

"He said I would be well rewarded," he said.

"And so you shall," said McPhee, bending down to him. "How much was spoken of?"

"One piastre," said the boy.

"Oh-h!" said McPhee, affecting incredulity. "A whole piastre?"

"Half a piastre," admitted the boy.

McPhee fumbled in his pocket. "Here is a half piastre," he said, "which you shall have when you have spoken. The other half I might let you have if I think you have told me correctly."

The boy nodded.

"Abdul Kassem says: Come quickly."

He held out his hand.

"Is that all?" asked McPhee.

"Yes," said the boy.

"Come quickly? Where to?"

"Give me another piastre," said the boy, "and I will take you."

They found Abdul Kassem waiting outside an old Mameluke house in the Haret el Merdani. Soon after they had separated he had had the same idea as Owen. He had remembered that there was a ruined mosque nearby with its tower still standing, had climbed up that and then had had a good view of the rooftop chase. He had seen Georgiades closing on his man, watched the man stoop and do something to the box, and then had seen the man run off in the direction of the Mosque Darb el Ahmah, whose distinct turquoise cupola had stood out among the other rooftop features. He had descended from his own tower and run to the mosque, arriving just in time to see the man slip out of the mosque itself and cross the square in front of it. While on the tower he had had a good look at the man and was sure that this was the same man. No, he had not been carrying anything, not in his hands, but Abdul Kassem thought he had something stuffed in the front of his shirt, for it bulged and hung rather than billowed. He had followed the man down a sidestreet and seen him slip through the door of this house. And then he had sent the boy.

"Good work!" said Owen.

McPhee was looking at him.

"OK," said Owen. "In you go!"

The great gate of the house was slightly ajar, probably to let a breeze blow through the courtyard. McPhee threw it wide open and the men rushed in. A porter, asleep in a recess of the entrance, opened his eyes as they went past, and then jumped up.

The men fanned out. They knew the structure of a Mameluke house and worked through systematically. The main reception rooms opened off the courtyard, and there were various recesses in there where a man could hide. The other rooms on the ground floor were either servants' rooms, mostly cluttered around the main entrance, or storerooms. It took the men almost no time to work through them all.

Georgiades looked at Owen inquiringly. Nearly the whole of the upper portion of a Mameluke house was given up to the harem. There were no proper bedrooms in the Western sense of the word. Any room which was not being used for anything else would serve. Beds were just a few cushions, a pillow and a padded blanket, which was rolled up in the daytime and put in a cupboard.

The Mamur Zapt's traditional right of entry extended, uniquely, to harems but it was not one to exercise without thinking about it.

"There's no alternative," said Owen.

Georgiades shrugged and ran up the stairs, closely followed by his delighted men. As they spread through the upper part of the house there were startled shouts and screams.

McPhee remained below.

"I'll see no one gets out this way," he said, a little straightly.

Owen followed his men upstairs. The first room he came to, the main room of the harem, extended through the whole first floor of the house, from the old latticed windows at the front to the small oriels at the back. It was dark and cool, so dark that at first he could not see anything at all. Then his eyes picked out various women on divans, sitting bolt upright with shock.

Afterwards, when Owen was questioned at the club, he had to admit that he took in very little. He was looking for the man and as soon as he saw the harem was occupied he knew it was unlikely the man would be there. He had scanned the room to make sure and that had been that.

Required to furnish more detail, he had been at a loss. No, they were all dressed. They had not been wearing veils, true. No, he hadn't noticed their faces, it had been dark. What had they been doing? Chatting, as far as he could see. Oh, and one or two were embroidering or sewing or something.

"Sewing! You are a great disappointment, Owen!"

No, he had seen nothing erotic, or particularly exotic for that matter, either. His impression was they they were just having a good gossip.

"They must have been bored to death!" said someone.

"And you did nothing about it, Owen!" said someone else. "I begin to have doubts about you." Etcetera.

What he did not tell them was that he had seen someone he knew. He had been about to move on up to the next floor when his eye had picked out a face against the gloom.

It was Nuri's daughter, the one he had met at the party.

Her face had been rigid with anger.

"You!" she said. "What are you doing here? Don't you know it's forbidden?"

"I'm looking for a man."

"Here? You must be mad!"

"He came in."

"Into the harem?"

"Into the house," Owen admitted.

"He has not been in here," she said. "Nobody has come in here. No man would come in here."

"I am sorry, then," said Owen, turning away.

"You don't just go bursting into people's houses like that!" she said.

"Not even if the man we're looking for may have had something to do with the attack on your father?" asked Owen.

Georgiades appeared from upstairs and shook his head. He glanced round the room and pointed to a small door which Owen had taken to be the door of a kazna, a large cupboard in which such things as bedclothes were kept.

"Does that go anywhere?"

"Why not go in and find out?" said Zeinab.

Georgiades's hand was almost on the handle when the door opened of its own accord.

"What is the meaning of this?" said a harsh, unpleasant voice which struck Owen as oddly familiar.

Georgiades fell back.

A man came into the room, short, stocky, bare-chested, dressed only in red silk pantaloons.

It was Guzman.

Chapter 9

"You have offended the Sirdar," said Garvin. "You have offended the Khedive. You have offended the Agent. And you've bloody offended me."

He picked up a piece of paper from his desk.

"I've even had," he said, "a letter of complaint from the Kadi about your desecrating religious property."

He put the letter down.

"It takes some doing to offend *all* the powers of Egypt in the space of about two hours, but by God, Owen, you've done it. The Army, the Khedive, the Kadi—Not to mention me. And for what?"

"We've got the grenades."

"Not all of them. And you missed the man."

"How was I to know it was Guzman's house?" muttered Owen.

"You could have asked," said the pitiless Garvin. "The meanest beggar in the street outside would have told you. Instead, you went charging in. In fact, you spent the whole afternoon charging round, like a sort of lunatic McPhee. If I want a McPhee as Mamur Zapt," said Garvin, "I'll get a real one."

This was proving even more uncomfortable than Owen had expected.

"But I don't," Garvin continued. "I really don't. The Mamur Zapt isn't supposed to work like that. He's supposed to work behind the scenes, off-stage. Not front stage at the opera. The bloody comic opera!"

Owen felt this hit home. He sat there smarting but judged it best to keep quiet. Garvin obviously expected some reaction. When none came he was slightly off-put. His glare became half-hearted.

"It was a mistake, wasn't it?" he said, still aggressively but with rather less vehemence. "Raiding that Syrian? I thought it would be. The trouble with a raid is that it either works or it doesn't. If you don't wrap everything up it kills off all the leads. I told you it would be better to put a man on the shop!"

If we'd done that, thought Owen, we would not have got the grenades.

Perhaps Garvin guessed what he was thinking, for the glare returned, defying Owen to make his objection.

Owen sat there impassively.

Satisfied, Garvin relaxed.

"It was my fault," he said unexpectedly. "I shouldn't have let you."

Now it was Owen who was off-put. He found himself wanting to demur.

Garvin was taking no notice, however. He was following his own train of thought.

"Maps!" he said suddenly. "Maps!"

"What?" said Owen, startled.

Garvin turned to him.

"Maps," he said. "That's what you need. You need to build up your own set of maps. The Mamur Zapt is different from the police," he went on. "The police are interested in catching the criminal and punishing him. You're not interested at all in seeing he gets punished, and not even interested, really, in him getting caught. What you're interested in is seeing that certain things don't happen. You may have to catch people, you may have to keep them in prison, but that's all incidental.

You may be able to do your job without it. In fact, it's better if you do do your job without it. You've got to anticipate, to know in advance what's going to happen and then to stop it. To do that you need information. Contacts. Maps."

He looked at Owen.

"I shouldn't have let you raid that Syrian, should I?" he said. "We should have used him to help you build up one of those maps. Syrian connections throughout the city. It would have been worth it."

"Even at the price of a box of grenades?"

"Even at the price of a box of grenades," said Garvin seriously. He considered a moment. "At the price of something going wrong at the Carpet, though—" He broke off. "Well," he said, "it's never straightforward in this business."

"Did I tell you," he asked, "that the Old Man wants you to be in charge of security arrangements for the Carpet?"

"Still?"

Garvin smiled wintrily. "I would think so," he said.

As Owen went out Garvin said: "The Carpet's always a pig. There were riots all over Cairo when I was doing it."

Owen knew the words were meant encouragingly.

☙

Nikos came in, unusually agitated.

"There's a woman to see you," he said.

"What sort of woman?" asked Owen. "Do you want me to come out?"

It was rare for a woman to come alone to the Mamur Zapt's offices, or, indeed, any other offices for that matter. Usually if a woman had business with an office she sent a man on her behalf or a male relative. In the few cases where she came herself she came accompanied. Occasionally, though, a countrywoman would come to see the Mamur Zapt with a petition. She would wait self-effacingly outside, not venturing to come in, hoping only to catch the Mamur Zapt as he went past. Owen had left strict instructions that if a woman was seen waiting like that then he was to be informed. He would go down to her as soon as he could.

"No," said Nikos. He hesitated. Then he made up his mind. "I will bring her along to you."

Owen sat back surprised. He had very few visits of that sort.

Nikos ushered in an elegant woman, dressed in Parisian black. She wore a short, European-style veil but had bound her hair in an expensive scarf so as to reduce the offence to Islamic susceptibilities.

Owen rose automatically from his desk. Nikos withdrew. The woman came further into the room and lifted her veil so that Owen could see her face. It was Nuri's daughter, the one he had seen the day before, Zeinab.

"I wanted to see you," she said. "I thought I could be of some use."

Owen drew up a chair for her.

He felt unusually awkward.

For one thing, he had never before spoken to a young Egyptian woman alone. Arab Egyptian, that was. He had spoken to French Egyptians, Italian ones, Greek ones, but never previously to an Arab one. Even the Greek ones were pretty difficult to get to know. The Levantines were nearly as traditional as the Moslems where their women were concerned. Especially their daughters. Their wives were often restive and it was relatively easy to find a married woman with a taste for adventure. Their daughters, whether they had a taste or not, were seldom given the opportunity to indulge it. Young, single girls were kept as in purdah. And this was all the more true, of course, of Arab ones. You simply never saw them. Very occasionally you might meet a very Europeanized one in the most advanced of circles, as, indeed, he had done, but even there they hardly ever detached themselves from the crowd. Your only chance was someone as Europeanized, independent, unconventional and strong-minded as Nuri's daughter evidently was. If, of course, she was single.

For another thing, there was this unfortunate business of the harem.

"I really must apologize," he began. "I had no idea you were—" And stopped.

"A member of the harem?" she finished for him icily. "I am not. Any more than you are one of Guzman's eunuchs."

There was a delighted intake of breath in the corridor. Owen wondered who was listening. Indeed, now he noticed it, there was such a silence along the corridor that probably *everybody* was listening.

He got up and shut the door. That made it almost unbearably hot, so he turned on the fan. That levitated the papers on his desk. He made a grab at them and weighted them down with a couple of files. Some of them, however, escaped on to the floor.

He felt he was being excessively clumsy; in all ways.

He looked up and found large dark eyes regarding him with definite amusement.

"Anyway," he said firmly, pulling himself together, "I am sorry."

"It *was* a little unexpected," she said.

"It was a mistake," said Owen. He felt an urgent need to explain. "We were chasing a man. One of my people thought he came into the house."

"Perhaps he did," she said cooperatively. "It's a favourite trick in Cairo for pickpockets being chased to run into the courtyard of an old house. There's usually a second entrance. They run in one and then straight out the other."

"My man's experienced," said Owen. "He ought to have looked out for that."

"How could he? Unless he had run into the courtyard himself."

"He had to be careful. The other man had grenades."

"Yes," she said, "so I heard."

It must be all over Cairo now, he thought bitterly.

There was a little silence. Then she said: "But that didn't stop you from sending your men in."

"No."

"I was in the house," she said. "So were others."

"It was a risk," he admitted.

"Yes," she said. "It was. For us!"

"I had to take it," said Owen.

The dark eyes regarded him soberly. Then, suddenly, again there was the flicker of amusement.

"How definite of you!" she said drily. "And how British!"

Owen began to feel like McPhee again.

"I am sorry," he said again.

Then, feeling that he was being unnecessarily defensive: "You were in the house. I take it you were visiting?"

"Yes," she said firmly. Relenting, she added: "I wasn't really visiting them, but since I was in the house I thought I'd better call on them. It means so much to them when someone calls. They lead such boring lives."

Owen wondered if she had been seeing Guzman and felt an unreasonable pang of jealousy.

"You remember that girl? Leila? The one my father made pregnant?"

"Mustafa's wife's—"

"So that's his name, is it?" she said. "Yes. That one. Well, my father is not such a monster as you think. He always looks after the women. He asked Guzman to take her in as a washerwoman. Guzman is an old friend of his. They worked together for the Khedive even before my father became a minister. I was coming to see how she was."

"I thought she was staying with relatives?"

"She is. She comes in daily. They live not far from here. They are very poor. They couldn't manage if she didn't work."

"Mustafa spoke of others providing. Did he mean your father?"

"Surely not," she said. "He would never accept anything from my father. That's why my father had to be indirect."

Sometimes it seemed to Owen that the whole of Egypt was bound together by intricate, interlinked systems of obligations, favours and rewards, subtle reciprocities, often to do with family, which connected people in unexpected ways. It was an immensely powerful moral system and if you lived in Egypt you could not escape its pressure. "This is my brother's son," Yussuf had said one day, presenting a grubby little urchin, and Owen had known that he was expected to do something about it. McPhee had found the boy a place in the stables and Yussuf's standing with his family had been saved. For someone like Nuri the system's imperatives probably counted for more than those of the courts.

"I wanted to see you," said Zeinab, and then broke off.

"Yes?" said Owen, expecting it to be something to do with her father.

"It's about Aziz."

"Aziz? The Syrian?"

"Yes. The one whose house you raided yesterday."

"And rightly, too, this time," said Owen. "That's how we came upon the grenades."

She waved a hand dismissively.

"You know him, too?"

"His wife. She is Raoul's wife's sister."

Owen remembered Raoul from Fakhri's party and felt another pang of jealousy. He wondered what, among this web of relationships, was the nature of Raoul's relationship with Zeinab.

"She came to see Raoul this morning. She is very worried."

She hesitated.

"And what precisely is she worried about?" asked Owen, remembering the face he had seen at the door.

"Aziz has been foolish," Zeinab said. "She is worried that now you have found out about him you will pursue him. He will make another mistake and then you will put him in prison."

If only it was so simple, thought Owen. Out loud he said: "If he deals in grenades he must expect to be in trouble."

"He would like to stop. He only began it because he needed the money."

"That's what they all say."

"Yes, but in his case it was different. When he first came to Cairo, about ten years ago, he worked very hard and built up a legitimate business. Then one of his partners suddenly pulled out leaving him with huge debts. He had young children and did not know where to turn. The chance came up, he took it, it helped—"

"And then he couldn't stop," said Owen.

"He can stop. He wants to stop. Only…"

"Only what?"

"He's frightened."

"Of me?"

"Not of you. His wife is frightened of you."

"Thanks. What's *he* frightened of?"

She looked at him carefully, as if making a judgement. The decision was reached.

"One of the clubs."

"Which?"

"I don't know."

Zeinab pushed back the edge of the scarf where the heat was making it stick to her face.

"I know only what she told me," she said. "That's why she came to see Raoul this morning."

"And Raoul told you to come and see me?"

"No," she said. "Raoul does not know I am seeing you. She talked to me afterwards. I decided to come and see you."

Owen considered.

"What would Raoul's advice have been?"

"The usual, I expect," she said. "To pay and keep quiet."

"But you thought differently?"

"I am sorry for the woman," she said. "She is expecting another child. She has had two miscarriages already."

Owen was thinking about what Garvin had said. About building up his own map of Cairo.

"I might not pursue Aziz," he said, "if Aziz could help me occasionally."

Zeinab shook her head. "He's too frightened."

"No one would know."

"He would still be too frightened."

Owen nodded slowly. There was no need to press.

"I might leave him alone anyway," he said. "He's a small fish."

"Thank you."

"Was that what you wanted?" he asked. "What you came for?"

"Ye-es. And to give you the information."

"About the club? It's interesting," he said, "but I need to know more. Its name, for instance. Would his wife know?"

"You are not to approach her!" she said fiercely. "She is frightened enough already."

"Could you find out? She might talk to you."

"You are asking a lot."

"It was your father," he pointed out. "And he might still be at risk."

"She would be at risk if she gave you the name," Zeinab said. "And she's a very small fish indeed."

"I would like to help," said Owen, "only you'll have to tell me more."

Zeinab sat thinking it over.

Owen was content to wait.

Eventually she made up her mind.

"I will ask her," she said.

"Thank you."

"But you are not to speak to her. Even if I fail. Promise me."

"Very well," said Owen. "I promise."

అం

The next morning he received a phone call from her. She had obtained the information he wanted, she said. Better still, she had arranged for him to meet the lady in question.

He was to go to the Sharia el Mourani that evening about seven. There was a hairdresser's, Steffano's. It had an entrance from the rear, in the Sharia el Cheriffein. Next to a perfume-seller's. He was to go in that entrance. She would use the other one. Someone would be expecting him and would show him to a room.

"Steffano's," he said, "isn't that…?"

"Yes," she said. "That's why it will be quite safe. Everyone uses it. They will think it just another assignation."

One of the ways in which Cairene women evaded the constraints their husbands placed on them was through private appointments in apartments set aside for that purpose, usually above fashionable shops. Respectable ones allowed amateur partners only; but there was, too, a thriving trade in boys. Good-looking European boys were preferred. Steffano's was not a house of that sort, but the fact that Owen was European would fit.

He found the entrance without difficulty. A Greek girl was waiting inside. She looked carefully at Owen and then led the way upstairs.

He was shown into a room with a deep, soft carpet, divans and exquisite brocade drapings over the walls. The girl motioned to him to sit down on one of the divans and then left the room.

Owen heard a faint noise behind him and looked round quickly. Half-concealed behind some of the draping was a door. It opened fully and Zeinab came into the room. Behind her he could just see the figure of another woman.

"My friend does not think it proper to be in the room with you alone," Zeinab said, "or even with me present. She will stay in the room beyond and talk through the door."

"How will I know it is the woman I think?" asked Owen.

Zeinab looked at him sharply.

"You will have to take my word," she said. "I wouldn't have gone to all this trouble if it was another woman."

"Is she veiled?"

"She has her veil."

"I would like to see her face."

"You can't," said Zeinab flatly.

"For a moment," said Owen. "Through the doorway would be enough."

Zeinab turned and spoke to the woman. There was some debate. Eventually she stood aside. The woman beyond timidly dropped her veil, just for an instant. It was enough. It was the woman Owen had seen in the Syrian's house.

He indicated that he was satisfied. Zeinab walked across and sat down on the divan opposite him. If he talked directly to her he would have his back to the other woman. He compromised by sitting half round so that he could both address Zeinab and keep an eye on the door behind him. It was just a precaution.

"The society," said Zeinab, "is Tademah."

"How does she know?"

"She has seen a letter."

"Signed Tademah?"

"Yes."

"Addressed to her husband?"

"Yes."

"What did the letter say?"

Zeinab looked over his shoulder. The woman began to speak, hesitantly and so softly that he could hardly hear her.

"It spoke of guns," she said.

"Which your husband had? Or was going to get?"

"To get, I think." The woman was almost inaudible.

"The note asked him to get them?"

"Yes," the woman breathed.

"Did it say how the guns would be collected?"

"I do not remember."

"Or how they would be paid for?"

"I do not remember."

He heard a little sob.

"It does not matter," he said. "But you are sure it was from Tademah?"

"Yes," she whispered. "It said at the bottom."

"Just Tademah? No other name?"

"No."

After a moment she said: "It was at the top of the letter, too. It said, 'Greetings from Tademah.'"

"Did it threaten your husband?"

"Not this time."

He could barely catch the words.

"There have been other letters?"

"Yes."

"How do you know? Have you seen them?"

"No. My husband has spoken of them."

"He is worried by them?"

"Yes," she said, "yes."

"Do they come often? How often do the letters come?"

There was a pause.

"I don't know," the woman said eventually. "He does not always tell me."

"But he worries about them?"

"Yes," she said, "always. He always worries about them. He does not sleep."

"You know when he is worried," Owen said. "How often is that? Once a month?"

"No," she said. "Not as often. Three months, four months perhaps."

"Have you ever seen any of the men?"

This time he could not hear the answer at all. He looked at Zeinab. She shook her head.

"Does your husband go out to meet them?"

Again he could not hear.

Zeinab shook her head again.

"You'd better stop," she said.

"One question more," said Owen. "How long has your husband been receiving these letters?"

This time he heard the answer clearly.

"For two years," she said. "For two years we have had this badness with us. Two years of not sleeping at night, of worrying about my husband, about what we would do if...if..."

Zeinab stood up.

"You see?" she said.

The woman's voice steadied.

"Of worrying about the children," she said.

Owen stood up, too.

"Thank you," he said to he woman behind him. "You have been very helpful. You have told me what I needed. I shall remember this and be a friend to you."

Zeinab went into the room with the woman and shut the door behind her. Owen left by the way he had come.

༄

He went home to change before going out to dinner. There was a message waiting for him. He rang the office at once.

"You'd better come in," said Nikos. "There's been an attack on Ahmed."

Chapter 10

"I thought we had a man on him?" said Owen.

"We did," said Georgiades.

"Then what the hell was he doing?"

"Watching," said Georgiades, "as he was told to."

"Yes, but not to watch him being half-killed."

"I'll kick his backside," said Georgiades. "Tell you what. You kick his backside. It will have more effect."

He went to the door and bellowed. "Ya Hamid."

Bare feet padded along the corridor and a subdued man in a dirty white gown came into the room.

"Effendi!" he said, and touched his heart.

"Hamid!" said Owen sternly.

"Yes, effendi?"

"What is all this?"

"Tell him the whole sad story," Georgiades directed.

Hamid studied his toes.

"I was watching the boy," he said in a low voice. "He came out of the college with his friend and walked along the Sharia el Torba. They crossed the Sharia Mohammed Ali and went into the Sharia es Souekeh. They stopped at a lemonade-seller and sat there for a long time. Some other young joined them and they talked a lot. Then the others left and the boy and his friend went on towards the Sharia Khalig el Masri.

Just before they came to the Mosque el Behat some men fell upon them."

"How many?"

"Four, effendi. They were big, strong men with clubs. They knocked the boy down and beat him sorely. Then his friend ran away and I heard him calling for the police."

"Did the men try to rob the boy?"

"No, effendi. They just beat him."

"No knives?"

"None, effendi. Just clubs."

Owen looked at Georgiades.

"They just wanted to scare him," said the Greek.

"Looks like it, doesn't it?" said Owen.

He turned sternly on Hamid.

"And all this time," he said, "you watched and did nothing?"

"Yes, effendi," said the man humbly.

He rubbed one foot against his shin. As the horny sole scraped up and down there was a distinct rasp.

"There were four of them, effendi," he said, "and they were all bigger and stronger than I."

"You ought to eat more," said Georgiades, inspecting him critically.

"You could have shouted for the police," Owen said to Hamid, still sternly but softening.

"Then they would have beaten *me*," said Hamid.

He put the foot back on the ground and examined it carefully.

"Besides," he said, "the friend was calling for the police. And, besides, I was told but to watch."

It was hardly fair to expect heroics from a man paid a few milliemes an hour. Owen looked at Georgiades and shrugged. Georgiades grinned.

"Our friend keeps his feet on the ground," he said, "in one sense at least."

He turned to Hamid.

"So you watched," he said. "Tell us what you saw."

"The men went on beating the boy until they tired. Then one of the men said: 'That is our work well done. Let us go now to the bath house and claim our reward.'"

Owen interrupted him.

"'The bath house,' you said? The hammam?"

"Yes, effendi. They said they would go to the hammam to claim their reward."

"I don't suppose," said Owen, discounting the possibility even before he had said it, "that you followed them to the hammam?"

Hamid traced a long circle with his toe. Reluctantly he raised his eyes to Owen's.

"Effendi," he said. "I did."

"What?"

"The boy was all right," Hamid pleaded. "I heard him groan. There was a woman by, with onions, and I said: 'Stay with the boy. His friend comes shortly with aid.'"

"Hamid!" said Owen, awestruck. "You have done well."

"It was all right to leave the boy?" asked Hamid anxiously. "Not to watch?"

"On this occasion," said Owen, "it was all right."

"He would not have been able to do anything," Hamid reassured him. "He had been well beaten."

"It does not matter," said Owen.

It did, however, matter to Hamid.

"I would not have left him otherwise," he assured them.

"On this occasion," said Owen, "it was justified."

Hamid was inclined to pursue the point further but Georgiades laid his hand on the Arab's arm.

"Tell us, ya Hamid," he said conversationally, "what happened at the hammam?"

Hamid, happier now, stopped tracing patterns on the floor with his toe and looked up brightly.

"When we got to the hammam," he said, "the men went in."

"Yes?" said Owen, with sinking heart.

"I waited outside lest they suspect I was following them."

"You did not go in?"

"Oh no, effendi!" Hamid was shocked. "They would have seen me. Besides, it would have cost two piastres."

"So you waited outside."

"Yes, effendi." Hamid beamed.

"And then?"

"Then the men came out," said Hamid, "and went away. But I did not follow them this time."

A thought struck him.

"Should I have followed them, effendi?" he asked anxiously.

"No," said Owen, resigned. "No, Hamid. You had done your best."

"Thank you, effendi," said Hamid, bursting with pride.

Owen took a deep breath.

"So you did not see the man they talked with," he said, more in confirmation than in hope.

"Only when he came out with them," said Hamid.

"You saw him, then?"

"Yes, effendi?" said Hamid, surprised.

Owen fought to keep himself in control.

"What did he look like? What did he say?" he snapped.

Then, realizing that two questions at a time were probably too much for Hamid, he calmed down.

"Tell me, ya Hamid," he said, in as relaxed a tone as he was capable of, "did you by any chance hear him talking with the men?"

"Yes, effendi," said Hamid, beginning to worry that he had said or done something wrong.

"Can you remember what was said?"

"The men were grumbling. One said to another: 'Fifty piastres is not enough.' Another said: 'He promised us more.' The man said: 'That is all you get until I know you have done your work properly. Come to me tomorrow and I will give you the other fifty.' The men went on grumbling but he would not give them more. 'We will come back tomorrow,' they said. Then they went away."

Georgiades patted Hamid on the arm.

"You have done well," he said, "to remember all that. Has he not?" he appealed to Owen.

"He has done very well," Owen agreed, "and shall be rewarded for it. I do not suppose," he said, looking at Georgiades, "that he also heard where these bad men were going to meet."

"At the hammam," said Hamid promptly.

"At the hammam? Indeed!" said Georgiades. "And I don't suppose," he went on, "that they said when this would be?"

"Oh yes they did!" said Hamid, confident again now. "At sunset tomorrow."

"Would you know the men if you saw them?" Owen asked.

"Oh yes, effendi," said Hamid fervently.

"And that other? The one they talked with?"

"Oh yes, effendi!"

"Then you have done well!" said Owen, patting him on the shoulder.

"You have done very well!" said Georgiades. "And I shall speak to the senior orderly about you and he will see that you eat well and drink well tonight. Then tomorrow you will help us and for that you will receive double pay. Which you richly deserve!"

He shepherded Hamid off along the corridor. A little later he came back mopping his brow.

"Sometimes," he said, "I feel as if the heat is getting to me. I have this dream: I am the one sane man in a world of madmen. Or vice versa."

"For God's sake don't let him lose himself," said Owen.

"I won't!" Georgiades promised. "Not till after. Then I'll let him lose himself quick."

"Keep him here overnight."

"And all tomorrow as well. I've told Osman not to let him go out, not even for a pee. I've told Abdul Kassem not to let him out of his sight."

Owen went across to the window and pushed open the shutters. The cool night air came in. He kept his face there for a moment.

"There is a faint chance that he won't mess it up tomorrow," he told the shutters. "Only faint. I've been in Cairo long enough to know that."

"Faint," Georgiades agreed. "But a chance."

Nikos stuck his head in.

"There's a message for you to ring your friend in the Parquet," he said.

Nikos did not approve of such relations. He was a traditionalist as far as the department was concerned.

He looked pointedly at his watch.

"I am going home."

※

"It was a warning," said Nuri.

He had asked to see them when they arrived at the house the following morning. Their purpose was really to see Ahmed but Nuri's man had waylaid them.

He received them this time in a small downstairs room he evidently used as a study or library. The walls, unusually for Arab rooms, were lined with books, most of them in French. There was a desk with carved ivory paperweights, cut in the figure of nude women. There was a Persian carpet on the floor, and there were two deep, comfortable, leather armchairs.

Nuri motioned to them to sit in the armchairs. He himself used the high-backed wooden chair at the desk. This gave him the advantage of height. The squat, square form seemed to loom over them.

"You don't think it was a student quarrel, then?" said Mahmoud, who had asked for Owen's company. Owen sensed that Mahmoud found Nuri difficult to handle. They were both Egyptians but different kinds of Egyptian. Nuri was of the old, feudal society, a grand seigneur in a system that had been corrupt for centuries, aware only of the levers of pleasure and power, experienced, cynical, blasé, interested, a little, in Mahmoud as a bright, up-and-coming new man, but ultimately dismissive of the powerless. For Mahmoud, Nuri represented everything that stood in the way of a New Egypt: conservatism, venality, a disillusion which cut efforts to reform off at the knees before they even got started, power to block but not to do. There was, too, the social difference between them, which Mahmoud denied but could not help being sensitive to and which Nuri knew how to assert without lifting a finger. Mahmoud had not been at ease on their last visit and he was not at ease now. He needed Owen for assurance, or perhaps it was insurance.

"No," said Nuri, "I don't think it was a student quarrel."

"You think it was directed at you?"

"Of course."

He looked at them seriously. He was a different man today, more the elder statesman, less the old roué. Owen suspected, however, that Nuri was a man of many parts.

"Through striking at my son they strike at me. And they strike," he said somberly, "where I am most vulnerable."

Was this another part, Owen wondered: the loving father? Not entirely, he decided. Nuri genuinely seemed to have a soft spot for the boy; perhaps, in this male-oriented society, because he was a boy.

"We are doing what we can," said Mahmoud reassuringly.

"Yes," said Nuri sceptically. "And meanwhile?"

Mahmoud caught the tone and flushed slightly. He and Nuri always seemed to rub each other up the wrong way. Owen thought he saw traces of woodenness beginning to appear in Mahmoud's face. Nuri was exactly the sort of person he was likely to react against.

"Did you have anything in mind?" Owen asked Nuri. He thought it best to intervene.

"I hoped you would have something in mind," said Nuri. "Haven't you?"

"That depends," said Owen.

"Really?" said Nuri. "On what?"

Instead of answering, Owen said: "You could always get him a bodyguard."

"I have suggested that. He won't have it. For some strange reason he confuses a bodyguard with a nursemaid."

Owen could just imagine the touchy Ahmed's response.

"It is difficult being a rich man's son," Mahmoud put in unexpectedly.

Nuri looked at him quickly.

"Yes," he said, with a slight touch of surprise as if he had not expected Mahmoud to be so perceptive, or sympathetic. "Yes, I am inclined to forget that."

He turned to Owen.

"Couldn't you put a man on him?" he asked. "Unobtrusively, I mean?"

Uncomfortable visions of Hamid danced before Owen's eyes.

"It wouldn't necessarily help."

"If it's a question of money—?" said Nuri.

"It isn't. It's a question of men."

"As I said," Nuri picked him up with a flash of his old self, "it's a question of money."

Owen laughed, as he was expected to.

"You might do better than me," he said. "Still, I'll think about it."

"At least he wasn't badly hurt," said Mahmoud.

It was meant encouragingly, but again it came out awkwardly.

Nuri looked at him.

"This time," he said.

"Will there be a next time?" asked Owen. "If you're right about it being a warning?"

Nuri was amused.

"Will I heed the warning, you mean?"

"If you did, there might not be a next time."

"True," said Nuri.

"What exactly are you being warned to do or not to do?"

This time Nuri laughed right out. He put his hand on Owen's arm.

"Not to meddle, *mon cher.*"

"And are you meddling?"

"Of course!" said Nuri, with all his old ebullience. "Of course!"

⚭

Ahmed, however, was far from ebullient. He lay in a dark room, the shutters drawn, with a single sheet over him because of the heat and a Coptic nurse—female, and therefore borrowed from the European hospital—in attendance. He was lying on his side with his back turned towards them and remained like that when they came in.

Mahmoud went round to the other side of the bed, drew up a chair and sat down facing him, like a friendly doctor, and began questioning him about what had happened. At first Ahmed replied only in faint monosyllables but gradually, as he became involved in the recitation of his wrongs, his voice took on greater strength and he began to reply at more length, sitting up in the bed so as to emphasize his points indignantly. The sheet slipped off his shoulders showing the purple bruises on his back.

Owen had seen the doctor's report. There was nothing broken, no damage apparent other than severe external bruising. And all the bruises were on his back and limbs. That was unlikely to be an accident, Owen thought. The men had been instructed to give him a good beating and no more. His face was untouched.

But Ahmed's back was not the only thing bruised. His pride was very much dented. He could hardly bear to talk about the blows. Indeed, Mahmoud found it very hard to get him to say anything precise about the incident at all. He denounced his friend for deserting him, complained about the slowness of the police in coming and their general lack of interest when they got there, and criticized the hospital for its reception of him and treatment afterwards.

Mahmoud broke through the flood of rhetoric eventually: Did Ahmed think that the attack might be a warning?

Ahmed stopped in mid-flight.

"A warning?" he said. "A warning?" He seemed to freeze. "Why should it be a warning? Why do you ask me if it was a warning?" He regarded Mahmoud suspiciously.

"I thought—" Mahmoud began. But Ahmed interrupted. "It is not a warning," he said. "How could it be a warning? It was a criminal attack." His voice rose. "A criminal attack! That is all!"

"What was the point of the attack?"

"To rob me!" Ahmed cried excitedly. "Yes, to rob me! They were thieves! Robbers!"

Had they, in fact, stolen anything from him?

"How do I know? No, they took nothing! Perhaps the police stopped them! My friend came back in time! How do I know? Why do you ask me these questions?" he shouted.

The nurse gave Mahmoud a reproachful look and came forward. Ahmed threw himself back on the pillow and glared at them angrily.

Mahmoud patiently began again.

"He did think it was a warning, didn't he?" said Owen, as he and Mahmoud walked back beneath the pepper trees.

"He wasn't sure," said Mahmoud. "But the possibility was enough to scare him silly."

෴

Someone else thought it was a warning, too. Shortly after Owen got back to his office he received a phone call from Ahmed's half-sister, Zeinab.

"Have you heard?" she asked. "My brother has been attacked."

"Yes," said Owen. "I've just been to see him."

"Oh." Then, after a moment: "He's all right, isn't he?"

"He'll be all right in a day or two."

"Good," she said, relieved.

Owen was quite pleased that she looked to him for reassurance.

"It's linked with this, isn't it?" she said.

He wondered what she meant by "this." Her father or the grenades? Or both? The Nuri case was slipping into the background so far as he was concerned. It would have to wait till after the Carpet.

"I expect so," he said.

"Why would anyone want to attack Ahmed?" she asked. "Him of all people?"

"Why of all people?"

"I don't know," she said. "Because he's not worth attacking, I suppose."

"Your father thought it might be intended as a warning."

He heard the quick intake of breath.

"To him," Owen said.

There was a little pause. Then she said: "I thought it was a warning, too. To me." She laughed a little shakily.

"Because of last night? I doubt it. Unless they had advance knowledge. The attack on your brother happened at about the same time."

"That's what I worked out," she said.

"I wouldn't worry," said Owen. "If there was a message, it was meant for your father."

"Thank you!" said Zeinab tartly. "That is very reassuring!"

"Sorry!" Owen apologized. "I didn't mean it like that."

"No."

He tried again.

"Do you think your father was right? That it was a warning? Directed at him?"

"He's usually right in such matters," she said.

"I don't suppose you've any idea," said Owen casually, "what might have prompted such a warning?"

"No. He's always up to things."

"That's more or less what he said. Only it's not very helpful."

"It might be protection," she offered.

"That's what we thought."

"He is always getting demands for money. Usually he knows who to pay and who not to. Perhaps he got it wrong this time."

"You wouldn't know who's been doing some asking recently, would you?"

"No. Tademah?"

"I've looked through some of the letters he's received recently. Nothing from Tademah among them."

"Wasn't there?" She sounded surprised. "I thought there was," she said.

"Not among the ones I was shown," said Owen, remembering suddenly who had shown him them.

"Well, I'm not sure," she said, "but I thought there was. Perhaps it's just that they were on my mind. But it would fit, though, wouldn't it?"

"Yes," said Owen. "It would fit."

⟨ornament⟩

The hammam, like all the old hammams, had a façade of red and white stone. With its complex panelling and its fantastic arabesques it looked very like a small mosque, Dervish perhaps, except that its entrance was unusually narrow and had its door recesses painted green. If it had been a bath for women it would have had a towel hung across the sunken entrance.

Owen ducked down and entered a pleasant, spacious room with several broad, marble-topped couches on which patrons were sitting in various stages of undress, already embarked on the main purpose of their visit, which was not to bathe but to chat. Owen went over to one of the couches and began to undress. An attendant brought him towels and clogs and stood by to receive his clothes and valuables. Owen wound one of the towels about his waist and the other around his head and went through into the next room.

This was the first of the warm chambers and in the winter when the Cairenes thought it cold, bathers would undress there and not in the outer room. Today, however, it was empty and he went straight on into the main bath room.

This was a large, square room with a marble-paved depression in the middle in which there was a beautiful fountain of white marble. From it shot a high jet of very hot water, all around the depression, at the sides of the room, were low, marble-covered couches. The couches were set back in Moorish arches which pointed in to carry the central dome, and there were other, smaller domes directly above the couches with little glazed holes in them through which the light came.

Several customers were already in the bath room, lying on the couches being scraped or massaged by the attendants, or else sitting with their feet in the central sunken area talking to their friends. One of the towel-swathed figures, Owen did not know which, was Mahmoud.

When they had talked this over beforehand, they had wondered how to cover all the rooms. If any money changed hands it would almost certainly be in the outer room, either before or after bathing. It was more likely to be afterwards. The men would meet in the baths and leave together. As they dressed, the balance of the money would be handed over and then the parties would leave separately. Or so they thought. Whether they had guessed rightly remained to be seen.

Owen and Mahmoud had agreed that it would be best for them to be in the bath room. They would try to spot their men, wait until they left and then go with them into the outer room. If they missed them it should not matter too much; the normal attendants in the outer room had been replaced for the day by Owen's men.

Owen went across to one of the marble couches and lay down. A huge Berberine attendant, naked except for a loin-cloth, approached and seized him. Without a word he began to work systematically over him, kneading the flesh and cracking the joints. Whenever he applied pressure he would give a little grunt. From all over the bath room came similar little grunts, both from the massagers and from the massaged. Mixed in with them was another sound which Owen could not at first identify. When the Berberine turned him over he saw that it came from the slab next to his. A man was having his feet rasped. If you always went barefoot or half-slippered your feet developed large, hard callosities. The rasps were made of Assiut clay and shaped like crocodiles, and as rough as breadcrumb graters.

The Berberine removed the towel from Owen's head and began to twist his ears. When they cracked, he transferred his attention to the neck, twisting the head first one way and then the other. Little drips of sweat fell from the Berberine on to Owen's body. Everyone in the room was sweating profusely. The bath room was heated with hot air and the water which played from the fountain was only just below boiling point. In two of the corners of the room were further tanks of extremely hot water. Occasionally, helped by an attendant, a man would plunge into one of these.

The Berberine finished with Owen and moved on to someone else. Owen lay for a few moments recovering. Then he went to a separate water-tank for cleansing. The attendant lathered him with soap using a large loofah and then washed it off. When the real work was done the attendant went away and Owen was allowed to play with the taps and spray himself with water which he considered to be at a more reasonable temperature.

The attendant returned with four fresh towels. Owen wrapped himself in them and wandered back into the first of the warm chambers. It was cooler in there, though still too hot for the singing birds. Owen could hear them next door in the outer room. He chose a couch and sat down. An attendant brought him cushions and coffee and he made himself comfortable.

From where he sat—he had chosen the spot deliberately— he had a good view into the bathroom. Mahmoud, he knew, was still in there. Between them they would cover the two rooms.

He sipped his coffee and waited.

Hamid had given descriptions of the men but that was not what helped him to spot them. Two brawny men wandered in a lost fashion through the warm chamber, came to the doorway of the bath room and stood sheepishly, obviously never having been in the place before. One of them muttered something to the other and they walked to the far side of the sunken area and sat down with their feet in the water and their backs to one of the slabs.

Two only of the men had come, one to watch the other, Owen supposed. The others would be waiting outside. And outside Georgiades would be waiting, too, along with Hamid and a few other men.

The man they had come to meet did not appear for some time. Owen would have worried, had he not seen the men worrying, too.

Eventually he appeared. His head was screened in towels and at first when he came in he did not go anywhere near them. But then, watching from under his own towel, Owen saw him make his way as if by chance across to them and sit down beside them. He spoke to them. The men's faces cleared and they sat waiting docilely while he went over to the water-tank for his soaping and washing.

As the attendant removed the towels Owen had a good look at the man.

It was Fakhri! Fakhri, the so-helpful editor! Fakhri, who had started the whole thing with that first eyewitness report!

He could not believe it! He must have made a mistake! It just could not be.

But then the man turned his face and Owen could see so clearly that there was no possibility of error. It was indeed Fakhri.

Fakhri completed his washing, took his towels and then sauntered round the bath room chatting to various other patrons. Eventually, as if by accident, he came to rest near the two men.

Owen's mind was whirling. The various pieces of the pattern that he had detected and fitted so cleverly together suddenly sprang apart, jumped into the air, somersaulted and crashed down all over the place. For a moment or two all he could do was contemplate the ruins. Then, one by one, unbidden, the pieces rose up again in his mind and each one, seen in a new light, was totally transformed. Things taken for granted moved round before his eyes and pointed in a completely new direction. Things new fitted in with a click. And underneath, slowly, realization dawned.

He had been duped. From the start he had been fooled. From the very moment Fakhri had walked into the office with the testimony which had set everything in motion. How much of that original testimony was true, Owen wondered now. Probably enough to confuse! And then the solicitous inquiries into Nuri's health at the café! And, also in that conversation at the café, now he came to think about it, there were other things as well, deliberately planted no doubt. It almost made Owen groan to think of them. Denshawai, Nuri's past. And then Ahmed! It was Fakhri who had directed him to that number of *al Liwa*, the one that had led on to the Nationalist meeting and Ahmed's connection with the Nationalists, and his presence at the village, and his possible

links with Mustafa. He had seen things the way Fakhri had
meant him to see them. And even when Fakhri had been
taken by surprise, as when Owen had turned up unexpectedly
at his party, he had turned it to his advantage!

Owen thought back over the party. The introduction to
Daouad, the firm pointing at *al Liwa*, the apparently incidental analysis of Nationalist politics, the pinpointing of key
factions. Oh yes, Fakhri had been obliging, all right. He had
told him, or had seen that he learned, everything he needed
to know. Everything he *wanted* to know. Because Fakhri had
probably seen the drift of his thinking and carefully fed him
things which would confirm it and distract.

Fakhri was a shrewd political operator. And that was it!
Owen should have realized he was being operated on. Fakhri
was part of Egyptian politics, he had a political position of
his own. He was not just an independent commentator. He
had his own game to play.

Whatever that game was, he played it very well. Fakhri's
innocent brown eyes and chubby, sympathetic face floated
before him. The convivial chatter, the apparently unconscious
giveaways, the way he made you feel that you were in control
and he was just a clumsy, fat pigeon struggling unavailingly
in your grasp.

God, Fakhri had run rings round him. He had round everybody. Especially the British! The British thought they were
in control and all the time Fakhri, apparently accepting, per-
petually deferring, forever giving way, was doing exactly as
he pleased.

And to think they'd got on to him through Hamid! The
super-subtle brought down by the super-simple! It was the
kind of irony Cairo would relish.

It would relish even more, he thought uncomfortably, the
story of how Fakhri had made a monkey of the Mamur Zapt.

Never mind. There would be one person at least who
would not be sharing in the general enjoyment.

Owen waited grimly.

Eventually Fakhri rose to his feet, said his farewells and came into the warm chamber. After a dutiful interval the two men followed him.

On their way they nearly collided with a figure so densely wrapped in towels it was evident he could hardly see. The man apologized profusely, stepped aside to let them pass ahead of him and then followed. Owen guessed that it was Mahmoud.

Fakhri went over to the other side of the room and sat down with his back turned to the two men. They found a couch some way off and sat down, very obviously waiting.

They had to wait some time.

Fakhri, clearly enjoying his pretending, called for coffee and then more coffee. He seemed to know everyone in the hammam. Everyone, that is, except for Owen and the morose, densely towelled Mahmoud who had planted himself down on the couch next to that of the two men.

After a while Owen himself stood up and walked on through into the outer room, where he collected his clothes and valuables. There was no need to hurry through. He could linger as long as he liked. Here, too, one could sit on cushions and drink more coffee, and enjoy the singing birds suspended from the pillars in their fine gilt cages. Here, too, the main object appeared to be conversation. Owen fell into earnest discussion with his neighbour, a portly gentleman who, it appeared, supplied chestnuts to half the stands around the Ezbekiyeh Gardens and was more than happy to describe at length both their virtues and the problems he had in getting them there. Owen listened with rapt attention, a towel draped over his head to soak up the last drips of moisture.

Out of the corner of his eye he saw Fakhri come in and collect his clothes. The two men came in close behind him. They all three went over to one side behind a pillar and he lost sight of them, though he noticed that Mahmoud, towelling his head vigorously, had placed himself where he could see them.

The three emerged from behind the pillar and soon afterwards the two men left.

Fakhri himself took his time. Even when he had finished dressing he did not leave at once but fell into conversation with a newcomer. He then spent some time tipping the attendant.

When, finally, he left, Owen and Mahmoud were just behind him. As they stepped out into the warm evening air they drew alongside.

"Hello, Fakhri," said Owen.

Chapter 11

"No," said Fakhri. "No. It wasn't like that at all."

"You arranged the attack," said Owen. "Are you telling us you didn't?"

"I arranged the attack," Fakhri admitted, "but I didn't mean him to be hurt."

"No?" said Mahmoud sceptically.

"It was a signal. That was all."

"Who was the signal to?" asked Mahmoud.

"Nuri, of course."

"What was it saying?"

"You know," said Fakhri. He looked at them almost appealingly. "You know it all," he said.

"Tell us."

They were in Owen's office. The others were in the cell below. Hamid had identified both the men and Fakhri as they entered the baths. When the men came out they had been followed. They had gone straight to a small square a kilometre or so away where the other men were waiting. Georgiades had arrested the lot. Now he was questioning them.

"I didn't want to hurt the boy. Really. The men were told—" The brown eyes regarded them anxiously. "They didn't make a mistake, did they?"

"Go on," said Owen, refusing to be drawn.

"I wouldn't want you to believe—"

He read the message in their faces and shrugged his shoulders.

"Very well, then," he said quietly. "Nuri had been meddling. He is always meddling. Trying to create new alliances. His own faction, which is very small now, and other moderates usually. This time he was after the Nationalists. He was trying to do a deal with Abdul Murr. He thought that if he could get Abdul Murr to go in with him the Khedive might see them as a possible government."

"Never in a million years!" said Owen.

"He might!" Fakhri insisted. "If he thought he was securing a new base of popular support."

"The Nationalists would never go along," said Mahmoud.

"They would," said Fakhri, "if they thought there was power at the end of it."

"Jemal?" said Mahmoud sceptically. "El Gazzari?"

"Not them," Fakhri conceded. "But others would. Abdul Murr."

"Never!"

"He might," said Fakhri. "He's got very fed up with Jemal and el Gazzari lately. Understandably," he added.

"Fed up is one thing," said Mahmoud. "Going in with a man like Nuri is another."

"It's not just that," said Fakhri. "Abdul Murr is no fool. He thinks that if the Nationalists could once get into power and show they could govern, then the Khedive wouldn't be able to do without them."

It was plausible. Certainly Owen felt so, and probably Mahmoud felt so. Mahmoud, however, clearly had a distaste for the whole thing. It ran counter both to his strong dislike of Nuri and his equally strong sympathy for the Nationalists.

"Nuri in a Nationalist government?" he said. "I don't believe it."

"It wouldn't be a Nationalist government," said Fakhri. "The Khedive won't agree to that. It would have to be a coalition and Nuri would have to lead it."

"Lead it!" cried Mahmoud.

"The Khedive won't agree on any other terms," said Fakhri. "That's why Nuri is in such a strong position."

"They won't go along," said Mahmoud.

"You'd be surprised!" said Fakhri.

There was a little silence. Owen could see Mahmoud struggling to come to terms with what Fakhri had said. He was still reluctant to accept it.

"You say these things, Fakhri," he said, "but how real are they?"

"Very real."

"How real?"

"Real enough to worry all the other political groupings. Real enough," said Fakhri, with a glance at Owen, "to worry the Mamur Zapt apparently. When I saw you taking an interest," he said to Owen, "I guessed that the British suspected something."

Owen let it pass. Sometimes there were dangers in being oversubtle.

He noticed Mahmoud look at him, however, and wondered if he would have some explaining to do.

"It could be a powerful combination," he said, "the Nationalists *and* the Khedive."

"That's just it," said Fakhri. "It worried us, too."

"Us?"

"Everybody, really. There are various factions around the Khedive, rivals of Nuri. They don't want it to happen. Then there are the Nationalists themselves. Plenty of them are opposed to it. Jemal and el Gazzari for a start. And then, of course," said Fakhri, "there are moderate groups, like my own, who are worried about being left out in the cold."

"And you were worried especially."

"Not especially," said Fakhri. "Why do you think that?"

"Because you did something about it."

Fakhri was silent for a moment.

"Not especially," he said again. "It was just that someone had to do something."

"And that someone just happened to be you?" said Owen sceptically.

"Yes," said Fakhri defiantly.

Owen let the pause drag on.

"So you decided," he said at last, "to send Nuri a signal?"

"Yes. We thought that if we sent him a direct warning—"

"By killing Ahmed?"

"Killing?" Fakhri looked shaken. "No," he said, "how could you think that? We wanted to give him a good thrashing. That was all."

"Why pick on Ahmed?"

"Because he's Nuri's son. Because Nuri loves him. Because Nuri has been using him as a go-between."

He looked at Owen.

"I did try to tell you," he said, almost reproachfully. "I've been trying to point you in his direction. I thought if you knew how far things had got, you might find a way of stopping it."

"How far had they got?" asked Owen.

"Further than we thought they would. Nuri is a cunning old devil. He seemed to be persuading Abdul Murr. It suddenly looked as if things were coming to a head. As if he might succeed."

"Was that the point of Nuri's visit to the *al Liwa* offices?"

"Yes. That was part of it, though the real fixing was to come later, in private. Anyway, we had to do something. I wanted to let Nuri know that we knew. So—" Fakhri shrugged. "I hired those men. They didn't overdo it, did they?"

Again the sympathetic brown eyes regarded Owen anxiously. Again Owen did not reply. The longer Fakhri was kept on the hook the better.

"I am sorry," said Fakhri softly. "It was just one of those things. Just politics."

༄

Even the coffee did not help. Sensing the mood that Owen was in, Yussuf entered silently, filled the mug and withdrew without saying a word. The shutters, which had been opened first thing to air the room, had long since been closed. Owen had been in for three hours already, and all the time he had been thinking about what Fakhri had said the evening before.

They had got nowhere, nowhere on anything really important. Ahmed's thrashing, his and Nuri's visit to *al Liwa*, what Nuri was up to, all this had been explained, and it did not seem to have advanced matters one little jot. The original attack on Nuri, the grenades, the Tademah connection, if there was a Tademah connection, they knew no more about now than they did before he and Mahmoud had gone to the hammam.

He had thought for a moment, the moment when Fakhri had revealed himself, that everything had suddenly tumbled into place. It had been a shock but once he had recovered he had felt that he had grasped the true pattern. The man behind had finally declared himself.

But it was not true. Fakhri was not the man behind, or if he was behind anything, it was only the most trivial parts of the pattern. At first in his fury Owen had thought Fakhri capable of anything. Now he had simmered down he realized that Fakhri was not really like that. The trouble was that Owen believed him. He believed what Fakhri had said the previous night. That Nuri was scheming along those lines was completely credible, knowing Nuri. That the Nationalists, or some of them, were tempted, was entirely likely, despite what Mahmoud might think. That the Khedive would play along, distinctly probable. That the other parties would be worried, certain. Even that Fakhri, who was definitely not a man without resource, would take it upon himself to do something about it.

And if he did decide to intervene, it was not at all unlikely that he would act in the way he said he had: choosing the gentler path of issuing a warning, picking his target with perception and ensuring that things did not go too far. No knives. Owen had noticed it himself.

The nub of it was that he did not believe Fakhri was a killer. He had only his feelings to go on, and he had already been deceived by Fakhri. Still, he stood by his feelings. He did not believe Fakhri was a killer.

But then, how did he know there was a killer involved? No one had been killed yet. The attempt on Nuri's life had not succeeded. It had been bungled. If someone like Mustafa had been chosen to perform the actual act, that did not exactly argue for someone behind the scenes who really knew his business, a cold, calculating killer by proxy.

All he had to go on was the whiff of fear in the Cairo air. He smelt it himself.

Not just that. The grenades. They were what chilled him. If you went for grenades you meant business. In a crowded city especially. The attack on Nuri was one thing. At the end of the day it was not very important, and anyway he could leave that to Mahmoud.

But the grenades were quite another thing. And that he could not leave to anybody else. They were his pigeon. Now that he had been put in charge of arrangements for the Carpet, his pigeon only.

But then, were all these things related to each other anyway? They might all be separate, nothing to do with each other. The attack on Nuri, the grenades, Ahmed's thrashing— they might all be entirely unconnected, just brought together in his mind because by chance they all came over his desk in the same week. The last of them, Ahmed's thrashing, was almost certainly nothing to do with the other two. Perhaps the other two were not connected either. They were all separate. The only thing they had in common was that he had to solve them.

It wouldn't do. He knew what was bothering him. The grenades. The Carpet. The only way he could set his mind at rest about the arrangements for the Carpet was by finding out who had those missing grenades: finding out and catching them. And the only lead he had to that was the Syrian, the gun and the attack on Nuri. And on that front he had made absolutely no progress at all.

As the morning wore on he became more and more conscious of the Return of the Carpet hanging over him like a heavy black cloud.

⚬⚬⚬

As soon as Mahmoud spoke, Owen knew that something was wrong.

"Are you going to be holding Fakhri?" Mahmoud asked, without preamble.

"Yes," said Owen, surprised. "I think so."

"On security grounds?"

"Yes," said Owen. "Why?"

"I would challenge your decision. There seems no security issue. It is a straightforward criminal offence."

"So?"

"So Fakhri should be transferred at once into the custody of the Parquet."

Owen held the telephone away from his ear and looked at it. What was wrong with Mahmoud this morning?

"What's the matter?" he asked.

"Nothing's the matter. It's just that I would like Fakhri transferred at once, please."

"Is this official?"

"What do you mean?" The voice sounded slightly puzzled.

"Are your bosses on to you or something?"

"No one is on to me at all," said Mahmoud stiffly.

Owen found it hard to believe. Unless—unless something had happened to upset Mahmoud. Perhaps at their meeting yesterday. He racked his brains to think of what it could be. Something he had said? It was obviously only too easy to touch off the sensitive Mahmoud. But he was not aware of having said or done anything which could have this effect. Something Fakhri had said?

"I was thinking of questioning him again later today," he said into the mouthpiece.

"If you will see that he's sent round immediately," said Mahmoud, "I will ensure that he is properly questioned."

It was the "properly" that did it; that, and the lingering, rankling memory of the "amateur" remark earlier.

"I am afraid I am unable to release the prisoner for questioning by the Parquet," Owen said coldly, and put the phone down.

If it had not been for Mahmoud's tone he might well have been willing to transfer Fakhri. Fakhri was of no real interest to him. But Mahmoud had irritated him. He had thought Mahmoud a person he could get on with, but if he continually blew hot and cold in this way he would be a strain to be with; and Owen was beginning to wonder this morning whether the strain was worthwhile.

He wondered what it was that had rubbed Mahmoud up the wrong way. Had it been that remark of Fakhri's, no, perhaps he'd not actually said it, just implied it: that Owen had known all along what Nuri was plotting? Owen had not had a chance to deny it and he had seen Mahmoud look at him. That was just the sort of thing to touch Mahmoud off.

He shrugged his shoulders. There was nothing he could do just now to put the matter right, if that was the matter. That was supposing he even wanted to try. And right now he wasn't too sure about that.

He returned to his brooding. The heavy black cloud was still there. If anything, it was even heavier and blacker than before.

⊙〰〰⊙

Worse.

Guzman rang.

"That's all I bloody need!" said Owen. "Tell him I'm tied up in a meeting."

A few moments later Nikos came back.

"He doesn't believe you," he said. "I can't think why. He says get you out of the meeting."

Owen picked up the phone resignedly.

"Yes?"

"Guzman here."

"Yes? What can I do for you?"

He hoped he sounded preoccupied.

"The Khedive is concerned—"

"Yes, yes."

"—about the arrangements for the Return of the Holy Carpet. *Really* concerned. I understand you have been put in charge of security?"

"Yes," said Owen, "that is correct."

"In that case," said Guzman, "it becomes all the more important for me to check the arrangements beforehand."

"I'll send you a copy."

"I need a briefing."

"There's a general briefing tomorrow morning," said Owen. "Do come."

"Why was I not invited?"

"You are invited. Do come."

"I need a personal briefing. I would like to go through the arrangements with you in some detail."

"Difficult—" began Owen.

"Before the meeting tomorrow," said Guzman. "It might save you embarrassment if I have checked it through privately beforehand."

He put the phone down.

Owen was left holding his end, seething with fury. First Mahmoud's "proper" questioning, then Guzman's checking beforehand. He gave his anger full rein. At least it was a distraction from the sick feeling of impotence that overtook him whenever he thought about the Return of the Carpet.

He made up his mind and reached for his sun helmet.

"Going out?" asked Nikos, affecting surprise.

"Too bloody right I'm going out!" said Owen.

"In case anyone else rings?" asked Nikos.

⟶⟶

Owen had intended to go to the Sporting Club but as he came out on to the Bab el Khalk he changed his mind. If he lunched at the club he would be sure to meet someone who would ask him about the Carpet and just at the moment that was the very last thing he wanted to talk about. Instead, he decided to find a quiet restaurant and dine alone.

As he crossed the top end of the Kasr el Nil, where there was a little cluster of fashionable European shops, he saw Zeinab come out of an expensive perfumery.

"Hello!" she said. "This is fortunate. I have something for you."

"That's nice," he said. "Why don't you give it me over lunch? I was just looking around for somewhere."

"I never eat lunch," she said. "Perhaps some coffee?"

They were standing near one of the large European restaurants. Normally Owen would not be seen dead in such a place. It did, however, follow the European style with respect to women. They could talk without attracting attention.

At this hour in the morning, late for coffee and early for lunch, the restaurant was far from crowded and they found a small table in a corner cut off by potted palms from the main concourse. Zeinab sat down with relief.

"Shopping!" she said.

Her veil this morning was three-quarter length, a decent concession to Moslem susceptibilities. She had bound her hair again in a scarf. Hair as well as face was an offence to strict Muslims.

She rummaged in her handbag and produced a small sheet of folded notepaper.

"This is what I have to give you," she said.

Owen took it and opened it.

An address was written down.

"It's from Raissa," said Zeinab.

"Raissa?"

"You know. You've spoken to her. Aziz's wife."

"I didn't know that was her name."

"She wants to be helpful. You said that if he was helpful you might not punish Aziz."

"Yes," said Owen.

He looked down at the address.

"What is it?" he asked.

"Aziz has gone there sometimes. After a letter."

Owen put the paper away in his pocket.

"Thank you," he said. "And thank her. Tell her that she has indeed been helpful and that I will remember it."

"Do not tell anyone else," said Zeinab. "She is terrified, poor lamb. You have no idea what it took for her to do this."

Owen nodded.

"You can assure her," he said, "that her husband is safe so far as I am concerned."

"Good!" said Zeinab with satisfaction.

He would see that no action was brought. Garvin would make sure of that. He was keen on maps.

They sipped their coffee.

Owen thought Zeinab deserved a reward. He told her about Fakhri.

Zeinab was astonished.

"Fakhri!" she said. "I thought he was a friend!"

"I don't think it was too hostilely meant," said Owen.

He wondered why he felt the need to justify Fakhri.

"Not hostilely meant? When he thrashes the poor boy within an inch of his life?"

Owen noticed that Ahmed was now a poor boy. It may have rung a little hollow to Zeinab, too, for she added hurriedly: "Though he may well have deserved it."

"It was meant as a warning," said Owen. "As your father supposed."

"Oh-ho!" said Zeinab. "So it was political, then. Well, Fakhri wants to watch out. My father is not likely to take this lying down."

"He did try to see that the beating was not taken too far," said Owen conciliatorily.

Again he wondered why he was putting in a good word for Fakhri.

"Did he?" said Zeinab, unplacated. The veil stopped above her mouth. The lips tightened into a straight line and the jaw became even more prominent. Owen suspected that Fakhri would find he had Zeinab to reckon with, too,

"Pas si formidable!" he protested mildly, and touched her hand.

Zeinab was startled but did not withdraw her hand.

Owen wanted to ask her about Raoul but decided that would be a mistake. Perhaps he could do it obliquely.

"How long have you know Raissa?" he asked.

"A year," said Zeinab, "maybe two."

"She seems to trust you a lot."

"She doesn't have anyone else."

"Not her husband?"

"Her husband, yes."

"I would have thought," said Owen, "that she would have known other women in the Syrian community."

"She does," said Zeinab. "She doesn't go out much, that's all. It's all those children. Besides, Aziz is very strict."

"He has conventional views about women, does he?"

"Normal views," said Zeinab.

Owen wondered how he could get there.

"What about her?" he asked. "What's her own family like? She's Raoul's wife's sister, isn't she?"

"Yes," said Zeinab. "Raoul brought her over once he had settled down."

"How long ago was that?" asked Owen.

"Seven, eight years ago. I don't know. Why do you ask?"

"Just curious," said Owen. "It's the usual pattern isn't it? One person goes to a place, does well, then brings his family over. The boys get jobs, the girls get married, usually to friends. And so a little community develops."

"Yes," said Zeinab. "Cairo is full of communities like that."

"But how do you fit in?" asked Owen. "Usually they're very tight little communities. They keep to themselves. The Greeks to the Greeks, the Syrians to the Syrians."

"Are you asking about me and Raoul?" demanded Zeinab. She pulled back her hand.

"Why," she said, "you sound just like the Mamur Zapt."

ᕫᜌᜌᜁᕬ

Arrangements for the return of the Holy Carpet were being finalized. A large street-map of Cairo had been spread out on a table and the area between the Citadel and the mosques of Sultan Hassan and Al Rifai'ya marked out with red ribbon. Nikos and the Army saw eye to eye on these matters.

The Khedivial Pavilion was indicated by a little green flag. Neither the Sirdar nor the Agent had pavilions on this occasion, since this was a purely Egyptian affair. They would be guests of the Khedive. However, Nikos had marked out a place for the band and thoughtfully indicated in bright orange where the Army—the Egyptian Army—would be drawn up. All was clear to the Army officers who were present and to John and Paul who were looking at their watches and fretting.

The Return of the Holy Carpet was one of the two great processions of the Cairo year. The other was the Departure of the Carpet. The Carpet departed with the annual caravan of pilgrims and returned from Mecca some months later, usually well after the pilgrims had returned, the actual date depending less on position in the religious calendar than on how far behind administrative arrangements had fallen.

It also depended on the desert tribes between Mecca and the coast, who were still inclined to harass the pilgrimage and had been particularly difficult this year; so much so that the Sirdar had sent an escort of half of the Fourth Battalion, a troop of cavalry and two machine-guns, not to mention the famous screw-gun battery which Lord Kitchener had wanted to buy for the Boer War.

The Carpet, of course, was not a carpet. It was a piece of tapestry made to go round the Kaaba stone at Mecca. It was of the stiffest possible black silk—black because that was the colour of the Abbasid dynasty—and embroidered heavily with gold. Making it was a hereditary privilege of a certain family, necessarily well to do; and a new one had to be made every year, since the Khedive cut up the old one, or the part of it that was returned to him, to present pieces of it to great Mohammedan personages.

The Carpet might, or might not, have been carried in the Mahmal, which was a beautifully ornamented frame of wood with a pyramidal top, carried by a single tall camel, which was afterwards exempted from any other labour for the rest of its life. The camel brought the Mahmal all the way from the coast, entered through the old gates of the city and then proceeded in triumph to the Citadel, where it would describe seven circles and be received by the Khedive.

"Seven?" said one of the officers incredulously. "Christ!"

"Can't you cut that down a bit?" asked another officer.

"Certainly not!" said McPhee firmly. "Seven is what is prescribed."

McPhee took a great interest in Arab ceremony.

"Seems excessive to me," one of the Army people said, "and damn dangerous, too. All that milling about just in front of the Sirdar."

"In front of the Khedive," said Nikos, who was a stickler for accuracy.

"It *is* a bit close," said Paul.

"No, it's not," said Owen. "The circles are described in the centre of the square. The pavilion is set well back. The Khedive comes out to receive the Carpet."

"Bit dangerous for the Khedive, isn't it?"

"He's got to kiss the Mahmal," said Owen. "You can't do that at a distance."

"As long as it's him coming out and not the Sirdar," said someone.

"Where exactly will the Sirdar be while all this is going on?" asked someone else.

"For Christ's sake!" said Paul. "We've gone through all that."

"Left-hand side of the Khedive's chair, four paces left, half pace back," intoned Owen. "The chair will be marked."

"How will he connect up with his horse?" asked someone who had not spoken before.

"Horse?" said Owen. "What bloody horse?"

"The Sirdar always leads the Army off afterwards."

"Can't he do that in a car?" asked Owen. "Does it have to be a horse?"

"Yes," said John. "I'm afraid so."

"He rather fancies himself on that bloody great white charger of his," said Paul.

There was a moment's disapproving silence from the Army.

"Doesn't security become a matter for the Army at that point?" asked Owen hopefully.

"No," said John and Paul together.

"It's all part of the arrangements," said John. "Anyway, what *are* the arrangements for afterwards?"

"The Khedive goes off at some point," said Paul. "Usually early because he's bored."

"He goes off independently," said Owen, "by car."

"Is that a good idea?" asked one of the officers. "Wouldn't it be better if they all left together?"

"We could put a proper guard on them that way," said another.

Paul shook his head. "It won't do," he said. "The Khedive will want to do his own thing."

"He'd better look after himself, then," an officer said.

There were grunts of approval.

"What about the Agent?" asked John.

"He'll go one minute after the Khedive goes," said Paul.

"Will he want an escort?"

"No," said Paul. "Williams will drive him home."

"Is that OK?"

"It's been OK so far," said Paul tartly.

Owen decided that it was time to assert himself.

"What will happen," he said firmly, "is this. At some point the Khedive will leave. He will go in a car with his usual escort, one car in front, one car behind. He will be accompanied by a mounted troop, who will ride on both sides of the car, allowing people to see him but at a distance, and obstructing possible aggressors. The convoy will proceed to the Palace via the Sharia Mabdouli. Shortly afterwards, the Agent will leave, in his own car, with Williams driving, two guards, and another car escorting. Those cars will proceed independently by another route back to the consulate. At some point later, when the ceremony has been adjudged to have been finished—"

"Who's adjudging it?" asked John.

"I am. The main body of troops will move off down the Sharia Mohammed Ali, turn left at the Bab el Khalk and make their way along the sharias Ghane el Edaa and el Khoubri back to the barracks where they will disperse. The Sirdar will ride with them."

"Will he have an escort?" asked Paul.

"He'll have the Army," said one of the officers stiffly.

"Yes, but if he's riding at the head of them, won't that leave him a bit exposed?"

"There will be an advance party," said John reassuringly.

"Good," said Owen briskly. "Then I'll leave that bit of it to you."

He looked at Brooker, who had been noticeably subdued throughout.

"Why the Sharia Mohammed Ali?" asked one of the officers. "Isn't that rather a long way round?"

"It's the broader street," said Owen, "the best for a procession and the safest from the point of view of grenades."

"Grenades," said one of the officers, who hadn't heard. "Bloody hell!"

"That OK, then?"

The party began to break up. Paul and John collared Owen to go for a drink.

"You can have another when this lot is all over," said Paul. "In fact, you can have dozens. And I will join you!" he said fervently.

෴

Although the encounter with Zeinab had not gone entirely satisfactorily and had ended, in Owen's view, prematurely, it had restored him to a more balanced view of the world. He had even gone so far, the previous evening, as to instruct Nikos to transfer both Fakhri and the other men held in connection with the attack on Ahmed into the custody of the Parquet.

Because he was busy it was not until the next evening that he received a response.

"I've been trying to reach you all day," said Mahmoud.

"Sorry!" said Owen. "I've been tied up pretty well the whole time."

He thought he had better explain in case Mahmoud disbelieved him.

"I have a briefing session this morning. Two briefing sessions," he said, remembering Guzman. "It's the Return of the Carpet."

"Oh," said Mahmoud. "The best of luck. Glad it's nothing to do with me."

"That's what they all say."

The responsibility of the Carpet still hung over him. He knew its leaden weight would not go away until the affair was over.

"I wanted to apologize," said Mahmoud. "I shouldn't have gone on like that yesterday."

"It's all right."

"I don't know what got into me."

"I thought it might be what Fakhri had said. You know, his helpful suggestion that I had been aware all the time what Nuri was up to and hadn't bothered to share it with you." There was a silence.

"Something like that," Mahmoud mumbled.

"Well, I hadn't been aware."

"Of course you hadn't!" said Mahmoud warmly. "That's what I told myself. But it was too late then."

"It hadn't been a good morning."

He told Mahmoud about Guzman.

Mahmoud commiserated.

"I think we were both disappointed that the Fakhri lead didn't seem to be getting us very far," he said.

"That's right," said Owen. "For a moment I thought it was all falling into place. Have you got anywhere with him today?"

"No. I think he really has told us all he knows."

"Pity."

"Yes."

"Not very helpful."

"Not in itself," said Mahmoud.

"What do you mean?"

Mahmoud hesitated.

"I had an idea," he said. "Suppose somebody else wanted to stop Nuri's little deal? Only they were not so concerned to limit themselves to beating."

ᎶᎷᏖᎤ

Owen was still thinking it over when Zeinab rang.

"In answer to your question," she said, "the one you did not ask: Raoul loves me dearly. Which is very sad for him."

And rang off.

ᎶᎷᏖᎤ

Owen now had two things to think about. Between the two he became very confused.

He summoned Georgiades.

"Mean anything?" he said, showing him the address Zeinab had given him.

"Yes," said Georgiades instantly.

He went back to his office and returned with a file.

"It's a printer."

He took out a leaflet.

"You've seen this before," he said.

He laid it on the desk in front of Owen. It was the leaflet Georgiades had been given by Ahmed.

"He printed that?"

"Yes. And other things."

Georgiades put the file on his desk. Owen opened it. Inside was a selection of handbills, leaflets and pamphlets.

"All his own work," said Georgiades.

They were of a violent, inflammatory kind, similar in tone to the one he had already seen.

Owen picked one out.

"They seem to have a thing about the Sirdar," he said.

"About the British generally," said Georgiades.

He showed Owen some more.

"About most people," said Owen, turning them over.

"Not about Greeks," said Georgiades. "They've left me out of it. So far."

"Anti-Turk?" asked Owen.

"Why should he be anti-Turk? He's a Turk himself."

"Well, isn't that interesting?" said Owen, thinking about other Ahmed connections.

"There's a room over the shop," said Georgiades. "Two men live there. Others go there."

"You've got a man on the place?"

"I've got someone who calls in. Regularly."

"Better have someone on it full time from now on. At least for the next week."

The next day a vendor of religious knick-knacks took up position in the street where the printer lived. He suffered badly from ophthalmia and was almost blind. The little boys of the street could easily have stolen the things from his tray had it been worth it. The women took pity on him and brought him bowls of durra, especially when, in the heat of the afternoon, he stopped his fruitless patrolling and sat down in the shade with his back against the cool stone of the wall and his tray in front of him in the dust. There were similar figures along the street and another representative of God's afflicted was not noticed.

The day before the Carpet returned, when the workmen were putting the final touches to the pavilions in the big square before the Citadel and the small shopkeepers along the Sharia Mohammed Ali were decking their shops with bunting, the two men moved out.

Chapter 12

The Khedive's pavilion stood far down in the open space below the Citadel. From there the ground sloped upwards, first to the Market of the Afternoon and then to the Meidan Rumelah. After that it rose steeply and became the giant rock of the Citadel itself. At the top of the rock were the massive towers and ramparts of Saladin's castle; and at the utmost top of the castle was the Mosque of Mehemet Ali, with its obelisk and soaring dome. From that great dome, built only a century before, a host of smaller minarets and domes descended in a sweep like the curve of a scimitar to the two other great mosques which stood left and right where the chief thoroughfare of the city, the Sharia Mohammed Ali, came out into Citadel Square.

In the early morning sunshine the Mameluke domes took on the colour of pearl and rose. Pageants were early in Egypt to avoid the fierceness of the noonday sun, and the people had been gathering since before six. Many of them had brought seats, not so much to sit on—the ground would do for that—as to stand on when the procession went past. They were kept well back from the Khedive's pavilion by a fence of soldiers. Whenever they encroached beyond the fence they were turned back by mounted policemen on white horses.

The soldiers, too, had arrived early. First, the foot soldiers of the Egyptian Army, in their sky-blue, with white spats and scarlet tarbooshes. Then the artillery with their horse-drawn guns to fire the salute. The guns were ranged in line, the horses detached, and the crews set to preparing the pieces. Last came the cavalry, again in light blue, the staff conspicuous in white and gold.

Notables and foreigners arrived some time after. A space had been roped off for their carriages not far from the Khedivial Pavilion. Lesser notables stood in front of the pavilion, and there was a sort of tribune for those members of the diplomatic corps who had not been able to find an excuse for leaving Cairo that weekend. The pavilion itself was filled with chairs for the dignitaries, and soon they began arriving. The pashas had gold bands around their turbans, and among them, in robes of sacred green, was the Sheikh el Bekri, the Descendant of the Prophet. There were ministers and politicians and a number of officials in court dress. Among them, too, was the British Agent, in morning dress, and the Sirdar, resplendent in full dress uniform.

The Khedive himself did not arrive until the last moment—indeed, after the last moment, for the ceremony was due to start at nine and he did not arrive until nine-fifteen. The band played the Egyptian anthem, the guns thundered out, and the Army stood at salute. A car dashed up to the pavilion and the Khedive got out to be greeted by the Prime Minister, dressed in a green sash, and countless other officials, all in vivid sashes of one kind or another.

Immediately afterwards a burst of Oriental kettle-drums and hautboys from the entrance of the square announced that the procession was approaching.

At the head of the procession, nodding gravely on its camel, was the Mahmal, a square tent twelve feet high, of crimson and cloth-of-gold, with gold balls and green tassels. Because of the nature of a camel's gait it was very seldom upright, but jogged jauntily along, surrounded by religious banners gorgeous with Arabic texts. It was followed by a standard-bearer and five drum-beaters mounted on fine camels with splendid trappings, the same band probably that had played into Cairo every important pilgrim who had lately returned from Mecca. The camels were led by men in picturesque dresses, who did not at all look as if they had been to Mecca. They did not even look respectable. They looked as if they were men who did odd jobs about the bazaars, hired for the occasion. Their business, it was clear, was to lead the band camels, not to have been to Mecca. There was also a jester, but he was a holy man and had been to Mecca.

Behind it was the escort, burned black by the sun of the Arabian desert, incongruous in its Britishness and with its modern artillery, marching with precision, competent, necessary.

When the Mahmal came abreast of the Khedivial Pavilion it went through various evolutions while it performed the required seven circles. Then it advanced right up to the pavilion steps.

The Khedive came down the steps to receive it.

Owen could almost hear the officers' intake of breath as a mass of people in brightly coloured dress swarmed around the plump figure. But Owen was not watching them; his eyes were on the motley about the camels.

His men did as they should and formed an inconspicuous, informal screen between the enthusiastic crowd and the officials, and after a few moments the Khedive turned back up the steps and returned to his chair.

The procession resumed. The Mahmal nodded away, appearing to toss on the sea of supporters which closed in uncontrollably now on every side. With a final blaze of hautboys the camels disappeared.

The Khedive was already getting into his car. The escort took up position. At the last moment Owen had been persuaded to include a detachment of the Camel Corps, on the grounds that with their tall cocks' plumes, they were especially picturesque and the Khedive would love them. He had wondered whether to station them in front of the Khedive's car so as to force the Khedive to slow down and keep within the wall of his escort. That would be dangerous, however, should the Khedive need to make a quick getaway, and he had settled for the rear. He was determined to have the more mobile horses guarding the sides.

As soon as the Khedive's party had moved off there was a general rush for carriages. Owen saw Paul and the Agent waiting quietly until the first burst had subsided and then making their way in the opposite direction to where an open tourer had drawn up unobtrusively. They stepped in and were gone.

Officers barked orders and the soldiers began to form. Owen could not see the Sirdar at first but then picked him out. He was already mounted and talking to a group of officers, similarly mounted.

The soldiers were ready to move off. The Sirdar took up his position at the head of the column. There was a trumpet call, a pause and then another trumpet call. The column moved off and turned up the Mohammed Ali.

The sharia was broad and its lower end lined with trees. Bunting was draped between the trees, and many of the small shops were festooned with brightly coloured flags. The crowd here was less tumultuous than the one which had threatened to overwhelm the Mahmal and at first the applause was dutiful rather than enthusiastic. Few Cairenes, however, could resist a spectacle and before long the crowded pavements were a-buzz with delight at the tall soldiers.

Some of them were indeed very tall. Following the triumphant conclusion of the Sirdar's campaign, many Sudanese had been recruited into the Army. You could tell them by their darker skin. They were much taller and fitter than the average fellahin. In their splendid tarbooshes they looked gigantic.

Police lined the route throughout, keeping the onlookers well back from the marchers. McPhee had had to raid the forces outside Cairo. For some of the country police it was their first visit to Cairo and they were both impressed and bewildered. The police were spaced more widely than McPhee would have liked. It was easy to break through the cordon—small boys were forever doing so—though when anyone did they were soon chivvied back by mounted police with rhinoceroshide whips.

Owen began to move up the column, keeping his horse well out to one side, unobtrusively close to the long line of policemen.

He had chosen to ride because of the extra mobility but it also gave him a better view. From where he sat he could see over the heads of the policemen into the crowd. Occasionally he saw faces he recognized: journalists, minor civil servants with their families, even middling notables who had been at the Khedive's Pavilion, picked out by their sashes, ostensibly on their way home but reluctant to miss any of the fun. He even thought he saw Guzman, but that was almost certainly a mistake.

He looked back down the Mohammed Ali. At the far end was a dense cloud. The street had been heavily watered that morning but already the sun was drying it out and the wheels of the gun carriages were stirring the dust.

The whole of the column was in the Mohammed Ali now and the front of the procession—he could just see the mounted figures—was about half way along, approaching the point where the street suddenly narrowed and ran between blocks of residential houses. Owen urged his horse. It was here if anywhere that there might be trouble.

It was to a house in that part of the sharia that the two men had moved when they left the room above the printer's.

They had taken a room on the first floor with heavy latticed windows hanging over the street. The edge of the procession would pass directly under them.

Georgiades would have all that well in hand. In fact— Owen looked at his watch—he would already have acted.

The head of the procession was about level with the house now. Owen stood up on his stirrups to see better. Yes, it was almost exactly parallel. Nothing happened. It was now definitely past.

He relaxed back into his saddle. A small boy squeezed between a constable's knees and ran out into the street. Scandalized, the constable grabbed him and thrust him back into the crowd.

Owen had had to rein in. He paused now and looked along the crowd. It was intent on the spectacle, relaxed, enjoying itself. The sweet-sellers, sherbet-sellers, lemonade-sellers and souvenir-hawkers were doing good business. A few youths were distributing political leaflets. One of them seemed familiar. The boy turned and Owen saw that it was Ahmed. He was thrusting leaflets into the hands of the onlookers. They took them blindly, their eyes on the soldiers.

I don't think you'll do a lot of trade today! thought Owen, and urged his horse on up the line.

And then suddenly, right on top of him it seemed, there was an enormous bang.

დოოდ

For a moment or two he could not quite take in what had happened. He became aware that his horse was shying and twisting. Almost automatically he brought it back under control. Then he grew conscious of the ringing in his ears and of that distinctive after-echo and realized.

There had been an explosion, a bomb had been thrown. A grenade.

And yet the procession was marching on as if nothing had happened.

An acrid cloud of smoke drifted across him. He looked round, bewildered.

And then he saw.

Behind him, a little way down the sharia, a horse, one of the police horses, was on its knees in a pool of blood. Its rider lay to one side in a crumpled heap, and everywhere, all over the pavement, people were lying. Police were running towards them, and children were crying, and the soldiers went on marching past.

Someone was plucking at his stirrup. It was one of the policemen.

"I saw him, effendi!" His eyes were round with shock. "I saw him! He threw something!"

The horse dropped its head and turned over on its side. Great shudders ran along its flanks and each shudder widened the gap in its belly from which blood and something else was pouring out. A leg seemed to have become detached from the horse and lay at a strange angle as if it did not belong to its owner.

Owen took a grip on himself.

"You saw him?" he said.

The constable was still clinging to his stirrup.

"Yes, effendi," the man almost pleaded.

"Who was it?" Then, seeing the man was not taking it in, he gestured towards the crowd. "Which one?"

The constable had to force himself to look.

"I don't know," he said. And then: "He ran away. I saw him."

McPhee appeared, distressed, efficient.

"You straighten things out here," Owen said harshly. "I've got to see what's happening up front."

McPhee began at once to issue orders.

Owen called to him.

"This man says he saw who did it." He indicated the constable beside him. "Get someone after them if you can."

"Right," said McPhee, and came across.

Owen had to prise the constable's fingers open to get him to release the stirrup.

As he prepared to ride away, Owen caught sight of Ahmed. He was sitting among the people on the pavement, his head on his knees, weeping.

Owen called to one of the policemen.

"Get that one!" he said, pointing.

He did not wait to see what happened but touched his heels to his horse's sides and cantered up towards the front of the column.

It was proceeding as if nothing had happened. The heels clipped in smartly, the arms swung, the faces were as impassive as ever. And up here, seeing only what they expected, the crowd, which obviously had heard the explosion, assumed that it was somehow part of the procession and cheered and shouted and waved as before.

Georgiades stepped out into the street.

"What's happened?" he said.

"Did you get them?"

"Yes."

"The grenades?"

"Two of them."

"That was the third, then," said Owen.

"Anyone hurt?"

"Yes."

Georgiades grimaced.

"It was probably intended as a decoy," he said, "to distract attention from what was going to happen up this end."

"You got the men?" asked Owen again.

"Sure thing," Georgiades soothed him. "Two men and a boy."

"A boy?"

"A walad. To run messages, perhaps? Anyway, we've got them."

Owen cantered on.

Two horses detached themselves from the front of the column. One of them turned back to meet him. It was Brooker.

"What's gone wrong?" he said.

"Sirdar OK?"

"Yes." Brooker looked at him. "Why shouldn't he be?" The other horse was John's.

"Christ, Gareth!" he said. "What's up?"

"Decoy—we think. The main business was to happen up here."

"Bloody hell."

John prepared to speed back to the Sirdar.

"We've got them," said Owen. "The ones who were to do the business up here."

"The grenades?"

"All three accounted for. That was one of them you heard."

"The others—"

"We've got. With their owners."

"Thank Christ for that, anyway."

He and Brooker rode back to the Sirdar.

The procession was approaching the Bab el Khalk, where it would swing left into the Sharia Ghane. The streets were wider here. There was less likelihood of an attack. Owen watched for a moment and then cantered back the way he had come.

The rear of the column was passing the dead horse now. Some of the horses shied a little as they sensed the carcase.

The pavement was clear. People were being helped into ambulances.

"No one much hurt, actually," said McPhee. "Concussed, shocked, but nothing more. So far as we can tell. OK up front?"

"Yes. All according to plan."

"Up front, yes," said McPhee.

The horse was still. The blood was dark with flies, and other flies were dense about the entrails.

The rider had been moved.

"What about him?" said Owen, gesturing.

"Concussed. Just, we think. Alive, anyway."

It could have been a lot worse.

They were enveloped in a great cloud of dust as the artillery went by. They emerged coughing and choking.

"Did Georgiades get the others?"

"Yes."

"We've got this silly bugger," said McPhee, waving his hand, "if he had anything to do with it."

Ahmed still sat on the ground, hunched up, his head buried in his arms. The thin shoulders were shaking.

Owen dismounted and walked across to him. Ahmed became aware of the boots and looked up.

"I never thought it would be like this!" he said, weeping.

"Like what?" said Owen.

Ahmed's eyes traveled out to where the horse was lying and then were quickly drawn away again.

"This!" he said, burying his head in his arms again.

"Bombs do this," said Owen. "Didn't you know?"

Ahmed shook his head.

"They didn't tell you, did they?"

"No," said Ahmed.

"Who gave it you?"

"What?" said Ahmed, uncomprehending.

"The grenade. The bomb."

Ahmed raised his head and looked back at Owen, shocked.

"No one," he said. "No one. I swear!"

"Where did you get it from?"

Ahmed looked blank.

"You threw it," said Owen. "Where did you get it from?"

"I didn't!" Ahmed almost shrieked. "I didn't! I didn't! I swear!"

"Who gave it you?"

"No one! No one! I swear!"

Someone touched Owen on the arm. It was the constable who had held on to his stirrup.

"Effendi," he said. "It wasn't him. I saw."

"Not him?"

"No, effendi. The man ran away."

The man had recovered from his shock but the eyes were still wide, horrified.

"Yes," said Owen. "I remember. You said."

"I saw," said the man. "I saw."

Owen looked at McPhee, who led the man aside and began talking to him quietly.

Owen turned back to Ahmed.

"I didn't know!" Ahmed groaned, rocking his body from side to side. "I didn't know!"

"What didn't you know?" said Owen, bending over him.

"That they would do this. They said—"

He burst into tears.

"What did they say?"

Ahmed was unable to speak. He just rocked to and fro.

"Come!" said Owen, slipping into Arabic. "Something terrible has been done and I need to know."

Ahmed brought himself under control.

"They said—" he whispered, "they said it was leaflets only."

"You were giving them out on the pavement," said Owen.

"Yes, I would give them out. And they—"

"Yes?"

"They would throw them on to the ground. In front of the policemen and soldiers."

"You would do this at the back?" said Owen.

"Yes."

"And someone else would do it at the front?"

"Yes," said Ahmed. "In front of the Sirdar."

"It was not leaflets," said Owen.

"No," Ahmed whispered. "No."

He buried his head in his arms. Owen touched him gently on the shoulder.

"Who threw it?"

"Farouz."

"Where will I find him?"

"At Guzman's. We were to go to Guzman's after."

"Guzman's?" said Owen incredulously.

"Yes," said Ahmed, looking up. "Didn't you know?"

Chapter 13

Afterwards, Owen understood. At the time he just had to act. He sent one of the policemen for Georgiades. With the others he headed straight for Guzman's.

Georgiades reached him just as they got there.

"Here we are again," he said. "What is it this time?"

"The same as it was last time," said Owen savagely. "Only then we missed it."

He told Georgiades.

"I always knew he was a bastard," said Georgiades, "but that didn't make him stand out."

They went straight in. Farouz they caught almost at once. He was drinking water in the kitchen. He wasn't even armed. Guzman got away. He was in a room upstairs and had more time. Later they learned he had taken refuge in the Syrian consulate.

McPhee exploded.

"Sir, I really must protest!" he said to Garvin.

"You don't think I like it, do you?" asked Garvin.

They were in Garvin's office later that afternoon. The soldiers were back in quarters, the Mahmal resting in a mosque, and the population at its siesta. In the evening they would come out on to the streets again and there might be trouble. Owen had police everywhere, though, and there were double

guards on all military installations. He had great hopes of
the day passing off without further incident.

John had rung him to give the Sirdar's congratulations.

"He thinks you're great," said John. "He thinks he's pretty
great, too. Steadfastness under fire. Firm as a rock, cool as an
iceberg. That sort of thing. Oh yes, and nothing actually
happened."

"To him," said Owen.

"Well," said John. "That's what counts, isn't it? Or isn't it?"

The Agent's praise had been more muted.

"He's glad you got the men," said Paul. "So am I. It might
have become a habit."

Garvin's reaction was hard to tell. It was still unfinished
business to him, probably, and he was waiting to see how it
turned out.

"Can't the Agent do something, sir?" asked McPhee.

"Like what? Protest?"

"I was hoping for something more, sir," said McPhee.

"You mean ask the Sirdar to send in a regiment or something? He wants to do that already."

"Well, we do run the country, sir," said McPhee doggedly.

"Sometimes I wonder if anybody runs the country," said
Garvin. "I certainly don't."

"Couldn't he put pressure on the Khedive?"

"The Khedive's delighted by the whole business. Anyway,
Guzman is a Turk."

"What's he doing in the Syrian consulate, then?"

"He's there because he's a Turk."

Since Egypt was still, legalistically, a Turkish possession,
the Turks did not need diplomatic representation. If they
could not work directly through the Khedive they drew on
the services of friendly powers.

"You mean we can't get at him at all, sir?" asked McPhee.

"That's right," said Garvin.

"I'll get at him," said Owen.

Ahmed was interrogated that evening. Interrogated, or questioned. Owen claimed that he was being interrogated, since he was held under security provisions and this was a military matter. Mahmoud pointed out that he was also being held in connection with the attack on Nuri, that this was a civil affair, and that the Parquet intended to question him. In the end they agreed that Ahmed was to be both interrogated and questioned.

Ahmed gave his answers in Owen's office. He was no longer in a state of shock. Nevertheless, it was a very subdued young man who was brought in. He sat in a chair, looking down with unseeing eyes at his feet, waiting numbly for Owen to begin.

Owen, deliberately, did not begin at once. He had some papers on his desk—the estimates, alas, were still with him—which he pretended to go through, marking them with a pencil. Eventually he put the pencil down and said matter-of-factly:

"Did they tell you to stand there?"

Ahmed looked up startled.

"Outside the Beyt el Betani? That's where you were, weren't you?"

"Yes," said Ahmed.

"Giving out leaflets?"

"Yes."

"Right by the water-cart?"

It was the water-cart which had taken the main force of the explosion, shielding the people on the pavement and accounting for the low level of serious injury.

"I think so," said Ahmed.

"They told you to stand there?"

"Yes."

"While someone else was going to stand further up the Sharia Mohammed Ali, just where the road narrows?"

"Yes."

"You knew that, did you?"

"Yes."

"Were they going to be in the street, do you know, or in a house?"

"There was talk of a room."

"This was at the meeting before, when you were planning what you would do?"

"Yes."

"Who was at the meeting?"

Ahmed hesitated.

"I don't know," he muttered finally, looking down.

"You were at the meeting, weren't you?"

"Yes," Ahmed admitted.

"Who else was there?"

Again the long hesitation. Owen was just making up his mind to press harder when Ahmed spoke with a rush.

"I was late," he said, almost tearfully. "I had an essay to write. It had to be in the next day. He said it would be all right."

"Guzman?"

"Yes."

"If you came late?"

"Yes. They had nearly finished. Well, they had finished really. They were just waiting for me."

"You couldn't help being late."

"No," said Ahmed. "I had run all the way."

"Were they angry?"

"No. They just—sort of joked." He flushed and looked down.

"What were they talking about when you arrived?"

"Nothing really. They were just waiting."

"OK," said Owen. "So what did they say to you?"

"They told me where to stand."

"By Farouz?"

"Yes."

"And give out leaflets?"

"Yes."

"That was all?"

"Yes." Ahmed looked at him. "I swear it," he said.

Owen kept his face quite blank.

"And Farouz," he asked, "what was Farouz to do?"

"To give out leaflets," said Ahmed. "I thought…"

Owen waited.

"Really!" Ahmed insisted. He seemed suddenly on the verge of tears. "He had a bag over his shoulder. Like mine. I thought—I thought—" He stopped.

"Yes?" said Owen.

"That he had leaflets in it," said Ahmed faintly. "I wondered why he wasn't giving them to people. I thought perhaps he was saving them to throw before the soldiers."

His voice faded away and came to a stop. Owen was beginning to think he had stopped for good when he started again.

"He didn't throw," Ahmed said. "Not for a long time. I kept wondering why."

Again the voice faded.

Owen let the silence drag on for some time before he prompted.

"But then he did throw."

"Yes," said Ahmed.

"You saw?"

"He put his hand in the bag and took something out. I couldn't see. The crowd was very thick. He tried to throw, but the crowd—he was all hemmed in. It went up in the air. Not very far."

Tears began to run down his cheeks.

"As Allah is my witness," he whispered, "I did not know."

Owen waited for him to say more. When he did not, he said: "Let Allah be your witness still: surely you knew what these men would do?"

Ahmed shook his head decisively.

"No," he said. "No. No."

"You knew they were Tademah."

There was a long silence.

"Yes," said Ahmed at last. "I knew."

ᏭᎢᎥᎥᎥᏫ

At this hour in the evening the office was completely quiet. There were a couple of orderlies at the end of the corridor and occasionally Owen could hear their low voices. The constable who had brought Ahmed up was probably with them. The only other noise was the buzzing of insects around the lamp.

Owen got up, walked across the room and poured himself a cup of water from the large earthenware jug standing in the window where the night air would cool it. All the offices had water. Yussuf refilled the jugs every morning. At this time of year, when Cairo was so hot, it was necessary.

He poured out a cup for Mahmoud, and then another for Ahmed, which Ahmed took without looking up.

"When did you first learn they were Tademah?" he asked, and then, as Ahmed did not reply, "At once, or later?"

Ahmed's lips tightened.

"At once?"

There was a half-nod, suppressed.

"When you got back from Turkey?"

This time Ahmed looked up in surprise. "Yes," he said. "How did you know?"

"You were given someone to contact?"

Again the half-nod.

"Guzman?"

The shake of the head was definite.

"Who, then?"

Ahmed made no reply.

"Farouz?"

No indication. He had obviously made up his mind to say no more.

Owen sighed. He would have to work harder.

"You knew they were Tademah," he said. "Are you saying you didn't know they would kill?"

Ahmed's lips remained tightly compressed.

"Not even," said Mahmoud, coming into the conversation for the first time, "when they ordered you to kill your father?"

Ahmed looked up thunderstruck.

"No," he said. "No. How could you think—It wasn't like that."

"Wasn't it?" said Mahmoud. "What was it like, then?"

He pulled his chair forward so that he was confronting Ahmed. Owen moved a little to one side to let him take over.

Ahmed started to say something, stopped, looked from one of them to the other and then said: "It wasn't like that."

"You heard Mustafa at the meeting."

"Yes, but—"

"You spoke to him afterwards."

"Yes—"

"You gave him hashish. Too much. More than you were supposed to."

"No—"

"You found him a gun. They gave it you."

This time Ahmed was silent.

"And you gave it to him."

Mahmoud paused deliberately and then followed up with concentrated ferocity.

"To kill your father."

"No," said Ahmed. "No."

Mahmoud sat back in his chair but did not relax the pressure.

"Yes," he said. "Yes."

"It's not true!"

"All those things are true," said Mahmoud. "I've checked them."

"Yes, but—"

"Are you saying they're not?"

"They're true," said Ahmed, almost in a shout, "but not—"

"Not what?"

"Not the last."

"No?" said Mahmoud disbelievingly.

"It was to frighten him!" cried Ahmed. "That was all. I swear it!"

"Mustafa does not say so."

"I told him!" said Ahmed, weeping. "I told him!"

"What did you tell him?"

"I told him it was to frighten only. That it would be wrong to kill. It was right to punish Nuri for what he had done, but not to commit another wrong! I told him. I swear it!"

"And Tademah," said Owen sceptically, "did they want to punish him, too?"

"No," said Ahmed. "That was different."

"What did they want?"

Ahmed was silent.

"Money?"

"No," said Ahmed. "Not money."

"There was a note."

"I wrote that," said Ahmed, surprisingly.

"You wrote it?"

"Yes. To frighten Nuri. To make him think Tademah would avenge."

"Avenge? Denshawai?"

"No, no," said Ahmed. "The girl. Mustafa."

"It was just part of your personal campaign?"

"Yes."

"What did Tademah think?"

Ahmed lowered his head. "They thought it was foolishness," he said.

"They weren't really interested?"

"No."

"What were they interested in, then?"

Ahmed was mute.

"Nuri's deal? With Abdul Murr?"

Again Ahmed was surprised.

"You knew?"

"They wanted to frighten him off?"

"Yes," said Ahmed. "They weren't really interested in the girl, but when I told them what I planned, they said they would help."

"So they gave you the gun?"

"Yes. They said it would serve a double purpose."

"'They,'" said Mahmoud. "You are always saying 'they.' Who are they? What are their names?"

"I daren't tell," said Ahmed. "They would kill me."

"You realize," said Mahmoud softly, "that if you instigated Mustafa to commit a crime, whether Mustafa planned to kill your father or not, then you bear responsibility?"

Ahmed went ashen.

"I did not mean…" he whispered.

"Whether you meant to or not," said Mahmoud.

"Who are 'they'?" asked Owen.

Ahmed licked his lips. "I dare not," he said. "They would kill me."

"I will start you," said Mahmoud. "Guzman. Farouz. Ismail. Abu el Mak."

The last two were the men Georgiades had arrested.

He waited.

"I do not know any others," Ahmed protested.

"Were there others?"

"I do not know," said Ahmed wretchedly.

"Did you ever see any others?"

"No. The printer," he remembered.

"That was all?"

"Yes, I swear."

"Did you hear any other names mentioned?"

Ahmed thought hard.

"No," he said. "I do not think so."

It was possible. Some of the societies were very small. It was possible this was. That would account for its success in going undetected.

"They would kill me," said Ahmed.

"You will be safe," said Mahmoud, "in prison."

"If what you say is true," said Owen, "we hold them."

"Guzman is free," said Ahmed.

☙

Owen and Mahmoud went round the corner to a Turkish restaurant. As they approached it the smell of charcoal lay pleasantly on the night air.

Mahmoud said to Owen: "What will you do with him?"

"After? Let him go. Hand him over to you. He's no use to me."

Mahmoud was silent.

"Hand him over to you, I expect," said Owen. "At any rate the Nuri part is solved. You will be able to write it up and get it to court."

"It will never get to court," said Mahmoud. "It will be quietly dropped. Nuri will see to that."

Now it was Owen's turn to be silent.

"I'll be put on another case tomorrow," said Mahmoud. "Nuri will already be pulling strings."

"What about Mustafa? Will they set him up instead?"

"They might not. They'll probably just let him out after a time. Otherwise Ahmed might not go along with it."

"To do him justice," said Owen.

"He's all right. Just young."

"Want me to keep him? For a bit?"

"No," said Mahmoud. "He's learned his lesson."

They walked a few steps further. The restaurant came into view.

"On second thoughts," said Mahmoud, "perhaps you'd better keep him. Until you've taken care of Guzman."

☙

"Suppose we do catch him," said Georgiades, "what then?"

"What then?" said Owen. "I'll bloody well see he's tried and convicted, that's what's then!"

"You'll be lucky," said Georgiades.

"Lucky? The case is cast-iron."

"If it's ever heard."

"What do you mean?"

"It depends on Ahmed," said Georgiades. "Will he testify?"

"He'd better!"

Georgiades eased himself on his chair. Although it was still very early in the morning the heat was intense.

"Is he going to be tried himself? Ahmed, I mean?"

"Mahmoud thinks not," Owen conceded.

"There you are!" said Georgiades.

"He may not be tried," said Owen, "but he can bloody well testify."

"He'll be out of the country. His father will pay for him to have a long vacation. Far away."

Owen, who was hot, too, had not expected Georgiades to take this line.

"Are you saying we can't make this stuck?" he said with irritation.

"I'm saying it will never get to court. Guzman is one of the Khedive's staff. He will look after him."

"Even if he's tried to blow up the Sirdar?"

"Especially if he's tried to blow up the Sirdar. And that's another thing: Guzman will be a popular hero. Have you thought of that? He's done what every Egyptian would like to do: blow up the Sirdar. Or at any rate try to. Bring him before a court and there would be a wave of popular feeling. I can just see it."

Owen could see it, too.

"What are we going to do, then?" he said. "We can't just let him go scot free."

Georgiades shrugged.

"You could kick him out," he said. "Encourage him to use his talents somewhere else."

"Send him back to Turkey? That's just what he wants!"

"Is it?"

Owen looked at him.

Georgiades spread his hands.

"Well," he said. "Think! A Young Turk. Is that going to make him popular with the Sultan? Practising assassination. Do you think the Sultan would like that? It might be him next time. Secret society, revolutionary, conspirator. Wonderful! Just the chap the Sultan needs! I'll tell you one thing. Guzman may be popular with the Egyptians. He might be popular with the Turks for all I know. But one thing is for sure: he won't be very popular with the Sultan!"

⚭

When Georgiades had gone, Owen sat there thinking. Gradually his chair tipped back. He put his hands behind his head and closed his eyes. His feet found their way on to his desk. The chair tilted even more, so much so that Owen came to with a start. He pushed the chair back so that his shoulders rested against the wall. Feet went back on to desk. He shut his eyes again and blotted out everything except what he was thinking of.

He was still like this when Georgiades reappeared. He took one look at Owen and then padded away again without disturbing him.

And he was still like this one hour later when Nikos went in. Nikos, too, might have left him, but Nuri was waiting outside. This was an honour and Nikos was impressed.

"His Eminence, Nuri Pasha," he announced grandly as he ushered Nuri into the room.

Nuri, quite recovered now, came forward with outstretched hand, all geniality.

"It is good of you to see me, Captain Owen," he said. "I know you must be busy."

Nikos looked at Owen reproachfully and then retired, leaving the door conveniently open, for the sake of coolness no doubt.

Nuri sat down on one of the hard wooden chairs which were all that Owen had. He placed his walking stick, a different one from the one Owen had seen previously, ivory-topped this time, between his knees and folded his hands over the top. The heavy torso and massive neck and head were thrust forward slightly in eager anticipation of Owen's words and the face sympathetic, friendly, amused. The eyes were as shrewd and watchful as before.

Nuri came straight to the point.

"What shall I do about my foolish son, Captain Owen?"

Owen had half-expected this, both because it was the custom of the country and because he knew Nuri could never refrain from politicking.

"He has done wrong, I know, and must be punished for it. But," said Nuri, "as I am the only one who has suffered—"

"Mustafa?"

"Mustafa must be looked after," Nuri acknowledged. "I will see to that. But apart from him—" He stopped. "Of course, there is the danger to the state. I recognize that. But somehow I do not see Ahmed as a major threat to that."

He smiled, inviting Owen to join in. Owen, carefully, did not. Nuri registered the lack of response and changed the note.

"Besides," he said sombrely, "it is, in part at least, my fault."

"Why?" asked Owen.

"I should have taken him more seriously. Though that is hard to do. Especially when his political ideas are so naïve. He badly needs a lesson in realism."

"This is it," said Owen.

"Yes," said Nuri, "but the lesson comes costly. No parent likes his child paying the price. Have you any children, Captain Owen?"

"No," said Owen. "I am not married."

"Not even in India?"

"No."

"Ah," said Nuri, a little wistfully. "Then you will not know what it is like."

"What do you want?" asked Owen.

"I do not want the charges to be pressed."

"That is a matter for the Parquet."

"Not entirely," said Nuri, "and in any case I have seen to that. He is held by the Mamur Zapt."

"He is held under security provisions."

"Of course." Nuri held up a hand. "I am not objecting to that. I, too, have an interest in security. What I was wondering, however, was whether Ahmed constituted such a threat that giving him a good scare would not suffice. He would have to leave the country, of course. He has been a nuisance to you and I would have to ensure that he was no longer a nuisance. I recognize that. But I think I could guarantee that to your satisfaction."

"Where would you send him?"

"To Paris. To the Sorbonne. To study law."

He caught Owen's eye and grimaced.

"I know," he said. "He hasn't the brains. But he thinks he has, and I don't want to be the one to undeceive him. Frankly," he said, "I have not been altogether skilful in my relations with my son."

"I'll think about it," said Owen.

Nuri stood up, beaming.

"That is all I ask," he said, stretching out his hand. "It is good of you even to consider it. As Sir Eldon said only this morning, Ahmed is a damned nuisance."

Owen took in with amusement the reference to the British Agent. Nuri believed in letting people know how the cards were stacked.

As Nuri went out he said: "You have met my daughter, I believe?"

"Zeinab," said Owen. "Yes."

"I'm pleased about that," said Nuri. "At least you won't think that the whole family is imbecile."

ॐ

"So what do you want me to do?" asked Garvin.

"I'd like you to get a deportation order signed," said Owen, "and handed to me for execution."

"We don't want anything to happen on the way to the docks," Garvin warned.

"Not my style. I just want to make sure he gets on a particular boat. So that I can arrange a reception committee at the other end."

"He'll smell a rat."

"He won't even know it's me. They'll be just ordinary officials."

"Not too ordinary. Otherwise he'll get away."

"He won't get away."

Garvin mused.

"This reception committee you're organizing," he said. "I don't know that I go along with that sort of thing. Especially in a foreign country. Especially in a foreign country like Turkey."

"I'm not organizing it myself," Owen explained. "I'm just tipping off someone else so that they can organize it."

"Friends?"

"The authorities. The Sultan."

Garvin looked surprised. Then he understood.

"It may come unstuck," he said. "There are plenty of Young Turk sympathizers in the police and among the Sultan's own men. They may see it doesn't happen."

"I've thought of that, too. I think I know a way of getting a special word to the Sultan personally. After that it's up to him. Entirely," said Owen.

"That's it, is it?" asked Garvin, looking at him. "You're not involved in any other way?"

"Cross my heart and hope to die."

"I shouldn't hope to die," said Garvin. "Someone might take you seriously."

"I'm not involved in any other way."

Garvin weighed the assurance dispassionately. Apparently he came to the conclusion either that Owen was speaking the truth or that it did not matter if he was not, for he said: "OK then. I'll see what I can do."

He shook the tiny bazaar bell on his desk and asked the orderly to bring him a form.

Owen was a little disquieted. He had not expected Garvin to envisage other possibilities. Having the law on their side, the English did not need to have recourse to such things, although Owen knew that most of the countries around them did. Perhaps it was just Garvin's chilly way.

Garvin made out the form.

"I shall take this to Harry personally," he said.

Harry was the adviser to the Interior Minister.

"The Minister himself has to sign it. Harry will get him to do that, but I can't answer for its confidentiality afterwards. Not five minutes afterwards!"

"Let me make a phone call," said Owen, "and I'll be ready to move."

Owen made his phone call. Garvin saw Harry and gave the deportation order into Owen's own hands. The order was served immediately on a Guzman who for once was taken by surprise. A handful of picked men escorted him to the docks and put him on an Istanbul-bound steamer where he was placed at once in a locked cabin with a man, again picked, outside the door. And within an hour the steamer was nosing out into the Mediterranean.

Owen and Georgiades watched it go.

"Suleiman will be all right," said Georgiades. "The problems will start at the other end."

"They'll be problems for Guzman," said Owen.

⌀

When Owen got back to Cairo he called in Nuri to see him. That was twice in two days and Nikos was doubly impressed. Nuri, however, was not surprised.

"It's always best to move fast in these matters," he said.

"How fast we move depends on you," said Owen.

"Ah?"

Nuri settled himself back in the chair to hear the terms of the deal.

"In things like this," said Owen, "the pawns are not important."

"Just so," said Nuri, "the Mustafas."

"The Ahmeds."

Nuri was a little surprised at the classification but saw that it had potential and nodded polite agreement.

"What matters," said Owen, "are the persons moving the pawns."

Nuri looked at Owen quickly but said nothing. Perhaps he feared that this extension of the classification was directed at him.

"Take the attack on you, for instance," said Owen. "Mustafa was only a tool. So was Ahmed. A more complex one, possibly, but still only a tool. He took some things on himself—"

"Foolishly."

"Foolishly," Owen agreed, "but generously. He wanted to put the world to rights—"

"He's young," said Nuri, but looked pleased.

"—but basically he was being used. It's the people who were using him that I'm concerned with."

"Yes?"

"I was wondering how you felt about Guzman."

Nuri took his time about replying. Owen knew that he was figuring out all the angles.

"Guzman is a dangerous man," he said eventually.

"Yes. Did you know how dangerous?"

Nuri shook his head.

"No," he said. "He's always been secretive. I knew he was fanatical and suspected he was extremist. But I did not imagine that he was so actively involved."

"You worked with him?"

"Well," said Nuri, "alongside him. We were never close."

"Rivals?"

"You could call it that."

"He let Ahmed have the gun. Is that his way with rivals?"

Nuri was silent.

"I'm not saying he meant Mustafa to kill you," said Owen, "but I don't think he would have minded if he had."

Nuri smiled wintrily.

"I think that is an accurate assessment," he agreed.

"Why is that?" asked Owen. "Is he like that with everybody or has he got something particular against you?"

"Both," said Nuri. "He is like that with everybody *and* he has something particular against me."

"And you're not going to tell me what that something particular is."

"No," said Nuri. "I am not."

They both laughed.

"It doesn't matter," said Owen, "because I think I know it already."

"Ah!" said Nuri, and laughed, but took it in.

"Your negotiations with Abdul Murr."

Nuri said nothing; but Owen saw that the remark registered.

"However," he said, "that is not my concern at the moment. What I want to know is this: is he going to try again? More seriously this time?"

"To kill me?" Nuri's eyes rested thoughtfully on the ivory carving of his stick. "Possibly," he acknowledged, looking up at Owen.

"I was wondering if it would be a good idea to take measures," said Owen.

Nuri's eyes met his unblinkingly.

"That could be arranged," he said quietly.

Owen saw that Nuri had misunderstood him.

"Not that," he said.

"Oh?"

"Guzman left the country this morning."

"Really?" said Nuri, surprised. "Already? How disappointing!"

"Not very," said Owen. "We pushed him. We put him on a boat. The *San Demetriou*. It left Alexandria this morning."

Nuri looked puzzled.

"Then—?"

"For Istanbul. He's in a locked cabin and will stay there until he arrives."

Nuri still looked puzzled.

"We thought the Sultan might like to know."

Nuri's face cleared.

"Ah!" he said. "I am beginning to understand."

"Someone, of course, would need to let him know. Privately. And without going through too many people."

"I understand now exactly," said Nuri.

He rose to his feet and held out his hand.

"A pleasure!" he said. "A real pleasure!"

As he got to the door he looked back.

"And my stupid son?" he asked.

"What you were suggesting the other day," said Owen, "sounds entirely reasonable."

෧෴෧

The next person to call on the Mamur Zapt was Fakhri.

He came at Owen's request and was more than a little nervous. Owen, however, held out a welcoming hand.

"I'm hoping you might be able to help me," he said.

"*You* want *me* to help *you?*" asked Fakhri.

"That's right," Owen agreed amiably.

Fakhri appeared even more nervous.

"I am, of course, at your service," he said cautiously.

"I'd like an article placed," said Owen, "somewhere where political people will read it."

"What sort of article?"

"Oh, just a review of the current political scene. It would, however, refer in passing to attempts by Nuri Pasha to form an alliance with moderate elements in the Nationalist Party and say that such attempts showed every sign of succeeding."

"Look," said Fakhri, "if we'd wanted to publish an article like that we could have done so months ago."

"I know," said Owen.

"But we didn't. And do you know why? Because of the harm it would do. It would play straight into the hands of extremists like el Gazzari and Jemal."

"I know," said Owen.

"You know?" said Fakhri, staring. "Then why do you want it? It would mean the end of Abdul Murr—of perhaps the last real chance of the Nationalists developing as a moderate Parliamentary party."

"I know."

"Then why—?"

Fakhri stopped as realization dawned.

"I see," he said. "You don't want a moderate Parliamentary party."

"Not a strong one."

"You'd prefer the Nationalists to be in the hands of the extremists because that would mean they would be discredited."

"And divided," said Owen.

"So that the British could go on ruling."

"The Khedive rules, we only advise."

Fakhri swallowed. "I don't like it," he said.

"Why not?" asked Owen. "Other moderates will benefit if the Nationalists become extremist."

"As you very well know," said Fakhri bitterly, "we are just as divided."

"This is your chance, then."

"You may find it hard to believe this," said Fakhri, "but I care more about seeing parliamentary democracy established in Egypt than I do about my own political career."

"Very fine," said Owen, "but not very realistic."

Fakhri sat quiet.

"I am sorry," he said at last, "but I cannot help you."

"With the article? A pity. It won't make any difference, you know. I shall find another way of placing it."

"I would prefer not to be involved."

"You're already involved," said Owen. "You involved yourself. Remember?"

"And this is the punishment?"

"Call it a warning," said Owen.

"I'd rather go to prison," said Fakhri with dignity.

"It would be a waste. A mere gesture."

"And the Egyptians are prone to gestures. I still think it's one I'd like to make."

Owen let him go and Nikos showed him out. Afterwards, Georgiades came into the room.

"I like that little man," said Georgiades, who had been listening outside. "What are you going to do with him?"

"Nothing."

"The article?"

"I'll place it somewhere else."

"How about *al Liwa?*" suggested Georgiades.

இ௯

John rang.

"What's all this? This chap Guzman getting away?"

"Not quite," said Owen, and told him.

"That's lovely," said John happily. "The Sirdar will like that. He really will!"

Then Paul.

"The Khedive's protested."

"He has?"

"Your action is precipitate and unjustified. He says."

"What did the Agent say?" asked Owen.

"That he was bloody lucky he didn't find himself on the boat, too, since the Sirdar was inclined to be even more precipitate."

They both laughed.

"Actually," said Paul, "the Old Man thinks it's neat. No fuss. No bother. Effective. Nice to have a Mamur Zapt who's got a bit of touch, he said. No, he really did."

The article appeared in a first-rate political weekly and was much read. Abdul Murr was discredited. The two extremist wings of the Nationalist Party turned on him and devoured the moderates. Afterwards, they turned on each other.

Nuri's plans, of course, fell through. Those plans. Being Nuri, he soon had others.

Ahmed was sent on a long course of study to France.

Mustafa was discreetly released, completely bewildered by the whole affair and content that matters should rest in the capable hands of his wife. Her sister was duly delivered and looked after.

When the *San Demetriou* docked at Istanbul there was a reception committee for Guzman, and Owen rather lost touch with what happened after that.

He himself took Zeinab to the opera.

About the Author

Michael Pearce grew up in the (then) Anglo-Egyptian Sudan among the political and other tensions he draws on for this book. He returned there later to teach and retains a human rights interest in the area. In between whiles his career has followed the standard academic rake's progress from teaching to writing to editing to administration. He finds international politics a pallid imitation of academic ones. Pearce lives in England.

To receive a free catalog of other Poisoned Pen Press titles, please contact us in one of the following ways:

Phone: 1-800-421-3976
Facsimile: 1-480-949-1707
Email: info@poisonedpenpress.com
Website: www.poisonedpenpress.com

Poisoned Pen Press
6962 E. First Ave. Ste 103
Scottsdale, AZ 85251